# Darned If You Do

# Darned If You Do

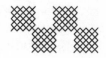

## Monica Ferris

BERKLEY PRIME CRIME, NEW YORK

THE BERKLEY PUBLISHING GROUP
Published by the Penguin Group
Penguin Group (USA) LLC
375 Hudson Street, New York, New York 10014

USA • Canada • UK • Ireland • Australia • New Zealand • India • South Africa • China

penguin.com

A Penguin Random House Company

Berkley Prime Crime Books are published by The Berkley Publishing Group.
BERKLEY® PRIME CRIME and the PRIME CRIME logo are trademarks of Penguin Group
(USA) LLC.

Library of Congress Cataloging-in-Publication Data

Ferris, Monica.
Darned if you do / Monica Ferris.—First edition.
pages ; cm.—(A needlecraft mystery ; 18)
ISBN 978-0-425-27010-3 (hardcover)
I. Title.
PS3566.U47D37 2015
813'.54—dc23                    2014035825

FIRST EDITION: February 2015

PRINTED IN THE UNITED STATES OF AMERICA

10  9  8  7  6  5  4  3  2  1

Cover illustration by Mary Ann Lasher.
Cover design by George Long.

# Acknowledgments

So many people help me with these novels that it's hard to thank them properly—I'm always afraid I'll leave someone out. (And too often I do!)

Attorney Rodney J. Mason of Saint Paul was very patient with me, explaining how to handle the relevant legal issues when a person suddenly is incapacitated and has an urgent problem in his home.

The Northwest Coin Club was excited about my idea of the discovery of a cookie jar full of Morgan dollars and gave me good hints about the mintages to look for. They also provided ongoing help in making sure that Rafael's knowledge of coin collecting is accurate (or, when necessary, inaccurate).

Leipold's is a real store in Excelsior, and LaVerna and Darel really do estimates of estates.

And dear Vivian Langford didn't know what she was getting into when she sent me that first handkerchief with a crochet-lace border. I challenged her to edge a handkerchief with a really big border—and she surely did!

Police services liaison Anne Marie Buck of the Hopkins Police Department is always willing to answer my questions about customs and procedures for the smaller police force.

# Acknowledgments

Thank you, Rev. Alison Bucklin and Joan Marie Verba—it took both of you to help me get the crochet parts right.

A big thank-you to Crème de la Crime, the best writers' group ever and anywhere.

And I owe everything to Ellen Kuhfeld, Nancy Yost, and Jackie Cantor.

# Darned If You Do

# Chapter One

### ✠ ✠ ✠

Tom Riordan often had trouble falling asleep, but once there, he slept like the dead. So he snored on, unaware, as a violent autumn thunderstorm roared down Highway 7, dumping three inches of rain onto the streets and lawns of the little town of Excelsior in less than an hour. Lightning lashed the clouds to greater effort, thunder cracked and banged and rolled. Trees, their leaves heavy with rain, swayed, bent, and danced under the onslaught of powerful winds. Now and again a branch would wrench loose to tumble through the air. When a bigger limb struck an electrical wire, snapping it, the dazzle of sparks was an echo of the lightning higher in the sky. Power all over town started going out.

Riordan, oblivious, slept on.

Then an ancient elm, its inside long rotted and its roots' grip weakened by rain, groaned under the wind's blast, twisted, and fell. It had given welcome shade to Riordan's house for many summers, but now it slammed into the roof, breaking through the shingles to thrust sopping leaves and wet and broken limbs into Riordan's bedroom, waking him at last.

Marianne Schultz, seventy-eight, was a retired school-teacher. A spinster, she was tall and thin, active and self-reliant. Now, at four in the morning, she stood in the wet, dark front yard of her house, using a powerful flashlight to look at the damage the storm had done. Power was out all up and down the block, she noted, and probably all over town. Several trees along the avenue were down, one blocking the street. Worst of all, the noble elm that had stood in her backyard for as long as she could remember—longer, probably, to judge by its great height—had fallen onto her neighbor's roof. It had broken through; shingles and boards littered the ground along with leaves and branches.

Marianne walked to the front of the damaged house, a brick structure two stories high, painted an unlikely rose pink that glowed under her flashlight's beam. All was silent within, blinds and curtains drawn—but that was generally the case. Mr. Riordan was a very private person, though not a recluse. He was seen everywhere but never invited anyone into his home. She wondered if he was in there.

She went up on the small porch, which felt a trifle insecure under her feet. A pillar missing at one corner had been replaced with a long board. She rapped hard on the front door.

"Mr. Riordan? Are you inside?"

No reply.

"Mr. Riordan? Are you all right?"

She leaned toward the covered glass insert in the door and cocked her head to listen. Was that a cry for help?

She rapped again. "Mr. Riordan?"

More loudly came the cry. "Help! Help me! There's a tree, a broken tree on me!"

She backed off the porch and looked up at a shattered window on the second floor. The voice clearly was coming from there.

"Are you hurt, Thomas?" she called.

"Yes, yes! I think my leg is broken! Ow, ow, I can't move! And my . . . arm . . . head . . . my head . . . Owwwww . . ." His voice faded, and soon all she could hear were incomprehensible sounds.

"Stay where you are! I'm going to get help!"

Marianne hurried back to her own house to call for assistance, but her landline was dead, and the impossibly complicated cell phone her niece had bought her had long since lost its charge.

So she pulled on a jacket—the post-storm air had turned chilly after a week of unseasonably warm weather—and started out on a swift walk toward the police station, six blocks away.

It was a trip complicated by downed trees and flooded streets. She met the occasional resident standing stunned in the ruins of his property or commiserating with a neighbor. She asked if anyone could use his cell phone to call emergency services, but nobody's cell was working—the cell towers had lost power, too.

In the distance she could hear sirens, and once she caught

a whiff of bad-smelling smoke, which meant a house was on fire, though she could not tell where it was coming from. She soaked her feet when she stepped into a gutter full of running water as she crossed the last street to the police station.

She walked into the low brick and stone building to find no one behind the thick glass window that separated the small lobby from the rest of the station. Next to the window there was a black wall phone without a dial, and beside it was a sign: TO TALK WITH A POLICE OFFICER, LIFT THE RECEIVER. Marianne lifted the receiver and heard a woman's voice say, "May I help you?"

"Yes, please, this is an emergency. A tree has fallen on my neighbor's house, and he's trapped inside, upstairs, and he's hurt."

"Where are you?" asked the woman.

"Inside the police station," replied Marianne.

"No, dear, where are you calling from? What city?"

"Oh. Excelsior. Where are you?"

"I'm a 911 operator in Minneapolis. What's the address of the house where the injured party is located?"

"Let's see, I'm 712, so he must be 710 Mitchell Avenue. A brick two-story, painted pink, with a big tree mashed into the roof. You can't miss it. And please hurry, it sounds like his injuries may be serious."

"You didn't go in to check on him?"

"I couldn't, his door is locked. I heard him calling for help through a broken upstairs window."

"All right, I'm sending help right now. Go back to the house to direct emergency personnel."

"Yes, all right," Marianne said. "Thank you."

\*　　\*　　\*

THE whole area around the south end of Lake Minnetonka was a nightmare. The storm had been a big one, sweeping across northern Iowa and halfway up the state of Minnesota, and had formed small pockets of fury. One of those pockets roared up from Saint Bonifacius through Excelsior and Shorewood and on across Lake Minnetonka to Wayzata. Power was out, trees were down, flash floods abounded, houses were damaged—two of them set on fire by lightning strikes.

Every member of the small Excelsior Police Department was out on the street—even the chief. The volunteer fire department was working hard; one of the houses on fire was in Excelsior.

Marianne, of course, didn't know any of this and had no way of finding out. She went back to her neighborhood and found others out on the street, some talking, some starting to clean up, some just standing and staring at the wreckage. Someone had set four camping lanterns in the middle of the street. They hissed faintly and gave off a brilliant light but also cast dark shadows into corners and behind bushes.

"Did any of you go in to help Mr. Riordan?" she called as she approached his house.

The three who heard her question turned to look at her. They all shook their heads.

"He never answers his door, you know that," said a balding stout man in robe and slippers.

"Yeah, so how do you know he's in there?" asked the equally stout woman standing beside him—Mr. and Mrs. Bond, retired grocers. They lived across the street.

"Because I heard him calling for help out that window," said Marianne, gesturing at the upper story of the pink brick house. "He said he had a broken leg and maybe a head injury and he's trapped up in his bedroom."

The couple stared up at the open window.

"I ain't heard nuthin'," declared the third person, a truculent man in his middle thirties, with the broad shoulders, big hands, and solid paunch of a truck driver. He was Paul Winston, the Bonds' neighbor, whose wife had walked out with their three children two months ago. Paul had not been completely sober since.

"We haven't, either," said Mr. Bond, "and we've been out here longer than Paul."

Mrs. Bond nodded. She would have said something, but a siren interrupted her. The quartet, and other people farther up the street, turned to face the flashing lights of a squad car headed their way.

Marianne lifted her arm to signal the driver and pointed to the Riordan house. The squad car's siren cut off, but the flashing lights stayed on as it pulled to the curb. A very large policeman in a dark blue uniform climbed out. He was about six four, very fit, with blond hair, gray eyes, and a lot of chin.

"What seems to be the problem here?" he called.

"Oh, Sergeant Larson, I'm glad you've come," said Marianne, hurrying to him. "It's Tom Riordan. My elm tree fell over in the storm and landed right on the roof of his house, breaking through. I came for a look and heard Tom calling for help. He's upstairs, probably in his bedroom."

"Did you go in to see if he's hurt?" asked Larson, looking thoughtfully up at the smashed roof and broken window.

"The door's locked," said Marianne.

"He always keeps his doors locked," contributed Mrs. Bond.

"I don't think nobody's ever been in his house," added Winston.

"Well, let's have a look," said Larson. He walked up onto the little porch and tried the door. It didn't open. He pushed on it, then stepped back and pounded on it with a mighty fist.

"Yo! Riordan! This is the police! You in there?" he shouted.

There was a pause, then, faintly, they all heard a voice wafting from the upstairs window. "Help me . . . Please, help me."

"Oh, dear God," said Mrs. Bond. "He *is* in there. Do something, Lars!"

Larson went back up on the porch, grabbed the doorknob, and slammed a big shoulder into the door. It trembled, but held. He hit it again. The third time, there was a loud crack and the door opened a few inches. Larson shoved it, hard, with both hands, and it opened the rest of the way.

He turned to the people standing on the sidewalk and said, "Wait here," in a voice that brooked no disobedience. Everyone took a step back to indicate compliance, and the big man went into the house.

# Chapter Two

❖ ❖ ❖

L ARS paused inside the door. The place smelled strongly of mold and seemed impossibly filled with stuff. He swept the room with his heavy steel flashlight and saw a narrow path marked on either side by metal barrels and rusty bicycles. A couch on the left was almost entirely obscured by cardboard boxes overflowing with all manner of objects: action figures, alarm clocks, teakettles, magazines, posters, and a stop sign whose letters were marked with faceted stones. On the wall over a wood-burning stove was a gigantic red Pegasus, the emblem of a certain brand of gasoline. There was much, much more, but Lars, remembering that there was an injured man upstairs, followed a narrow path through the heaps of stuff to a staircase toward the back of the living room.

The steps had been turned into bookshelves, with a narrow space in the middle for someone to climb them. The stairwell was, of course, completely dark, and smelled of dust and old paper.

At the top, the hallway was again piled nearly to the ceiling with just a slim passage down the middle. There was a crooked heap of elaborate birdcages, some without floors or doors. There were two cardboard cases of canned pineapple, and a stack of dinner china that looked like it might have been a complete service for twelve. Its gold trim glinted in the light from his flashlight, but only two of the cups had handles. There was a wheelbarrow full of boxes of tissue that had apparently been rescued from someplace wet. Two chest-high stacks of comic books leaned against each other in the corridor. Four antique steamer chests stood balanced on one another—precariously, because they all had humped lids.

"Riordan?" called Lars. "Are you up here?"

"Help . . . help . . . help," came a faint call from behind a door at the front of the house.

Lars went to the door and opened it carefully. This room, like the rest of the house, was packed floor to ceiling, in this case with mostly broken glass jars, several pickle crocks, myriad winter coats and boots, and magazines, all in wild disorder.

And then there was the wet, broken tree. Pieces of it—every size, from twigs to branches as thick as his arm—made a kind of sideways forest in the room. Back in a corner stood a narrow bed, and on the bed was a man in his sixties, long and thin, his eyes huge in the blaze of Lars's Kel-Lite. Blood covered half his face, and his blanket was soaked with it. He lay on his side, his lower legs trapped under a massive branch.

"Good gravy, man, are you all right?" A foolish question.

"Uh, no, I . . . I'm kinda . . . stuck. But, can . . . can you help me . . . up?" asked the man feebly.

"I dunno, Tom, you seem pretty well caught over there. Can you tell me how you've been injured?"

"My . . . my leg's broke." The man began a feeble struggle to rise.

"Here, lay still," ordered Lars. "You're only gonna hurt yourself more if you try to move. Listen, listen to me, you'll be all right if you hold still. I'll call for some backup, and we'll get you out of here real soon. Just hold on till I get more people up here."

"No, no, no . . . I think . . . I think I can get out of bed . . . if you'll lift up that end," Tom said, sounding alarmed. He began to struggle harder.

"Hold on, that's not possible. We got half a big tree in here with us. Have a little patience, man."

"No, please. I don't want . . . no people in my house." The man's voice was weak, but his desperate plea was clear.

"I'm sorry, but we don't have any choice. We've got to call for help." Lars reached for the mike attached to his shoulder. "Forty, this is one-three, we have an injured adult male trapped in a bed on the second floor. Lots of debris from a fallen tree. The house is very cluttered."

"Ten-four," replied a voice. "Sending a rescue squad."

"This is . . . wrong. Bad. I . . . can't . . ." The man struggled to a sitting position to push futilely against the massive limb imprisoning his legs, groaning with pain.

"Hold it, Tom! Listen to me!" Lars went to press gently on the man's shoulder. Tom was wearing a thin white T-shirt that had seen better days, and his bones were prominent under Lars's hand. "Lay down, you hear me? That's an order, lay back down."

Reluctantly, the man fell back. "You can . . . you can lift that tree, Sergeant Larson. You . . . you're big . . . strong," he said. "Please, lift it . . . so I can . . . get out. Then . . . you . . . help me down . . . stairs."

"Nothing doing. You're hurt too bad to be dragged off that bed and manhandled down a flight of stairs. If I try, it'll only hurt you more. So just take it easy."

Tom lifted a thin arm in a pleading gesture. "Please."

"I've called for an ambulance, they'll be here in a couple minutes."

"I don't . . . need no . . . amb'lance."

Lars, bemused and amused in equal parts, said, "Sure you do."

He squatted by the bed and took the man's big, calloused hand in his own. It was cold and clammy. Lars set his flashlight upright on the floor, and chafed the hand gently. "You're gonna be all right, but we need some help in here to get you freed up. Just hang on, okay?"

Through a thick lock of light-colored hair, Riordan searched the big cop's face. "All right," he muttered after a few moments, defeated. The room fell silent.

But it wasn't long before Lars said, "There now, hear that?" as a siren was heard coming up the street. "Help is here."

As the rescuers started arriving—firemen in big black coats and hats, emergency medics in white raincoats—their flashlights and lanterns made dizzying patterns in the clutter and destruction.

Lars, having done his part, left the house to go on other calls.

\*   \*   \*

EMERGENCY medical workers and a public works crew filled the space in the little bedroom. An IV line was slipped painlessly into Riordan's arm, and a thick bandage was applied to his head wound. No one said a word about the shocking amount of clutter in the house or the weirdness of finding a whole lot of broken tree in the bedroom.

Riordan was grateful for that, though his eyes flashed from face to face as he looked at the people assembled there to rescue him. What must they think? He was as ashamed as he was hurting.

But the men and women around him were kind and kept reassuring him that all would be well. It took a long while, but eventually a crane was summoned to drop cables into his bedroom from outside, and lift and support the broken tree while chain saws filled the room with a hideous racket as they cut through the tangle of branches. Tom was given a pair of ear protectors, which helped to muffle the noise.

It took over an hour to free him from his wooden prison after the crane arrived, and he was unconscious by the time they brought him down the steep and narrowed staircase and into an ambulance.

# Chapter Three

✦ ✦ ✦

I T was the quiet that woke Betsy. Not merely the quiet after the violent storm—which had brought both cats into the bed with her and Connor—but another kind of quiet.

As in dead silence.

The modern American home is full of a constant murmur of electric devices going about their business of chilling food, cooling or heating or refreshing the air, heating the water, washing the dishes or clothes, marking the passage of time.

When all that stops, the silence can be disturbing. So Betsy, who had awakened briefly when the storm was at its crashing, booming, flashing height, woke again when true quiet fell.

She lay still for a little while, wondering what had woken her up. Turning her head to look at the bedside clock radio, she saw nothing. The red numbers on its face had vanished.

*Ah*, she thought. *Power's out.* That sometimes happened during a violent storm. The outage usually didn't last long; in fact, power might be back before daylight.

Betsy rolled onto her back and lifted her left arm to press the little button on her Indiglo watch. Its cool green face lit up: 4:30 a.m. She sighed and dropped her wrist, letting it drift over to Connor's side of the bed—where it found empty space. Where could he have gone? she wondered.

Her live-in boyfriend, Connor Sullivan, was a retired sea captain. Betsy, an ex-WAVE, liked to jest that she had a weakness for anything nautical. For years he had been in charge of enormous cargo and even more enormous oil-carrying vessels as they crossed the Atlantic and Pacific oceans, responsible for both the cargo and the crew. A habit of responsibility, powerfully instilled, lingered in him. Doubtless his sleep had also been disturbed and now he had gotten up to see how extensive the outage was and if there was other damage to the building or in the immediate area.

Betsy waited for a few minutes, drifting on the edge of sleep. But he didn't return. Had he dressed and gone out?

She tried to decide not to worry about it, but the effort only made her concern grow until she was wide awake and now fully concerned. Annoyed at herself, she threw the blankets back and sat up. The red numbers on her bedside clock were flashing 7:12, 7:12, 7:12. That wasn't the right time, of course; the flashing indicated a break in the power source and the clock had made a random guess at the time.

Wait a minute.

She sat still and listened. Now she heard the tiny whir of the refrigerator in the kitchen, and the faint gush of the furnace pouring heated air into the bedroom.

The power was back on. Must've been a glitch, not a line down. *Whew!* She checked her watch again and adjusted the bedside clock to the correct hour, then lay back down.

But still Connor didn't return.

What was he up to? Maybe he really had gone outdoors. There had been a terrible storm earlier—she remembered waking briefly during the night as it raged outside. Maybe he had gone out to see if there had been any damage.

With an exasperated sigh—as much at herself for being foolish as at him for his too-strong sense of responsibility—she climbed out of bed. Sophie, the fat senior cat, voiced her displeasure with a high-pitched mew, but Thai, the young Siamese, said, "Yow!" in his deep voice and jumped down to come eagerly with her to the window. He stood up on his hind legs, forepaws on the sill, looking out just as if there were something to see.

But there wasn't. There wasn't a single light on out there. The big condo across the street was barely discernible as a darker blackness against the dark sky. Even the street-lights were out.

So why did their apartment have power?

She went into the living room and snapped on the lights, then went to the window in the dining nook. The little parking lot behind the building was very dimly lit by a single lamp over the back door, but the steep slope it faced was a featureless blackness. At the top of the slope were, she knew, several houses and a gas station. But had she not known that, she would never have guessed, because nothing of them could be seen. The lights were out all over the neighborhood—maybe all over town.

High overhead a half moon swam in fast-moving clouds,

disappearing behind them even as Betsy watched, making the darkness complete.

How weird that her building had power but nobody else did.

And where was Connor?

Sophie came to stand beside Betsy's left ankle. So long as she was up, Sophie seemed to be asking, how about some breakfast?

Betsy looked down at the big, fluffy animal with an exasperated sigh. Sophie, who was morbidly obese, had been found in a starving condition by Betsy's sister years ago and nursed back to health. But the cat retained a conviction that privation might suddenly reappear, and was in permanent preparation for that occasion. She spent her days down in the needlework shop curled picturesquely on a cushioned chair, cadging treats from the customers. Despite Betsy's efforts—which included a needlepoint sign hung on the back of the chair—NO THANKS, I'M ON A DIET—customers loved to slip the cat the occasional corner of a sandwich or half a potato chip or the tail end of a cookie. Betsy's veterinarian said that, despite the animal's weight, which varied from nineteen to twenty-three pounds, Sophie was healthy for a cat her age, which was probably close to fourteen years. So each morning and evening, Betsy fed her a little scoop of the healthiest dry cat food she could buy and let the chips fall where they may, including into Sophie's fat paws.

"No," she told the cat now, "because we're not really up, and you get fed when we get up."

"Meeeeeow!" argued Sophie. Her thin, high, plaintive cry sounded ridiculous coming from a cat her size.

"Ow-rah!" agreed Thai. His cry sounded eerily like that of a human baby.

"No," said Betsy firmly. She did not care to establish a precedent that any time a human in the house got out of bed, the cats got fed.

She heard the door to the apartment open and a baritone voice call, *"Machree?* What are you doing up?"

"Connor! Where did you go?" He must have noticed that the lights were on. She went to greet him with a hug. He was in a thick, sky blue terry robe and black leather slippers. So he hadn't gone outdoors.

"Down in the basement, starting the generator."

"You mean it actually works? It did all this?" She gestured around the warm, well-lit apartment with its humming mechanicals.

"Of course," he replied, his gentle tone belying the hurt in his eyes.

"Oh, Connor, I'm sorry! It was wrong of me to doubt you!"

The generator had become a point of contention when Betsy and Connor had attended a farm auction—Connor loved auctions—and he had raised his hand once too often while bidding on a big, old, dusty generator and found himself in possession of it. He had had to hire someone to truck the thing to the building Betsy owned and help him wrestle it into the basement. Then, after cleaning it of dust, dirt, and worse, he'd had to construct exhaust piping for it. It had taken him a week of tinkering to get its diesel engine to run in more than fits and starts, and when he did, it was noisy, and the piping leaked and filled the basement with noxious fumes. It had taken all Betsy's reserve not to declare the thing a failure and order it removed.

Why didn't she? Because he was so proud of having acquired, at a bargain price, a machine that he hoped never to need but would be priceless if he did.

Connor had the soul of a survivalist. In the basement he also kept a big, padlocked, waterproof chest filled with water treatment pills, a serious first aid kit, and enough canned goods and dried food to keep them both fed and watered for at least a month. He kept his car in top condition and rarely let the gas gauge go lower than half empty. He was a more-than-adequate plumber and electrician, and good—no, great—at first aid.

Betsy had found his pessimistic attitude toward civilization's durability aggravating at times. But now that awful old generator was chugging away at so great a distance its racket could not be heard, its leak long corrected, and she was warm and able to operate her well-lit kitchen, and even open her shop for business later—much later—that morning. And the same was true of her entire building, with two other tenants in the upstairs apartments and two other businesses on the ground floor.

"I think we're the only point of light at this end of the lake," Connor said now.

"You mean you did go outside?"

"Indeed not," he said, raising both hands, amused. "I got out my crank-powered radio and listened to the news. This whole end of the lake is without power, trees are blocking roads, and there is flash flooding all over the county. They're asking people to stay at home. My cell phone can't get a signal, since there's no power to feed to the towers out here."

"Wow," she said. Connor was not saying *I told you so* even with the expression on his face.

She laughed at his courteous reserve and embraced him again. "I love you," she said. "You are amazing. And thank you for buying that horrible, noisy, smelly, wonderful machine."

"You are welcome. Now can we go back to bed?" he said. "I could use another couple hours of sleep."

# Chapter Four

✠ ✠ ✠

A T midafternoon, the power was still out in Excelsior. Clouds had thickened again, and though the violent storms had passed, there was occasional heavy rain and a chill wind. Between that and some of the trees having been largely stripped of their leaves, suddenly it looked, and felt, like November, though it was not yet October; not a pleasant situation when houses and stores were without heat and light.

People had begun cleaning up their yards, whether just picking up debris by hand, raking up leaves and twigs, or, sick at heart, bringing out or borrowing chain saws to cut apart a favorite tree downed by the storm. Some had to borrow or rent pumps to empty flooded basements.

Word began to spread around town that the building that housed Crewel World, ISBNs Bookstore, and Sol's Deli over on West Lake Street had lights and power. And in that building you could get warm things to eat and drink. So now and again people would put down their tools and come to the needlework shop for a cup of hot coffee or tea, or drop into Sol's Deli for a hot bowl of soup and a sandwich. Even the two proprietors of ISBNs, who normally did not allow food or drink in their bookstore, bought some croissants from Sol's and borrowed a coffeemaker from Betsy's kitchen and offered rolls and coffee to browsers seeking a literary escape from their problems.

The talk in Betsy's shop was not only about whose favorite tree was down, whose roof was damaged, and whose basement was flooded, but about the strange accident that had befallen Tom Riordan. The top third of a big tree had fallen into his bedroom—while he was in bed! He had a broken leg, went one rumor. He had a concussion, went another. *And* a severely broken arm, *plus* broken ribs, *and* a bruised liver went a third. It was awful, they all agreed in shocked voices, and sad, and everyone hoped he would make a full recovery.

An ad hoc Monday Bunch meeting took place at around three o'clock that afternoon.

Everyone around the table—Alice, Bershada, Cherie, Phil, Doris, and Emily—expressed sympathy for Tom Riordan and exchanged rumors.

Listening curiously, but contributing nothing, sat a new member, Grace Pickering. She and her sister, Georgine, had come to Excelsior in the middle of August and rented a house on a month-to-month basis. They were from Jacksonville, Florida, experienced travelers, enjoying the novelty of living in the far north. Grace liked to crochet and was pleased to find the Monday Bunch. At thirty-five, she was the older of the two sisters, attractive, with sparkling green eyes and lots of dark auburn hair that fell in an artless tumble over her shoulders. She declared that she and her sister wanted to experience a white Christmas before they moved on, probably to Santa Fe. Betsy's store manager, Godwin, was sure there was something tragic in their background, because the two were so closemouthed about their past. All he knew about them was that they claimed to make a living buying antiques and collectibles and selling them on eBay. But Betsy told him not to be silly. No one who could crochet joyous fine lace like Gracie Pickering could have a secret sorrow.

"It's just too bad Jill isn't here with us today," said Bershada. "She could tell us the real facts about poor Tom."

"Why's that?" asked Grace. She was wearing thick magnifying glasses and using a fine pale blue thread to crochet a microscopic doily fit for a doll's house.

"Her husband was first on the scene in Tom Riordan's house," said Emily. Seeing Grace's puzzlement, she continued, "Oh, don't you know Lars is a police officer?"

"She used to be a cop herself," said Phil. He was nearly finished with a needlepoint canvas of a fat old witch riding a bicycle.

"No, really?" Grace looked up from her work, eyebrows raised in surprise. She'd met tall, fair-haired, quiet Jill.

Alice said in her usual blunt way, "She could've told us if it's true that his house is filled with garbage."

"Well, it's not," said Bershada. "There's no garbage in it, just . . . things. It's mostly old things, a lot of them not exactly useful, but it's not garbage."

Emily said, "I hear there are books stacked all up and down the stairs. I don't know how those ambulance people got Tom down from the second floor."

Bershada said, "Books, you say? I'd love a chance to sort those books." Bershada was a retired librarian.

"There's boxes of toys, too," contributed Phil in his loud, deaf-man's voice. "Oil cans. Birdcages. Cases of canned cat food. Sets of china. Audiotapes. Auto parts."

Grace asked, "So you've been in there?"

"No, but someone has, and he opened the curtains and lifted the blinds, so you can look through the dirty windows."

"I told him not to go over there," said Doris, his wife. "But he wanted to see."

"Why not?" said Phil. "And I wasn't the only one. I practically had to stand in line."

"I think it's rude to stare into people's windows," said Alice without looking at Phil, who snorted.

"There's a great big flying red horse on the living room wall," he added, unrepentant.

"'Flying red horse'?" echoed Betsy, who was working with Godwin on their Christmas window design.

Godwin smiled at her. "You know, the gasoline sign. Mobil used it years and years ago, and then stopped, but now they're using that old Pegasus again."

Grace said, "The old ones are very collectible. Some of them fetch hundreds even thousands of dollars."

"Really?" said Godwin. "And there's one on Tom Take's wall! I wonder where he got it?"

"Collectible!" barked Phil, snapping his fingers. "That's what Tom is, he's a collector. There's a TV show on cable about these two guys who drive all over the country looking for barns and sheds full of stuff these collectors have, er, collected. They'd purely love to visit old Tom."

"Are there dead birds in the cages?" asked Emily in a small, worried voice.

"No, of course not," said Phil. He grinned broadly. "But I saw a live mouse in the kitchen. He was bold as brass, sitting up on the edge of the sink, sniffing the air."

"Oh, ugh!" said Emily. "I hate mice!"

"Maybe he's Tom's pet," suggested Cherie.

"Naw, pet mice are white, this one's gray."

Alice asked, "Did you see anything of yours?"

"What kind of a question is that?" asked Grace.

"Didn't you hear me? His nickname is Tom Take," Godwin said to her. "Because he finds things, sometimes before people have lost them."

"Tom Take," said Cherie, frowning. "I've heard him called that, but isn't that also the name of a character in a children's book?"

"No, a character in a comic strip, *Little Orphan Annie*, from back in the thirties." For reasons that no one, not even he, understood, Godwin was a fan of old radio shows, old cartoons, old movies, and old comic strips.

Phil said, "I talked to some other people looking in the window. Morty Hanover said he recognized a rake he lost a couple months ago. Said his boy painted the handle with house paint and the rake in Tom's house had a handle painted the very same color."

Emily said, "Why don't they just unlock the doors and let people in to look for their stuff?"

Doris laughed. "And how would you keep people from just taking anything they want?"

Emily looked a little shocked at this jaundiced view of Excelsior's citizens, but then she nodded. "Well, I guess maybe you're right. But Morty should be able to get his rake back, at least."

Phil said, "Maybe he can buy it back at the garage sale."

Grace, interested, asked, "Who told you they're going to hold a garage sale?"

Phil snorted. "Well, they got to do something. That house is an epidemic waiting to start, the way it is."

Bershada asked, "Who is 'they'?"

"I don't know. Whoever winds up in charge," said Phil.

Betsy said, "The city will likely order Tom to clean it out."

Bershada said, "Since when is Tom one to take orders from anyone but his own self?"

That brought a chorus of agreement from everyone who had ever had anything to do with Thomas "Take" Riordan.

"So when do you think the power will come back on out here?" Godwin asked, bringing a fresh cup of coffee to Bershada, a handsome African American woman with dark skin, shapely lips, and a narrow, low-bridged nose. Her hair was covered with a deep red hat shaped like a turban.

The rest of the Monday Bunch had departed, but she was still seated at the library table in Crewel World, doing some hand stitching. Betsy was in the back, brewing a new urn of coffee.

Bershada was working on hemming a thick square of fabric about eleven inches on a side but with a deep, round indentation in the middle. "And what is that thing, anyway, a quilt square? And are you going to be able to make it flat, or is it ruined?"

"It's supposed to be shaped like this," said Bershada, holding it up with both hands cupped underneath. "When you heat up soup or stew in the microwave, you put the bowl in this, so you don't have to use pot holders to take it out. Plus, it keeps the soup warm while you eat it. Plus, if the soup runs over, it doesn't get all over the inside of the microwave. My friend Karen showed me how to make one, but I don't know where she got the pattern."

"Say, that's clever!" said Godwin, putting the mug of coffee in front of Bershada. He was a slim, handsome fellow, his blond hair a little enhanced, his skin a little smoother and fresher than nature intended at his age, which was coming up on thirty. "May I have a closer look?"

"Of course." Bershada tucked the needle across a corner and handed him the fabric square. He felt its thickness, about that of a pot holder, between his thumb and forefinger. She was using brightly colored material in a printed pattern of turtles and hedgehogs on the top side, and a deep, solid blue on the underside. Darts going from the corners toward the middle made it dished.

"What's the material?" he asked.

"A hundred percent cotton," she replied. "With the thinnest cotton batting available in between. You have to use cotton because artificial fabrics melt in the microwave."

"Could you make me one? I'm not all that fond of handwork, and we don't have a sewing machine."

"I'm going to make a batch of them to sell at our church's Christmas fair. This is my practice piece."

"Great, put me down for one—no, two—and bring them to me here." Godwin didn't go to church except for weddings. "Now, back to my original question: When do you think they're going to get busy here in town now? How long are we going to be kept freezing in the dark?" He looked around. "Well, in every other place but here. Rafael and I may bring our favorite blankies over tonight if the power's still out in town."

"I talked to the mayor, and he says it's possible we won't get electricity back in Excelsior until late tomorrow or even the day after. There's power out all over the county—in several counties, in fact. They're working day and night, but they'll bring the most densely populated areas back on line first, so that must mean people in Minneapolis are first in line and people out in the country are going to be without power for a week."

"Well, that's sucky," said Godwin. "Fair, but sucky for farmers. Especially the one who put his generator up for auction."

"They may call in people from upstate or even down in Iowa to help get it done sooner," said Betsy, coming out to the front. "Though there was similar damage down around Des Moines as a result of a storm like ours."

"How do you know that?" asked Bershada.

"Connor's paying attention to the radio news."

"That man of yours has been a real blessing, and not just to you!" declared Bershada. She checked her watch. "Uh-oh, I have to get on home. My grandson's got the grill fired up and we're cooking a lot of our meat from the freezer and having the neighbors in for a late picnic."

Godwin watched her go out the door and said to Betsy, "There's a great case of making lemonade when you're handed a whole bushel of lemons!"

# Chapter Five

✦ ✦ ✦

Tom Riordan figured that in a couple of days he'd be up and around. He was strong, still pretty young. If they'd just stop filling him up with those painkillers, he'd be all right.

Right now he was swimming in a dark sea of oxycodone. He knew he had a broken leg, but he'd seen people with broken legs walking around in a kind of boot. Why couldn't they give him a boot?

He was in a real mess, that he knew. He remembered a tree falling into his bedroom—he was pretty sure that hadn't been a dream—trapping him in his bed, and someone refusing to lift the tree off him—and he thought maybe that someone was Sergeant Lars Larson. But maybe not, maybe that part was a dream. Lars Larson was normally a good man, less inclined than many to pick on him.

He needed to get back home, to lock his doors and keep people out.

Lots of people had come into his house—into his own private house! And now they knew about his things. His very own, valuable things. They'd pick up his things, move his things, handle them, maybe damage them.

Steal them.

How long had he been here? A day or two. Or maybe longer? Maybe days and days and days. Surely not so long as a month, but too long. He had to get out of here.

That might be hard to do. He knew it wasn't just a broken leg. Despite the shots and pills, he hurt in many places. His leg was the worst. Or maybe his head. And it even hurt to breathe.

They said he had to stay here. But he could lie in his own bed and set an alarm clock to remind him to take pills, couldn't he? He had an alarm clock; several of them, actually. Maybe more than several—numbers had never been Tom's strong suit.

On the other hand, this bed was really comfortable. He hadn't realized what an uncomfortable bed he owned until he woke up in this one. Maybe they'd give him this bed.

No, probably not.

Maybe he could somehow take this bed and sneak it over to his own house. But there would be no way to get it up the stairs, so he'd have to camp out in his living room.

Though his living room was already crowded with his things.

His things. He could just see people walking through his house right now, picking up his things, handling his things, breaking his things.

Stealing his things.

He had to get out of here.

He could stay at home, take the pills they kept giving him. Set an alarm clock so he'd know when to take the next one. Couldn't they figure that out?

He needed to go home and run those people out of his house.

Those people were taking his things.

Maybe he could figure out a way to take this really comfortable bed home with him.

He was smart. He could think of a way.

His head hurt.

His leg hurt.

But maybe . . . sure.

Meanwhile . . . sleep awhile . . .

THERE were five people sitting around the oval table in one of the hospital's smaller meeting rooms.

"The one good thing about this case is that Mr. Riordan has health insurance," said Mr. White, the hospital administrator. "It's not really first-class insurance, but he's got solid catastrophic coverage. He was in good physical condition for a man his age when this happened, and it looks as if he'll make a good recovery. But"—he raised a forefinger in warning—"mentally, he's shaky. He doesn't understand how badly he was injured and insists he can finish healing at home. Even with a full-time nurse, which he's very unlikely to hire, I wouldn't release him just yet. And anyway, his house is not fit for human habitation."

"How about a nursing home or rehab center?" suggested Ms. Crowley, the RN in charge of his care.

"No," said Dr. Vandermay, Riordan's physician. "He insists he must go to his house, to protect it. He thinks thieves are eager to enter and steal his belongings."

Judi Mormon, the hospital's social worker, spoke up. "Mr. Riordan is a collector," she said, "or, as they're sometimes called, a junker or hoarder. I spoke with a psychiatrist who is knowledgeable about these cases. I told him that the team who rescued him reported that every room of that house is packed with junk. I spoke with Mr. Riordan myself, and he claims to know every item, where it came from, and how much it's worth. He's very symptomatic, according to Dr. Morrison. The house is probably unsafe; it needs to be emptied out, fumigated, washed down, and painted. In all likelihood, it will require rewiring and replumbing, too. But Mr. Riordan says it's fine and he has no plan to either fix it or sell it."

Dr. Vandermay said, "We can't possibly allow this patient to go back into that house until it's safe for him to live there."

Nurse Crowley said, "I can say with complete confidence, and in agreement with Judi, that he thinks his house is fine the way it is—well, except he plans to sue the neighbor whose tree fell on his house to force her to repair his roof. And he thinks she'll be glad to do it, because she's a friend."

"That right there tells you his state of mind," said Mr. White. "He needs someone to take the responsibility for his continuing care and to straighten out his domicile."

That suggestion brought immediate agreement.

Then Nurse Crowley said, "All right, who?"

"Doesn't he have any family?" asked Mr. White.

Ms. Mormon said, "No immediate family. He lists as next of kin a cousin who lives in Indiana. Her name is

Valentina . . ." She looked for and found a page in a thick file. "Shipp. Spelled with two *p*'s."

"Is this Shipp woman in charge of his trust?" asked Mr. White. "I assume he must have one. His family must know about his situation."

"He does have a trust, you're right," said Ms. Mormon. "But it's handled by an attorney in Excelsior, Jim Penberthy."

Mr. White asked, "Has Attorney Penberthy been notified of Mr. Riordan's condition?"

Ms. Mormon smiled. "I would think he knows by now. Riordan is a well-known figure in Excelsior, and the town has an excellent grapevine. On the other hand, I don't think he's been officially notified."

"What about Mrs. Shipp?" asked Dr. Vandermay.

"Unless Mr. Riordan contacted her—which is unlikely—she has no idea," said Ms. Mormon.

"In that case, it appears we have some communicating to do," said Mr. White. "Ms. Mormon, I'm appointing you to find out if Mrs. Shipp would be willing to serve as a conservator, and if not, who else Attorney Penberthy would recommend. I want you to expedite this, if you will, and report back to us via e-mail as soon as you have a name or names. This meeting is adjourned."

# Chapter Six

❖ ❖ ❖

Valentina Shipp was beyond tired. But her cousin, Tommy, was in deep doo-doo and needed her help. As in *now*. She pressed the accelerator down just a little bit more and glanced in the rearview mirror to make sure no state trooper was coming up behind her.

She was a tall woman in her early fifties, slat thin, with straight brown hair that had become mixed with gray of late, large, dark, intelligent eyes, a wide mouth under a proud nose, and lots of dark freckles. She wore a shapeless dark blue cardigan under a thin black Windbreaker, brown wool slacks, and tan desert boots. Her car was a fifteen-year-old compact with a barely functioning muffler and windshield wipers that needed replacement.

She was on the last leg of the journey, heading northwest on I-94, nearly done with Wisconsin, the Minnesota border less than ten minutes away if she didn't get stopped for speeding.

She had driven all night; the sun was giving pink warning of its rising into a clear sky. In a field near the highway a huge tree was lying on its side, its roots making cartoon-octopus silhouettes against the glowing horizon.

*That's right*, she told herself. There had been a big windstorm, with lots of rain, last week. That's why the tree had fallen on Tommy's house.

Dear old Tommy, the only cousin left. The only cousin that she knew of, at least. Her family members had a habit of dropping off the vine, either by moving away and not letting her know where they went, or by dying.

In a little less than ten minutes, Valentina found herself at the top of a great hill, with a broad river at the bottom. The river was, she knew, the Saint Croix, and marked the border between Wisconsin and Minnesota. Minneapolis and Saint Paul were just up the way. In Minneapolis there was a hospital called Hennepin County Medical Center, and in the hospital was her cousin, Tommy, poor thing.

She had a reservation at a cheap motel on the north edge of downtown in what she suspected was a rough neighborhood. But she was not afraid of rough neighborhoods; her house, without changing its location, had gone from being on the wrong side of the tracks to the right side and back again, and she had lived there serenely through it all. She smiled. Well, maybe not always serenely. Successfully, let's say.

The motel was not quite as bad as she feared. It was clean and one of the two beds was not uncomfortable. She took a shower, changed her clothes, and set off for the Hennepin County Medical Center, stopping at a McDonald's on the way for their largest cup of coffee and an egg and sausage McMuffin to go.

KASSIE Christianson waited in the lobby at the main entrance of HCMC for Valentina Shipp. Kassie had been Tom Riordan's social worker for several years, and brought into the recent mix by Judi Mormon. She was a short, slim African American woman, with short cropped natural hair, very large hoop earrings, and a no-nonsense face.

Kassie had spoken to Valentina on the phone, so she knew to look for a tall, thin woman with brown hair and wearing a tan sweater.

But she hesitated before stepping forward when she saw Valentina stride into the lobby like an inspector determined to find fault with the place. Valentina was wearing low-heeled suede boots, loose-fitting tan trousers, and a bulky tan sweater that looked hand-knit. Her light hair—brown mixed with gray?—was pulled carelessly to the nape of her neck with a rubber band. Her broad mouth was pressed into a straight line, and her dark, shapely eyebrows were pulled together forbiddingly over a hawklike nose.

Kassie could see a strong family resemblance to Tom Riordan, and since she'd first been introduced to him in the hospital, his face often showed a stronger emotion than he was actually feeling, so maybe Valentina shared that trait with him and wasn't feeling as aggressive as she looked.

"Ms. Shipp?" Kassie said, moving to intercept the woman's long strides.

The woman stopped short. "Yeah—are you Ms. Christianson?" Her voice was thin with a hint of twang in it. The tone was, however, mild rather than assertive.

"Yes. Could we sit down for a few minutes? I want to talk to you about your cousin, Mr. Riordan."

Valentina looked around at the various upholstered chairs and settees grouped in clusters around the large room. About half the groupings were occupied by one or more people. "Okay," she said, and smoothly led the way to an unoccupied cluster of four chairs a few steps away.

She sat down as gracefully as she walked—Kassie wondered if she was a trained dancer, or had been one in her youth.

"How is he?" asked Valentina.

"Doing well. The doctor thinks he'll recover completely—but it will take time. His right leg was broken in two places, and he's suffered some broken ribs as well. Plus he has a concussion, a bruised liver, and other internal injuries. He's not a young man, but he was in good health before the accident. It's just going to take some time."

"But he's not going home anytime soon."

"No. He's going to need some therapy on that leg. And . . ." Kassie hesitated, then plunged in. "I'm afraid his house is in very bad shape. He appears to be a . . ."

"He's a junker, right?"

"Junker?"

"He collects things. Like his dad, and his grandad. He buys things at garage sales, and will even take home things that other people throw out. Right?"

"So you know about that. And yes, but it's possibly worse

36

than you think. Every room of his house is full of things he's . . . collected."

"Oh yes?" But Valentina didn't sound surprised.

"That's not all," Kassie said.

"No?" Valentina's dark eyes looked directly at the social worker.

"The house itself is in bad repair. It's not just his bedroom—which is open to the elements where the tree came through. The kitchen and bathroom are infested with mold, and I believe the plumbing needs to be completely redone. Until it's been fixed, Mr. Riordan will not be permitted to live in the house." Kassie felt awful to be delivering such bad news; Ms. Shipp looked as if she had been struck in the face.

But she did not erupt; instead, her eyes closed for about thirty seconds while she seemed to be struggling to absorb what she was hearing. Kassie wondered if she would change her mind about helping her cousin.

"I'm sorry," said Kassie at last, trying for a reaction.

"Me, too," said Valentina, opening her eyes. Then, typically, she went on the attack. "You're his social worker. How did you allow the house to get into such a state?"

"Well, for one thing, he absolutely refused to allow anyone to come inside the place. He said he had some valuable things in there and didn't want anyone to know about them because he couldn't afford to insure them. I didn't exactly believe him—about having things of great value—but I wanted to respect his privacy. He's a nice man, but . . . sensitive. I didn't want to make him angry, I didn't want to hurt his feelings." Kassie was ashamed, because the excuses she was offering were pretty lame. Sometimes—often, actually—it was her job to hurt some feelings. She had let Tom Riordan down. Perhaps if her caseload had been lighter, she would have paid more attention. But Mr. Riordan had been polite and sweet and only a little strange, so she'd been content to visit him as scheduled, only at a restaurant or in the library or at her office rather than in his home. "I'm sorry."

Valentina sighed, trying to cool her temper. She looked around the big room, glanced at the nearest television set hanging from the ceiling, then looked at Kassie. "What are you expecting me to do?"

"What we're hoping you will do, first of all, is talk to him. Tell him what his doctor has been trying to tell him, convince him that he really can't go home right now because his injuries need more care, and because his home is not fit to be lived in."

Valentina looked at her some more and said, "What else?" Kassie almost smiled, because this woman was savvier than she'd hoped. Yes, there was more, or why had they summoned her all the way from her home in Muncie? They could have told her all this on the phone.

"Well, something needs to be done about that house, but I don't have the authority to do anything unless he agrees." She held up a hand against an objection she was sure was coming. "Nor does the person in charge of his finances."

"But I sure don't, either."

"Not right now, you don't. But there's a way you can get the authority. It's called an emergency conservatorship, and it's a whole lot easier to get if you're the next of kin. It's a legal option, it needs to be done by a judge after a hearing.

My understanding is that it can be done quickly, but the person to talk to about getting one is the man in charge of Tom's trust. He's an attorney named James Penberthy. His office is in Excelsior."

Again there fell a silence while Valentina studied Kassie's face. Kassie tried to look as sincere and hopeful and friendly as she could, while Valentina successfully concealed what she was thinking.

"Let me talk to Tommy first," she said at last.

V ALENTINA slipped into the hospital room feeling a little wary. She had not seen her cousin in years and wasn't sure of her welcome.

Tommy was asleep, or seemed to be. There was a big bandage on one side of his face, but she recognized him right away: the peaked nose, the dark freckles, the wide mouth, pursed a little in sleep. There was a deep crease between his thin, dark eyebrows; that was something new. Of course, he was somewhere around sixty-three, so it was time he got a few lines on his face.

The covers on his bed were awry, exposing the huge, complicated bandage on his right leg. His foot was bare, the toes lumpish and the nails needing to be cut. There were bruises on his hands and arms, some of them scabby. He looked shrunken; he must have lost weight—or maybe not. He'd been a skinny kid so why shouldn't he be a skinny old man?

She approached the side of his bed, which was cranked into a half-sitting position. "Tommy," she called softly.

His nose twitched and he reached up to rub it, but his eyes stayed closed.

"Tommy, it's me, Val. Are you awake?"

"Mph, yuh?" muttered Tommy. "Whosit?"

"Me, Val. I've come to take care of you."

"Who?" The dark eyes opened and wandered around a bit before coming to look up at her. "Oh, it's you, Val. I was just hopin' you might come." He swallowed thickly. "Can you take me home?"

"No, you got to stay for a while longer. You were hurt bad by that tree falling on you."

He smiled. "Yeah, that ol' tree did a job, all right. On me *and* my house. Say, Val, can you go out there an' check on it for me? I got this feelin' people been goin' in there and messing with my things."

"You still living in that brick house your dad left you? Out in Excelsior?"

"Well, sure, where else would I be livin'?"

"How should I know?" she asked, sounding aggrieved— her default position when she didn't know what to say. "You never write nor call."

"Ain't got nuthin' to say," he grumbled.

"That never stopped your tongue before!"

"Now lookie here, you gonna get an attitude, you can just go away!"

"All right, all right, let's not get our jammies in a wad," she said, gentling her tone. "'Cause now we do have something to say to each other. This lady I talked to, her name's Christianson—"

"I know who she is," interrupted Tommy.

Valentina bit down hard on her temper. "That's right, you do. Anyway, she says your house is a mess, a big mess."

"How does she know? Say, she been in there?" His expression hardened.

"Probably, probably. Or she's been talking to the people who have."

"Who all's been in there? They got no right! I keep my doors locked, how'd they get in?"

"Well, how were they supposed to get you out of there? Climb in a window?"

"Oh. Yeah. Well . . . Anyway, so what? They don't have to live in it. And it ain't that big a mess. An' there's good stuff in there, valuable stuff!"

"Really?" Valentina tried to turn a grimace into a smile. "That's your opinion. Hers is different. And her opinion is what counts; she's your social worker, your connection with the law, the person who's supposed to be in charge of you. She says the house ain't fit for human habitation, and that means they won't let you move back in there until it gets cleaned up to meet their standards."

"Why'd she decide that? I thought she liked me. I thought she was on my side!"

"She may or may not like you, but she's on nobody's side but the county's, you ought to know that. None of those folks are your friends. You're a job to her, not a friend, nor hardly even a real person. Her job is to make you behave, and you let that house get into a real state, she says, an' that it's got to be fixed. There's a law against filling up a house with junk." This was the hard part of Tommy's problems. Of all the problems in the world she most emphatically did not want, an entanglement with the law was number one.

"Well, how'm I gonna fix it when I'm laid up like I am?"

Valentina leaned closer and smiled. "They're gonna let me fix it for you."

Tommy fell silent for a few seconds, staring back into her eyes. "I can't figure if that's good or bad."

"Why, it's good, Tommy, it's real good! I'm family, right? I'll make sure not to harm you or your things." Val smiled as sweetly as she could. "Like they say, A spoonful of sugar helps the medicine go down."

And Tommy bought it, if grudgingly. "Well . . . Okay."

"Good, that's a good cousin. Now you can just relax and get yourself healed. I'll go take a look at it and see what has to be done."

"You come back here real soon—like once a day—you hear me? Tell me ever single thing you're doing out there. Don't throw nothin'—*nothin'*—away without askin' me first. I'm real serious about that."

"I hear you. And I promise, I'll come over here to the hospital and tell you everything I'm doing. Okay?"

Val wasn't quite superstitious enough to cross her fingers behind her back. But she thought about it, hard.

# Chapter Seven

### ◆ ◆ ◆

VALENTINA sat behind the wheel of her shabby little car, thinking. Tommy's house was in far, far worse condition than she'd anticipated, even after the description Ms. Christianson had given her.

Most noticeable, of course, was the junk. Every single room in the two-bedroom house, including the bathroom and the basement, was overloaded with stuff. None of the furniture in the living and dining room was even visible, much less usable, under the burden of things. Of stuff. Most of it, at first look, was without value—broken, rusty, torn, parts missing, you name it; it seemed as if every item had some problem or another.

But there were other problems that were not so obvious. There was a smell of mold, the kind that infests a house when there is water leaking inside the walls or under the floors. And there was visible mold on the wall tiles in the bathroom. When Valentina pressed a testing finger on a tile above the bathtub faucet, because it looked as if the grout was loose, the tile came off into her hand. Startled, she had dropped it and it broke into three pieces in the stained and dirty tub.

But perhaps the worst thing she saw was on the outside of the house, which she noticed when she stood alongside it. (*And why pink?* she wondered. Why on earth did Tommy think pink was a good color for a house?) The wall was crooked and bulging out near the bottom about halfway along, the bricks pushed just noticeably out of place. Not by a lot, but it was definitely crooked. When she looked down the other side, she saw more bricks pushed out a few inches, again near the bottom. That indicated a problem that probably couldn't be fixed with a little tuck-pointing. It was surprising that the house had not collapsed when the tree crashed into its roof.

Val put her head down on the steering wheel and closed her eyes. What was she going to tell Tommy? She had promised him she'd make his house livable again. She had promised Ms. Christianson, too. But this house had far, far, *far* more serious problems than she'd thought, well beyond her abilities. Maybe beyond anyone's abilities.

She started up the car. She was just too tired to think clearly about this. She would go back to her motel room and go to bed. Maybe tomorrow, after she'd caught up on her sleep, things wouldn't look so hopeless.

THE next morning, over breakfast at Denny's, things still looked hopeless, but at least Valentina felt less dismayed. She had faced seemingly hopeless dilemmas before, and, somehow, she'd found her way through them. So there was probably a way through this one.

She got James Penberthy's office phone number from the telephone operator—there was still a directory service via phone, which was reassuring to a troglodyte like herself. He said he could see her today at eleven if she cared to come out to Excelsior.

She did.

Penberthy's one-man office was on Water Street, the main street of the little town. There was a long, narrow reception area—no receptionist—and the room he worked in featured old-fashioned wood paneling, with the usual bookshelves filled with tan and maroon bound volumes. A watercolor painting of ducks flying over a marsh was the only decorative touch.

Mr. Penberthy was a man of indeterminate age with light brown hair cut short and intelligent blue eyes. His smile was pleasant, his handshake firm. He wore a business suit of conservative gray wool and a light blue silk tie. He did not offer Valentina coffee but sat down behind his plain wooden desk and got right to business.

"You are related by blood to Mr. Riordan?" he asked.

"Yes, his father and my mother were brother and sister. They're both gone now. His mother and father divorced, and she moved away, abandoned Tommy when he was ten or eleven. Remarried, I think, but then she kind of disappeared. I don't know where she might be." She paused to take a breath. "I'm Tommy's closest relative—in fact, as far as I know, I'm his only blood relative."

"I see. That would make you his next of kin, as he has claimed."

"That's right. My mother, his aunt, committed suicide nine years ago."

"Oh, how sad," said Mr. Penberthy, though he appeared more shocked than sorrowful. He looked at her as if to encourage her to go on.

"She thought she had cancer," Valentina said. "I don't know where she got that idea. Almost certainly not from a doctor; she was always scared to go to a doctor, afraid of what he might find wrong with her. My dad had left her right after she had me, and all she ever told me about him was that he was like a rat abandoning a sinking ship. I never could figure out what she meant by that—" Valentina pressed her lips together in an effort to stop herself from talking some more. Surely Mr. Penberthy did not need to know all this about her family history!

He continued to look at her with interest, but she nevertheless stayed silent to see what he would say.

"What you're telling me is very helpful, I think it gives me some insight into Mr. Riordan's personality."

Valentina shot him a hard look. *Was that some kind of slam?* she wondered.

But Penberthy continued, oblivious to her concerns. "Mr. Riordan is an interesting man, intelligent about some things and clever with his hands. He tells funny stories. I've enjoyed our conversations."

"What does he do to keep himself busy?" Valentina asked. "Has he got some kind of job?"

"Not a regular job. He often volunteers for town projects, such as our annual fall festival, Apple Days, and our summer festival, Art in the Park. He works hard, though once he feels he's done enough, he will vanish from the scene, usually without notice. There is some . . . lack of follow-through in him, an inability to make long-term plans. I believe the current jargon would have it that he is 'behaviorally challenged.'" He looked inquiringly at Valentina again.

She nodded. "He was an odd kid, and he grew into what my mother called a queer duck. But without a mean bone in his body."

Penberthy nodded back. "Yes, that sums him up in my estimation, too."

"So what are we going to do about him?" Valentina asked.

"I'm afraid the responsibility to solve this problem will fall primarily on you."

"Tommy isn't going to appreciate my help, you know."

Penberthy hesitated, then said with an apologetic smile, "I'm afraid we're counting on that. Those of us permanently responsible for him need to stay on his good side. By pushing off this difficult, but temporary, task onto you, we can stay in his good graces, and you can go home and get away from his wrath."

"So it's okay with you that Tommy will hate me for the rest of his life?" There was a bitter tone in her voice.

"I don't think that will happen. He'll be angry with you for a while, but when he gets his house back, cleaned up and in good order, a house the city cannot condemn, it will occur to him that you did him a great big favor."

Exasperated, Valentina threw her arms wide. "Have you seen that house?"

"No, he didn't allow me into the place. In fact, as far as I know, he didn't allow *anyone* into the place."

"I'm not talking about the inside, which is a filthy and unsanitary pigsty," Valentina said. "I'm talking about the outside. It's not just the mashed roof, either. The walls are crooked, bulging near the ground. That's probably caused by a serious problem with the foundation. Go over and have a look at it, Mr. Penberthy!"

He stared at her, his eyes at first startled, then sad. "I am ashamed to tell you that I have never gone to Mr. Riordan's house—have not so much as looked at it while passing by—or I might have noticed that it was getting into a very bad state. I'm glad that you came to see me and made me aware that things have gotten badly out of control.

"But we're moving at last in the right direction. With your help, we can get an honest assessment of the state of his house. Maybe it will even be possible to get it back in good order by making repairs."

Reluctantly, Valentina reined in her temper. "Kassie Christianson—do you know her?"

"Not well, but I have long known she's Mr. Riordan's social worker. Last time I talked with her, she mentioned your name."

"She says I should get an emergency conservatorship. She says then I would have the . . . the *authority* to go into Tommy's house and clean it out. But I don't want to make Tommy mad by throwing away some things he's really attached to—though I think he thinks he's attached to everything in the house."

"How much does it matter to you, since eventually you will be returning to your home in Indiana?"

Valentina sighed. "Do you know he plans to sue his neighbor over that tree that fell on his house? He wants her to pay for fixing his roof. And he's not mad at her. I'm not sure what he'd do to me if I made him mad. So I really don't want to give him a legal reason to be mad at me."

"If you get that conservatorship, there's no legal way he can stop you doing what needs to be done. And, let me tell you this: If Hennepin County condemns the house, it will be cleared out by county employees. They will be far less motivated to be careful with Mr. Riordan's possessions, and far more likely to enrage him by their actions. And he can tie things up in the courts for a long time. On the other hand, he will have no grounds to sue you. You can go back home with a clear conscience and no legal vulnerability."

Valentina sat silent for a full minute. Then she said, "All right, tell me what I need to do."

T HIS guy Penberthy wasn't a bad man, not really. He was just trying to get something fixed that never should have needed to be fixed in the first place, and it was partly his fault that things had come to such a pass. Valentina wasn't the sort of person who bad-mouthed people in the legal profession (or, for that matter, the police)—at least, not out loud—but she generally avoided them whenever possible. In her never humble opinion, they tended to be nosy and uppity.

However, Penberthy had kindly—and patiently—explained to her the path to an emergency conservatorship and said he would help her fill out the paperwork and represent her in court when she sought one. He was sure there would be no problem getting one but insisted they should begin the process as soon as possible.

So they spent half an hour filling out the form—which wasn't complicated—and Valentina gave him the name of the motel where she was staying so he could contact her when he'd made an appointment for the hearing. He'd expressed surprise that she didn't have a cell phone, to which she'd responded, "I never felt the need to have a leash on me." To her surprise, that made him laugh.

Then he had given her some good advice. First, and right away, she should find out who Tommy's friends were in Excelsior and talk with them. Second, she should recruit—a cool word, *recruit*—a working party from among them. Third, as soon as the conservatorship was approved, she should go into the house and start sorting things into three piles: valuables (to be sold or kept), good but useless stuff (to be donated to charity), and worthless (to be thrown away). There was going to be a series of quarrels if Valentina were to ask Tommy about the disposition of valuable or good stuff, so Penberthy's advice, to present Tommy with a fait accompli on her way out of town, was probably sound. She smiled to herself in the car; he had been ready to define the term, and she surprised him by knowing what it meant.

Judging by her first trip into the house, Valentina thought that Penberthy might have given her a fourth piece of good advice: to rent a Dumpster to hold that third bunch of things.

But Mr. Penberthy hadn't told her how to connect with Tommy's friends in town. Perhaps, since he was such a good thinker, she would call him and ask. Meanwhile, it was lunchtime.

There were some nice upscale restaurants on Water Street, but her purse was slender and her tastes plebeian, so she drove a few blocks farther and found a bar-restaurant called the Barleywine. The hanging sign was artsy, a painted barrel with a bouquet of wheat—no, it must be barley—stuffed in it, but there was a simple neon sign in the window: EAT. That reminded Valentina of signs on cheap cafés from her youth, where the food was unhealthy but plentiful and comforting.

She found a parking space and went in.

All right, it wasn't as shaggy as she had thought it might be at first glance. The floor looked like real stone cut into uneven slabs, which she knew was more expensive to install than even-sized blocks, and the bar was beautiful carved wood. And, most curious of all, the wall behind the bar was made all of glass, through which she could see huge steel cylinders that reminded her of a factory. But the smell that permeated the space, besides beer, was of low-cost fried food.

The restaurant's three booths were constructed of old-fashioned dark wood, each with a tall pole fitted with brass coat hooks. Nice—or as the kids say, sweet!

There were perhaps ten people in the place, six of them seated at the bar, the others crowded into a booth. They were varied in dress and age. Nobody was drunk or loud; the juke box was playing a big band tune.

Valentina chose the booth nearest the back and had hardly gotten around to the short, laminated menu before she was approached by a slim woman with long dark hair, lightly streaked with gray, and very intense dark eyes. The woman was dressed in a black turtleneck sweater under a tan cloth apron printed with the word *Barleywine*.

"Would you like to begin with a beverage?" she asked.

Jesting, Valentina said, "I think I'll have a taste of whatever you're brewing in those tanks back there."

"You'd have to wait a few days. The beer we're making right now isn't ready yet."

Valentina stared up at the woman, whose expression had turned humorous. "Oh, this place is one of those whaddya call 'em, microbreweries."

"That's right. On the other side of the menu is a list of what we're currently offering."

Valentina turned the menu over and found a list of beverages, including six beers, none of them a brand she recognized. "All homemade, right?" she said, and the woman nodded. "Well, what do you recommend?"

"What kind of beer do you normally drink?"

Valentina drew up her shoulders a little and confessed, "Actually, I don't much like beer. I'm more a lemonade and fruit juice sort of person."

"We have lemonade and fruit juices, too."

Valentina looked down at the rest of the beverage offerings on the menu's back side and, mindful of her wallet, said, "I'll just have water, thanks. And a BLT with chips."

"Coming right up." As the woman turned away, Valentina admired her dark hair, which was pulled into a very long braid down her back. She'd always wanted long hair like that but could never get it more than a little past her shoulders.

While she waited for her order, she began to eavesdrop on the quartet in the booth up the way. She couldn't hear everything, because they were speaking quietly and the music interfered a little bit.

". . . couldn't believe she repeated that to him!" one was saying.

"She's always been the type . . ." replied another.

". . . shouldn't have told her, you know what a . . . is."

"*I* heard he went to Phoebe and . . ."

"Well, can you blame him?"

Valentina smiled to herself. It sounded as if Excelsior was a whole lot like Muncie. She was tempted to go over and introduce herself to see if any of them might be a friend of Tommy's, but she couldn't think of an excuse to barge in. And, to be honest, she wasn't sure she'd like what they might have to say about her cousin. She was not in a mood to hear him bad-mouthed.

But he must have friends, or why would Mr. Penberthy have suggested she round them up?

A plate with a big sandwich on toasted whole wheat bread, ornamented with a lot of potato chips, suddenly landed in front of her. Valentina looked up and saw the dark-eyed woman studying her.

"Are you visiting family here in Excelsior?" she asked.

"Sort of. I'm here to help out my cousin, Tommy Riordan."

"Ah, I thought your face reminded me of someone," said the woman.

"Do I look like him?" asked Valentina, surprised.

"Yes, you do."

"Huh."

The waitress laughed. "I'm told my daughter looks a lot like me, though neither one of us can see it."

"Do you know Tommy?" asked Valentina.

"Sure. I think just about everyone in town knows Tom."

"Really? Are you sure?"

"Certainly. He's a friendly man, not hard to like. Why, is there something you're wanting from people who know Tom?"

Valentina blinked at the woman's keen perception. "Well, yes. I'm going to be clearing out Tommy's house, and I can't afford to hire a company to do it. So I need to connect with Tommy's friends who might be willing to help."

The woman frowned just a little bit and took a tiny step back.

Valentina said, "But I've been advised by Tommy's attorney, James Penberthy, to do this."

"Oh, well, that's different. If Jim thinks it's a good idea, then that's what you should do."

"The problem is, I don't know anyone in town, so I don't know how to connect with Tommy's friends."

"Are you staying here in Excelsior?"

"No, I've got a motel room over in Minneapolis."

"Hmm, that's going to make it a bit harder. Could you possibly relocate to Excelsior, even temporarily?"

"Well . . . to tell the truth, I can't afford the room rates out here. This business caught me kind of on the hop."

The woman said, "There's a little motel in Shorewood, which borders Excelsior, very good for the budget conscious." She named a rate that was actually a couple of dollars cheaper than what Valentina was paying now.

Valentina said, "Is it . . . I mean . . . is it . . . okay?"

"It's clean and quiet. No tubs in the bathrooms, but the showers have plenty of hot water. Ask for extra towels; theirs you can just about see through." The woman touched the side of her narrow nose with a slim forefinger while she thought and nodded. "They'll offer you a discount if you're staying for more than a week."

Valentina smiled. "Thanks."

She paid for her meal, left an adequate tip, and asked the waitress for the address and phone number of the motel. "What's your name?" she asked.

"Leona Cunningham. And I'm one of Tom Riordan's friends."

Valentina looked around the place. No one seemed to be signaling for service, so she decided to seize the opportunity. "Can I talk to you for a minute?" she asked Leona.

"All right, but make yourself comfortable, at least. Have a seat at the bar. Would you like a cup of coffee?"

Valentina hesitated—she didn't want to pay for something she didn't really need—but Leona added, "For free, of course."

How uncanny, reading something—accurately—in her face so easily.

"Thank you, yes, a cup of coffee would be nice. Just black, please."

The coffee came in a thick, heavy, old-fashioned mug designed to keep its contents hot. Valentina smiled as she picked it up; it was another reminder of the cafés of her youth. She took a sip. The brew was strong and flavorful. She hadn't had a good cup of coffee, not like this, in a long time.

She put the mug down, caressing it with two fingers.

"So, what did you want to talk to me about?" Leona asked.

"You said you were Tommy's friend. What do you know about him?"

"I don't think I understand the question," Leona said politely.

"Well," Valentina tried to clarify what she was asking. "He's my cousin, but I don't really know him. When he was a little boy he spent a couple of summers with us, but after that I hardly ever saw him. He's ten years older than I am, so I guess there wasn't any real reason for us to be close. And he was kind of a strange little boy—" Valentina stopped and gave a hopeful look at Leona.

Leona shrugged. "He's an interesting man," she said. "He has no enemies, but not everyone likes him, because he's still a little strange."

"What do you think, is he backward? You know, slow?"

"No, I don't think it's that. He seems to have some form of Asperger's, although he functions reasonably well. He's friendly enough, but he can be socially awkward. He knows everyone's name, however, and he loves to listen to gossip." Leona hesitated. "He also, on occasion, will take things that do not belong to him," she added. She looked inquiringly at Valentina.

Valentina laughed. "Is he still doing that?" she said. "We came to call him 'Klepto' when he stayed with us. He was a teenager at the time. After he went home the first time, Mom and I went into his room to clean it and found our missing stuff under the bed. The next summer, he did it again, and he'd gotten better at sneaking. It was never anything really valuable—we didn't own anything valuable back then—just things like Mom's thimble and my new sandals. And he didn't break them or light candles to them, or slobber on them. Just took them and hid them."

Leona said with a smile, "And as an adult he does the same thing."

"You mean, all those things in his house are *stolen*?"

"Oh, no, no, not at all! He buys some things, some things are given to him, and he brings home other objects that people have thrown away. A lot of people around here know about his collector's habit—just not that it has gotten so far out of hand."

"And Mr. Penberthy has put the responsibility of fixing this problem on me."

"Not completely. You don't have to fix Tom—nobody can fix Tom. All you have to do is fix his house. And you'd have to do that anyway, because look at how leaving it to him and Hennepin County has worked out."

"Yeah, the government is not your friend," sighed Valentina, and the two laughed, but not happily.

"So how do I connect with these people who Mr. Penberthy said would volunteer to help me?"

"When you get yourself relocated to Shorewood, get me your room number, and I'll hand it around so people can get in touch with you. Meanwhile I'll talk your problem up. Back when this place of mine was called the Waterfront Café, its nickname was Gossip Central, and it's still a good place to spread the word."

"Oh, so this place belongs to you."

"That's right. Another place you might consider visiting is Crewel World."

Valentina's eyebrows rose sharply. "Cruel World? What,

a store where you buy whips and handcuffs?" She did not think enlisting the aid of sadists was a good idea.

"Crewel—C-R-E-W-E-L, as in needlework."

"Oh. Of course. I should have known. Whew!"

Leona chuckled. "We have our dark side, but that's not it. Anyway, drop in there, introduce yourself, and ask the owner—her name is Betsy Devonshire—to pass the word."

Leona gave Valentina directions to the shop. "Go down the street toward the lake," she said, "just the one block. Then turn right and look for the sign on your right."

# Chapter Eight

❖ ❖ ❖

CREWEL World was the middle of three stores in an old, two-story redbrick building. On one side of it stood a used-book store, and on the other side a deli. Each had a big front window of plate glass with a narrow, diamond-paned window stretched above it. The needlework shop had a hanging wooden signboard painted with a needle pulling thread that spelled out *Crewel World*.

Luckily, there was a parking space right in front. Valentina pulled into it, then got out of the car into the bright September sunlight. She shivered a little, despite the sun, because there was a sharp chill in the air and her Windbreaker was inadequate against it. The previous day had been overcast, but at least it had been warm. "Almost feels like frost," she murmured to herself. Back home in Muncie the leaves were still on the trees and not even starting to turn. Here in Minnesota the season was far advanced.

She remembered what her cousin had scrawled on one of

his rare Christmas cards: *All thet is tween hear an the North Pole is a bob wire fence ha ha ha.*

Tommy never was good at spelling or grammar. On the other hand, his comment had been clever. And—she thrust her bare hands into her pockets—it had been right on the mark, too.

She stopped to look in the big front window of Crewel World, which had finished needlework projects displayed all over it. The theme seemed to be Christmas. Ugh, Christmas already? It wasn't even Halloween yet. There were samples, big and small, of needlework, but mostly big and mostly needlepoint. Valentina was not big on needlepoint, because the canvases it required were so expensive. Besides, for rich detail, she thought counted cross-stitch was the way to go. Like the piece in the window, right at eye level, which depicted a country cabin deep in snow with three deer looking at a Christmas tree in the cabin's window. The stitcher had used some sparkly white floss for the snow.

She noticed that there were no knitting models. Valentina loved to knit. Her house back in Muncie had knitted afghans on chairs and on the couch and bed. She had sweaters and mittens and shawls and table runners in wool and cotton and acrylic and blends, all of them knit by herself.

But wait a minute: Inside the shop she could see a counter, and on top of it sat a gorgeous fuzzy shawl and a sweater knit in a complex pattern.

Valentina drew a happy breath and went in.

As the door opened, she heard a silly tune on what sounded like a toy organ. Startled, she paused to listen. Wasn't that a song she recognized? She rather thought so but couldn't identify it.

From behind a spinner rack holding white cardboard squares of Very Velvet floss came a young man with blond hair and wide, innocent-looking blue eyes. He was dressed all in a medium brown, from his shoes to the thin, faintly shimmering sweater he wore. Silk? wondered Valentina.

"May I help you?" he asked.

"I'm looking for Betsy—uh—" Rats, she'd forgotten her last name.

"Devonshire?"

"Yes, that's right."

"She went to the post office to pick up a delivery. She should be back in a few minutes. Would you care to wait?"

"Yes, thanks." Casting about for something to say, Valentina asked, "Are you her husband?"

The young man's mouth fell open in surprised laughter. "Oh, my *dear*—!"

Enlightened, Valentina laughed back. "I guess not," she said.

"Not that she isn't a perfectly wonderful woman," the man hastened to say. "But . . . *que sera, sera*. Meanwhile, is there something I can show you?"

"I'm in town on . . . on business, I guess you'd say, but it's turning out I'll be doing a certain amount of sitting and waiting, and I need something to do with my hands . . ." She gestured eloquently.

"I know just what you mean. Waiting to be waited on, it's good to have some handwork with you. What kind of needlework are you most interested in?"

"Well, I like to knit, but the needles are too long and the ball of yarn too bulky to fit in this purse of mine—I don't want to have to buy a new knitting bag. I can't afford needlepoint and I'm too fussed right now to focus on counted cross-stitch. I used to crochet, but I'm not sure I remember how." She halted, embarrassed at this seeming attempt to anticipate and shoot down any suggestion he might make.

But he didn't seem to mind. He pressed a slim forefinger into the edge of his mouth, his head cocked a little sideways, and thought for a bit. Then he nodded once. "Crochet," he announced. "Once you know how to crochet, you can pick it up again very easily. It's just the thing. It will keep your fingers busy, and it takes just enough concentration to distract you from worry."

"But—"

"Just make squares and stitch the best ones into a scarf or, if you end up staying a long time, an afghan." He looked inquiringly at her.

But she refused to be drawn into any discussion of why she was in Excelsior. "All right, then, crochet it is. What do you have that won't empty my purse?"

He went at once to one of the big baskets scattered around the shop and pulled out a ball of bright yellow worsted-weight yarn that had its shabby original label—the one that had surrounded it back when it was a skein—safety-pinned to it.

"This is pure virgin wool," said the young man. "Betsy brought her other cat down here last week and he got into the yarn basket and killed three skeins before she could stop him."

Valentina smothered a laugh. "'Killed'?"

"He was trying to disembowel them." The young man

made a scratching motion with his fingers, his eyes alight with amusement.

Valentina released a laugh. Then she asked, "What do you mean, 'other cat'?"

"Here's the usual cat." He turned and gestured toward a chair at the far end of the long table in the middle of the room. Valentina took a step sideways and saw an enormous, mostly white cat lying on a powder blue cushion. Its head was raised, looking back at her with yellow eyes.

"That's Sophie. She's hoping you have something edible to share with her."

Valentina spread her hands. "Sorry," she said to the cat, and Sophie put her head down with a big, disappointed sigh.

The young man said, "The disemboweler is a Siamese named Thai. After that yarn incident, he's permanently banned from the shop."

"Small wonder. Now, how much is that beautiful yellow yarn?"

He named a price she would have expected to pay for cheap acrylic. "But this is wool, right?" she said.

"Yes, but it's been washed, so it's considered second-hand."

"I'll take it."

He said, "You'll need a crochet hook, too, right?"

"Yes, of course. In fact, give me a pair of them, size E—I lose small things, especially when I'm traveling. And do you have a how-to book?"

"We carry a pretty good selection." He led her to a set of white box shelves that reached nearly to the ceiling and

63

divided the front and back of the shop. About half the boxes held books and magazines; the rest held exotic and expensive yarns, magnetic needle minders, tubes of beads, tiny frames, and gadgets Valentina couldn't identify.

She was looking at *Simple Crocheting* by Erika Knight—a good-size book, profusely illustrated—when the door opened again. She turned to see a handsome woman enter wearing a royal blue trench coat and balancing a large box on one arm. Despite her youthful, curly blond hair, she looked to be in her middle fifties.

"Here, Betsy, let me take that," said the young man, hurrying forward to lift the box from her arm.

"Thanks, Goddy," said Betsy.

Goddy?

"Are you Betsy Devonshire?" asked Valentina, tucking the book under her elbow and coming toward her.

"Yes," replied Betsy.

"I'm Valentina Shipp, and Leona Cunningham said I should talk to you."

"Leona called a few minutes ago," Godwin broke in, as he was putting the box on the table. "She said she was sending a woman named Valentina over to talk to you. I told her you were out but would be back." He gave Valentina a look of mild rebuke. "This lady didn't tell me her name."

"You didn't look like a Betsy," Valentina shot back.

"Well . . . no," conceded Godwin, looking down at himself as if for reassurance. When he looked up, he had that mischievous look in his eyes again.

Valentina couldn't help it. She smiled. "You're quite a character!"

"You don't know the half of it," said Betsy, who was

shrugging off her coat. "Let me hang this up," she continued, heading for the back of her shop. "Then you can tell me what this is about."

"Do you want that book?" Godwin asked Valentina. "And these two hooks, size E?"

"Yes, please," said Valentina, joining him at a big old desk near one wall.

He quickly added up the charges, and, with a sigh she carefully suppressed, she swiped her credit card to pay them. Everything else was a bargain, but that book wasn't!

He had just handed her a large paper bag printed with purple flowers when Betsy came back.

"Now," said Betsy, "what does Leona want of me?"

"This is going to take a few minutes," said Valentina. "It's about my cousin, Tommy Riordan."

"Who?" said Godwin with a puzzled frown. Then his expression cleared. "Oh, Tom Take!" He drew up his shoulders and pressed the fingers of one hand against his mouth. "Sorry, sorry, sorry, sorry!" he mumbled, casting glances at both Valentina and Betsy.

There was a painful silence. Then Valentina said, in a chilly voice, "Is that what he's called around here?"

"Yes," asserted Betsy. "That's what a lot of people call him. Not being mean, not really. And Tom's not mean, either. We know he can't help it. He doesn't do it often and he doesn't take valuable things; it's more a nuisance. I understand that if you catch him in the act, he'll give the object back."

Godwin, anxious to make good, said, "I heard that if you think he's got something of yours and ask him if he's seen it, he'll say he thinks he knows where it is and will bring it back to you a day or two later."

Valentina's ire melted. "When he was a little boy," she confessed to the two of them now, "he came to stay with us twice, and when he went home, we'd go into his room to get our things back."

Godwin laughed. "So he was born like that!"

Betsy said, "So why are you here? What is it that you want from me? Here, come and sit down. Would you like a cup of coffee? Or tea?"

"No, thanks." Valentina followed Betsy back past the box shelves, into another, larger room. Here the walls were covered with stitched models, most of them framed, each with a three-digit number in a lower corner. Below them, slanted holders of counted cross-stitch patterns lined the entire room, and the floor was scattered with spinner racks holding everything from pretty scissors to different kinds of floss. In the center stood a small round table covered with a white tablecloth embroidered with winter scenes: snow-laden trees, sledding children, cross-country skiers.

Around the table were four delicate, pretty chairs with thin pink cushions on the seats. Betsy took one and indicated with a gesture that Valentina should take another.

"This is such a nice place," said Valentina. "Very cozy."

"Thank you." Betsy looked inquiringly at her.

Valentina took a deep breath. "Tommy's my cousin. I've been talked into taking responsibility for his house. He's going to be in the hospital for a long while, probably. He doesn't think the house needs anything but a new roof. But it does! It's in such bad shape that it might have to be torn down."

"I don't imagine Tom is happy about this."

"No, he isn't. But if I don't try to take care of things, apparently the county will. And he suspects—so do I, really—that they'll just send a crew in to throw everything away. Tommy says there are lots of valuable things in his house. And for all I know, that might be true. Those people might throw good stuff away with the bad—or, worse, steal the good stuff." Valentina winced. "I'm sorry, maybe I shouldn't have said that."

"No, that's a perfectly valid concern," said Betsy. "I have heard garbage collectors find valuable things in trash cans all the time. And not all the things are returned to the people who threw them away."

"The main problem is that I'm not rich enough to hire people to help—that house is too much for me alone. I don't know if you are aware of how awful the place is."

Betsy nodded. "Well, there have been some rumors lately . . ."

Valentina smiled grimly. "Well, it's probably even worse than you've heard. The house itself has something wrong with its foundation. The brick sills are bulging."

"Oh, I didn't know that! Was the foundation damaged when the tree fell on the roof?"

"I think it's been that way for a while. But before anyone can tackle that, the inside needs attention, and that's something I've been asked to handle. I talked to James Penberthy—he's Tommy's attorney, and he manages Tommy's trust—and he's going to help me get an emergency conservatorship. Then he says I should try to line up some volunteers from here in Excelsior to help me sort things out. I stopped for lunch at the Barleywine, and Leona Cunningham said I should talk to you."

Valentina looked around the shop, and a frown slowly formed on her face. "You do know her, right?"

"Yes, she's a good customer."

"But why did she think you could round up some help for me?"

"Probably because I can." Betsy smiled. "Her place and mine are two of the biggest carriers of gossip in Excelsior. I have a group that meets here every Monday, and between them and the regulars at the Barleywine, we can get the word out very quickly."

"Would you be willing to do that?"

"Of course. Why don't you give me a way to contact you, and I'll see what I can arrange. Would you be willing to come back here on Monday afternoon to talk to my regulars? You can tell us how many people you'll need and what you'll need them to do."

"Okay." Valentina nodded, feeling a sudden sting behind her eyes. Betsy's willingness to get involved was a huge burden off her shoulders. "I hope I'll have the conservatorship all fixed up by then. Oh, thank you, maybe this isn't going to be impossible after all!"

# Chapter Nine

❖ ❖ ❖

SEVEN members of the Monday Bunch sat around the library table in Betsy's shop: Emily, Doris and Phil, Jill, Bershada, Cherie, and Grace Pickering, who was only there temporarily. This time Grace had brought her sister, Georgine, with her. Georgine was a knitter; she was working on a bright red mitten. She looked like her sister but was a little taller and not quite as slim, and her blond hair was cropped short, a contrast to Grace's auburn locks, which tumbled in easy curls to her shoulders.

Betsy sometimes took a seat at the table, and she did so now, allowing a few minutes for the group's members to greet one another and bring out—and comment on—their needlework projects in progress.

She was herself working on a needlepoint canvas of red and pink roses from a counted cross-stitch pattern. Instead of wool, she was using size three perle cotton. She hadn't done any of the roses, with their leaves and buds, in the shop because counted cross-stitch was not her forte and the frequent changes of colors took all her concentration, but now she was doing the background in buff, using the basket weave stitch, which was easy.

"That thing you're stitching," said Bershada. "I just love those colors, so rich. What's it going to be, a pillow?"

"No," Betsy said. "It's going on the seat of a chair."

"Girl, if I put something as beautiful as that on the seat of a chair, no one would be allowed to sit on it."

Betsy, who had slaved over the piece for many hours, was inclined to agree that no one of lower rank than the Queen of England was going to rest her bottom on the stitching. She had spent countless hours frogging (or ripping out stitches—"rip it, rip it, rip it," hence the term); nearly as many hours as she'd spent stitching. But all she said was, "Thanks, it is nice, isn't it?"

The general sharing of needlework progress had subsided, and the gossip was about to begin, when Betsy spoke up again. "May I ask you all something?" she asked. "It's important, about Tom Riordan."

Tom Take's misfortune had been a hot topic since the night of the storm, and all eyes lifted to Betsy when she mentioned his name. "What about him?" asked Doris in her throaty voice.

"His cousin is in town, and she's been asked to clear out his house."

"By who? You?" asked Emily, not the sharpest knife in the drawer.

"Tom didn't ask anyone to do it, I'll bet," said Phil, grinning.

"Not Tom," agreed Betsy. "But his social worker and his attorney think that if this woman doesn't take on the task, Hennepin County will—and they might not be as careful of his things as she will."

"His cousin is a woman?" said Bershada. "Does she look something like Tom?"

"She looks a lot like him, actually. Why, have you met her?" asked Betsy.

"Not to speak to, but I saw a woman standing outside Tom's house last week, kind of looking it over, and she didn't look happy with what she was seeing. I thought maybe she was a real estate agent. That house might be a mess, but it's on a big lot only a block from the lake, and property values around here are staying nice and high."

There was a murmur of agreement.

"And this woman looked like Tom?" asked Cherie.

"Yes. Yes, she did. I almost went over to speak to her, but she was looking kind of mad, so I didn't."

"That was probably her," Betsy said. "Her name is Valentina Shipp. Leona sent her to me, because she thought maybe I could get some volunteers to help Ms. Shipp sort out the things in Tom's house."

"Write my name down," said Phil immediately. "I'll do it for free. In fact, I'd pay her for a chance to get a close look at the inside of that house."

"No need to do that, Phil," said Betsy, smiling. She sobered. "But this is a job for volunteers. There's no pay involved. Ms. Shipp is far from wealthy. She drove here all the way from Indiana to help Tom, because he's the last of her family."

Phil looked around the table. "What, I'm the only one who would like a chance to see just what Tom Take has piled up in there?"

Tall, fair Jill already knew some of the details about what had befallen Tom Riordan, since she was married to Sergeant Larson, who'd been one of the first responders when the accident was reported. "Put me down, too," she said now. "I wonder if that poor woman has any idea what she's in for."

Betsy said, "She's been inside the house, so yes, she has an idea. But she's hoping it will only take a week."

"She's a heck of an optimist, in that case!" said Phil with a laugh.

Emily said, "I'm afraid I can't volunteer more than one day, but I'll ask at my church if anyone else will come."

"That's a good idea," Betsy said. "I'll do that, too. And Leona is asking around as well. If we can get enough people, they can work in shifts, and maybe the cleanup will get done quickly."

"So you're volunteering, too?" asked Jill.

"I'm afraid not. I'm down to two part-timers right now, so I have to work more hours. But I'll ask Connor."

"Oh yes, please do that!" said Jill.

"Add me to the list," said Doris, and Betsy added her name to the list she was compiling.

"I can help out, too," said Cherie.

"What hat will you wear?" teased Phil.

Cherie liked hats, the more exotic the better. The one she was wearing today looked something like a squashed pot of dark red and orange velvet, with autumn leaves made from smooth fabric stuck carelessly on one side. She took the question seriously and thought for a few seconds. "I don't have a hard hat, but I have a sweet cloche that will keep the spiders out of my hair, at least."

"Oh, ugh!" said Emily.

"Scarves for everyone, even Phil," pronounced Doris.

Georgine said, "I know I'm a relative stranger, but I'd like to help, if I can. And maybe my sister will help, too."

"I don't think so," said Grace, wriggling her shoulders. "I'm afraid of mice. Bugs, too, for that matter."

"That's very nice of you, Georgie!" said Jill, and the others agreed.

"How many volunteers does she need?" Godwin, who had been eavesdropping while he restocked a spinner rack with overdyed silk floss, asked.

"I'm not sure," replied Betsy. "I should think at least four at a time, so it will depend on who can work when and for how many hours." She checked her watch. "Valentina said she'd come in today, and I hope she does."

"When does this volunteer help start?" asked Jill, the pragmatic member of the Bunch.

"As soon as she gets the legal right to start clearing," said Betsy. "If she doesn't come into the store today, I'll call her later to tell her the good news that she's already got some volunteers lined up. Now, when I read your name back, tell me what days you can work."

When Valentina arrived a few minutes later, she was apologetic and out of breath. "Oh, I'm glad you're still here!" she said. "I had a flat tire—I haven't had a flat tire in years and years. It took me a while to figure out how to change it."

"You changed it all by yourself?" asked Godwin, impressed.

"Sure. It's not hard, just a little messy." She looked at her hands, which were absolutely filthy.

"There's a restroom all the way in the back," said Betsy, "if you want to wash up."

And while she was gone, the Monday Bunch exchanged the opinion that she did, indeed, look a whole lot like her cousin, Tom.

# Chapter Ten

◈ ◈ ◈

"Tommy?" Valentina peered around the hospital room door.

"That you, Val? Come in, come in!"

"Wow, you're sitting up!" She came into the room. Riordan was sitting in a chair beside the bed, his leg propped up stiffly in front of him. His hair was combed, and he was freshly shaven, but his eyes were at half-mast. The big bandage on the side of his head had been replaced with a smaller one, but the thin, short-sleeved robe he wore showed still-bright bruises up and down his arms and on his hands.

"You look good, Cousin!" she said, and came to touch him on the shoulder. His slight wince told her that he still didn't like to be touched, just as was true in his youth, so she backed away.

"There's another place to sit over there," he said, pointing to the wooden chair with a cushioned seat back over near where another patient lay (or didn't; the curtains were pulled around the bed, so Valentina couldn't tell).

She went over and pulled the chair forward so she could sit facing him. "How are you feeling?" she asked.

"Better. I think they're going to turn me loose tomorrow or the next day."

"Not to go home," she said, alarmed.

"No, not yet. There's a place where they give you phy-si-cal thur-py"—he pronounced it carefully—"and I hafta stay there a week or two."

She nodded. "That's good, that's good." Then, seeing the look on his face, she added hastily, "I mean, good that you're still going to be cared for. They're not just handing you a pair of crutches and shoving you out the door."

"Yeah, I guess so. Have you been to the house again?"

She nodded. "Yes, I have. And I'm putting together several crews, people who are going to help me get it back in shape—so you can live there again."

His brows drew together and he asked suspiciously, "Who? Who's in these crews?"

"Well, there's Godwin DuLac—"

"That queer?" he said, laughing.

"Now, Tommy, you know you don't mean that the way it sounds."

He sat back, looking a little smug. "Maybe, maybe not. But I bet he don't lift nothin' heavier than a ashtray."

"Now, he's a good man, smart, and stronger than he looks, probably."

"Who else?"

"Connor Sullivan, Doris and Phil Galvin, Emily Hame, Jill Larson . . ." Valentina paused, counting on her fingers.

Tom's eyes closed, and he murmured, "They're people who hang out in that 'broidery store."

"Yes." She nodded. "That's where I was first told to go asking for help. The people I met in the store are asking around, rounding up more people, but they were the first to volunteer, so I'm putting them on the first crew."

"That Jill, she's married to that cop who broke inta my house."

"Yeah, after you were yelling for help," she pointed out drily.

"Well . . ." He shook his head slowly. "Yeah, well . . ." But he couldn't think of an argument and slouched a little in his chair. The movement made him suck air through his teeth.

"That leg still hurts, I guess," she said.

"Yeah, it still hurts, doggone it!" He slammed his hands feebly on the arms of his chair.

"Take it easy, take it easy," she counseled, holding a palm toward him. "It'll get better quicker if you don't wriggle around."

"Aw—!"

"An' there's another volunteer I just remembered, her name's Georgine, they call her Georgie."

"I don't think I know her," he said.

"Probably not. She and her sister, Grace, are new in town, been there a coupla months. Pickering's their name."

"Oh yeah, the twin sisters. I seen them around. They like antiques stores."

"They're not twins, but they do look kind of alike. But Grace is afraid of mice, and there are mice in your house, so only Georgie is coming. They buy and sell antiques and

77

collectibles, so it's good one of them is coming. She can keep us from throwing away something valuable."

"*What!?*" He rared up, suddenly furious. "*You're gonna throw my things away?*" Eyes wide and blazing, his voice rose to a shriek. "No, no, *no!*" Valentina tried to say something placating, but he overrode her. "You can't throw *anything* away! Them's my *things!*" He was leaning forward, trying to get his broken leg off its perch, his face twisted with rage and pain.

The pain won, and he fell back, panting. "I'll have you arrested if you throw *one thing* of mine away!"

The door opened and a nurse in pink scrubs came in. "What's going on in here? Mr. Riordan, are you all right?"

"No, I ain't all right, not so long as she's here. Take her away! Out, get out, get out!"

The nurse turned to Valentina, who lifted both hands in a gesture of surrender. "Don't worry, I'm going," she said to the nurse, and to Riordan, "You calm down, you hear? You'll do yourself a mischief, getting all mad like that."

He said between gasps of pain and fury, "Don't you . . . *never* come back!"

She smiled. The angry answer she wanted to throw at him was the one he wanted, so she made it gentle. "All right, honey, I promise."

G EORGIE knew it would be bad. She and her sister, always on the search for merchandise they could sell at flea markets and on eBay and craigslist and other web sites, had visited many hoarders' homes and barns and sheds, and, on one memorable occasion, they'd gone to a half dozen retired school buses bought for the express purpose of storing more stuff. Such visits were dusty and sometimes perilous—pulling out a find from a tall pile could set off an avalanche.

Though she and Grace loved finding wonderful things at least as much as selling them at a profit, the bad example set by the hoarders kept the two of them from allowing their own home in north Florida to fill up.

Seven volunteers had turned up late Thursday afternoon at Riordan's pink-brick house. They were all wearing clothes that they didn't mind getting dirty. The men all wore caps, and the women had covered their heads with a variety of scarves. Valentina ceremoniously opened the front door—a hasp and padlock had kept it closed after the police had broken in to rescue Tommy—and ushered them in.

A murmur of amazement came from the group as they entered the living room single file—it was impossible to do otherwise.

"Holy smoke!" said Phil. "This'll take us the rest of the year to clean out!"

"Now, maybe not," said Connor. "Is the rest of the house like this?" he asked Valentina.

"Oh yes."

"Still, have you hired a Dumpster or at least a pickup truck to haul things away?"

"Yes, Betsy gave me the number of the company that rents them, and they'll have it in the driveway first thing in the morning."

"Well done. Perhaps it's not as bad as we think. If every volunteer works hard, it could get done in six, eight days, tops."

"But we're not here to work today, are we?" said Emily. "You told us the actual digging out wouldn't start until tomorrow."

Valentina nodded. "We're going to do a walk-through, to see if you want to change your mind about volunteering. Also, I'd like you to point out anything you think is seriously valuable. Or something that might be dangerous to touch, or move. These rooms are too crowded for more than one or two of us to work in at a time, so we'll be splitting into small groups. Look around and choose which room you'd like to tackle. Ready? Let's go. Remember, just look, don't move anything, and meet back here in fifteen minutes."

It was clear that Tom Riordan had allowed his passion for acquisitions to literally cover other problems in his home. As the group trailed back into the living room, awed by the sheer size of his collection, Connor, bringing up the rear, agreed with Valentina that while the house's floors and windows were sound, the plumbing was all but defunct and the wiring probably dangerous.

Then he proposed that they all work together today to clear at least half the living room. That space would then be available to hold items that might have value or that were good enough to be donated to charity.

"Is that all right with everyone?" Valentina asked. They all nodded.

Valentina said, "Georgie, you're the closest thing we have to an expert. Help us sort now—and maybe when we come back tomorrow morning, you can stay here and look at things we're hauling out to the Dumpster, so we don't throw away something valuable."

But Georgie shook her head. "I can make some suggestions, but really, I'm not enough of an expert, especially on as many different things as I saw in here," she said. "I think you should hire someone to give you a professional opinion. I'll be glad to look at things, but please don't take my word for their value."

They set to work and quickly sorted out a great many obviously worthless things: a dried-up leather coat, old calendars, moldy clothing, shoes, and blankets, canned goods bulging in the middle, broken picture frames, filthy stuffed animals, alarm clocks with broken faces, three-legged chairs, and two small portable record players missing their insides.

They set aside an old coaster wagon, two flat-tired Schwinn bicycles, a big Chinese-style white vase with blue dragons on it, an enormous bowie knife in a crumbling leather sheath, three cast-iron frying pans, a rusty 30-06 rifle, a dozen institutional-size cans of baked beans, a coffee table, a beat-up metal detector, five dead cell phones, an antique wooden chest full of 78 rpm records, and an old, wooden, pendulum-powered wall clock.

"So, I guess it's not all worthless junk," said Valentina, looking over the objects.

"I could sell that wagon, as is, on eBay for a hundred dollars, like that," said Georgie, snapping her fingers.

"Well, that gives me hope," replied Valentina. "So now we're set up to tackle the rest of the house tomorrow. See you all here at nine."

IT was the middle of the next morning. Phil was working alone in Riordan's bedroom. The heavy blue plastic liner over the smashed roof cast an eerie light, as if the room were underwater. Under a pile of broken glass, which Phil was scooping up with a dustpan, he found a crushed box of Handi Wipes.

It looked empty, but when he picked it up, it rattled. He stuck a finger into the opening and encountered small, solid objects with bumps all over them. Peach pits, he thought. He began to toss it into a trash can, but something about the varied feel of the objects changed his mind, and he turned the box over to shake its contents into his palm.

"Great jumpin' horned toads!" he murmured (although not exactly in those words). In his hand were three pieces of jewelry, two rings and a brooch. "Naw!" he corrected himself, annoyed. Stones that size couldn't be real. One ring was a kind of dull silver set with a big piece of deep blue glass; the other was gold with two big clear stones flanking a large dark gray cabochon stone that shifted in color as he moved it in his hand, showing glints of electric blue. The brooch was nearly three inches across, also gold colored, with lots of filigree; it featured a green center stone the size of his thumbnail, flanked by four clear glass stones.

The pieces were a bit ostentatious, Phil thought, but maybe Doris would want them. He dropped them into a pocket and went back to work.

Meanwhile, down in the kitchen, Jill and Georgie were busy. Georgie was clearing a counter of empty fruit and vegetable cans and cocoa mixes when she came upon an old cookie jar shaped like a buxom African American woman with a red scarf around her head and a long green skirt. The word COOKIES appeared in raised lettering near the hem. The figure wore a big, red smile.

"Hey, look at this!" said Georgie. "What a great find!"

Jill looked up, surprised. "You're kidding!" she exclaimed.

"No, I'm not. These things are very collectible."

"By who, the women's auxiliary of the Ku Klux Klan?"

"No, I'm serious. Collectors love them; even African Americans buy them. Look at it, no crazing, no chips, and the colors are strong. Probably worth sixty, even seventy dollars." Georgie reached to pick it up, but to her amazement it was too heavy to lift one-handed. She picked up the top—it came apart at the waist—and saw a glint of silver inside. She reached in and pulled out a coin. It was large, bigger even than a silver dollar, thick and heavy. On the front was the profile of a woman with a hint of double chin, lots of wavy hair swept back, and a serene expression—good heavens, it was a Morgan dollar! It was worn, but the lettering on it was very clear, and the date on it was 1884. Georgie gave an exclamation of surprise and delight.

"What kind of coin is that?" asked Jill.

"It's a Morgan." Georgie handed the coin to Jill, then reached in and pulled out three more. She put her hand in a third time and pulled out four more. Again, they were all old Morgan silver dollars. Most were in pretty good shape.

"Are these real?" asked Jill, hefting them in her palm.

"Yes, they're real. And they're valuable." Georgie leaned over to look into the jar. "There must be dozens in here."

Jill went to the door leading into the dining room. "Valentina! Valentina, come see what we've found!" she shouted. She came back to Georgie. "How valuable?"

"I don't know for sure; it depends on the date, the mint, and the condition. Some might be as low as thirty dollars, some worth hundreds, a very few could be a lot more. I don't know which dates are the most valuable." She held up two coins. "See, this one is in really good shape, but not this one."

"What is it? What have you found?" Valentina came into the room. There was a smudge on her prominent nose, and the white work gloves she was wearing were filthy.

"This old cookie jar—"

"Yes, I saw it the first time I came through. I can't believe Tommy had that racist thing in his house. Toss it."

"First of all, it's not considered racist anymore," said Georgie, "and it's worth maybe seventy dollars to a collector. But second, it's full of Morgan dollars, which could be worth thousands of dollars."

*"Each?"* Valentina's voice came out in a squeak.

"No, no, not each. In total. Possibly."

"Still," said Jill, "that's a lot of money."

Connor, who had followed Valentina into the kitchen, said, "We can't leave those in the living room. We'll have to find someplace secure to put them. A safe deposit box, maybe."

"I've never seen a Morgan dollar," Valentina said. "What do they look like?"

Georgie handed over two of the coins. "They all have that face on them, with an eagle on the back," she said.

Valentina turned them over and back in her gloved hands. "Pretty woman," she said, rubbing one with a thumb. Then she added, awed, "Say, this one is like a hundred and fifty years old!" She looked around the still-filthy kitchen. "I bet we don't find anything else in the whole house as wonderful as this."

\* \* \*

AFTER some of the others had a look at the hoard of silver dollars, the pairs broke apart and re-formed.

Emily ended up working alone in the little dining room, feeling near despair.

"Oh, sweetie, what's the matter?" Emily looked up to see Georgie standing in the doorway.

"I don't know what to do next," cried Emily, feeling tears stinging her eyes. "It's all so—so *complicated*!"

"You're absolutely right, and you shouldn't be in here alone. I'll help. We start in this corner, okay?" Georgie's brisk, take-charge attitude put heart back into Emily.

"Bring that big plastic trash barrel over here. Now, pick up the thing nearest to hand. What is it?"

Emily lifted a box with six cans of tuna fish in it, all with rust on the lids.

"Toss it," Georgie said. "My turn, here's a big glass ashtray with a corner broken off. Toss. Your turn."

Emily picked up an old cigar box full of campaign buttons. "Ooooh, lemme see those," cooed Georgie. "Here's one for JFK and LBJ, and it's nice and clean. Here's one for LBJ and Hubird—did you know that's the nickname Lyndon Johnson gave Hubert Humphrey? LBJ's wife was called Lady Bird, and so he took to putting 'bird' onto folks' names."

Emily giggled. "How do you know all this stuff?"

"It's part of doing what I do, finding things worth selling. Besides, it's fun to learn about so many wonderful things. These might be worth something. So we'll put this box of them on top of this other big box."

With Georgie's encouragement and information-loaded chatter, and Emily's now-cheerful cooperation, both of them filled and carried out the trash can four times. In less than an hour they had cleared a quarter of the room. There was a small heap of things remaining, and they moved them into the living room.

"What's next?" said Emily, brushing a cobweb off the sleeve of her old blue sweatshirt. She was feeling fresh and cheerful—Georgie was terrific!

"Let's see if we can clear the table. Then we'll have a better place to put the stuff we're not throwing away."

"Good idea."

Soon Emily was sorting a dozen old glass bottles by shape—whether they had held wine or milk—and then by whether they were whole or chipped. They had cleared enough of the floor around a big silver milk can to discover that it was not ornamental but functional—it was holding up one corner of the table.

She had come to the center of the collection, where a circle of dark wine bottles surrounded something she did not recognize. "Say, Georgie, what's this?"

"What's what?" asked Georgie, who was sorting so swiftly through a heap of old issues of *Look*, *Life*, and *Saturday Evening Post* magazines that they were fluttering out of her hands like startled birds.

Emily was looking at a large mother-of-pearl goose egg attached to an alabaster base. A stem a few inches long rose out of the top of the egg, surmounted by a small tarnished silver pelican. "This," she said, and put a forefinger on the pelican—and the stem went down and the egg split open. "Whoops!" said Emily, releasing the stem. The egg closed.

"Hey," said Georgie, dropping the magazines she was holding to the floor. "Do that again."

Emily did.

Both women bent over the object for a closer look. Inside the egg were a tiny pair of scissors, a small pick, three needles thrust through a scrap of silk, a thimble, and two small, empty spools of thread, all made of tarnished silver.

"It's a kind of chatelaine, I think," said Emily, poking the spools. "You know, a stitcher's helper. But I've never seen one like this. It's beautiful."

"Yes, it is, but I don't think it's a chatelaine," said Georgie. "There's another word—I can't think of it . . ."

"Holy *cow*!" came a loud male exclamation from somewhere in the house. It was followed by a shout. "Hey, everyone! Come and see this!"

# Chapter Eleven

❖ ❖ ❖

THERE was a second extremely narrow and dark staircase off the back porch. It had been clogged solid with jars and canned goods but was now cleared. Georgie had vanished up it, and Emily could hear other voices coming from upstairs—Valentina's and Jill's among them. She hurried up.

Connor was in the back bedroom, where an ancient sagging bed was half out from under piles of tools, lanterns, pots and pans, clock radios, and empty Coke bottles. The rest of the floor was partially cleared, but Emily could not get into the room, since it was already crowded with Connor, Jill, Valentina, and Godwin, standing shoulder to shoulder amid big plastic bags filled with God knows what, and Georgine blocking the doorway.

Georgine stood behind Doris and Phil, looking eagerly between their shoulders. "What is it, what's he got?" asked Phil in his loud, old-man's voice, as Emily came up behind them.

What Connor had was a classic leather mailbag, the sort carried over the shoulder by an old-fashioned mailman. He was holding it so they could look inside and see that it was about a third full of letters and small packages.

"Why, it looks as if a mailman was interrupted while he was still delivering!" said Valentina. "How did this get up here?"

"Tom Take took it," said Godwin with a laugh.

"How old is the mail?" asked Doris. "Maybe it can still be delivered."

Connor reached into the bag and picked up a brown envelope with several postage stamps on it. He looked at the cancellation and said, "August 1996."

*"August 1996?"* echoed Phil.

"Heavenly days!" exclaimed Godwin. "I was a mere child in 1996."

"Oh, I think you were a bit more than that," said Doris, laughing.

"Well, barely," he grinned, with an abashed shrug.

"It appears that Mr. Riordan has been taking things for a long time," said Georgie.

"And his father and grandfather before him," said Valentina. "But what are we going to do with that mailbag?"

They all looked at Jill, the person present who stood closest to the law.

"I imagine it belongs to the post office," she said.

"Couldn't we at least look at what's in there?" urged Godwin. "Maybe there's an old *Vogue* magazine; we can laugh at the clothes."

"It's still a crime to interfere with the mail," Jill said. "Even old, undelivered mail."

"Who's interfering?" said Connor, making a show of putting the brown envelope back—but he stopped just as he was about to let go of it.

"Look, this one's addressed to Crewel World," he said, turning it in his hand to show the neat printing. "I could take it with me."

"Drop it," said Jill in that cop's voice she could summon at will.

Connor did, looking up at her in surprise. Then he mock-snarled, "You got me, copper."

She laughed, a little surprised at herself. "Maybe the post office will deliver it."

"What else have you found up here?" asked Valentina, anxious to get things back on track.

"Nothing as good as this."

Phil put his hand in his pocket. "That reminds me, I found some costume jewelry that's kind of pretty. You want it, Dorie?" He pulled out the rings and brooch.

"Ooooh," said Doris, picking the brooch out of his hand. "This one I like."

"Hold it," said Valentina. "I may have to charge you fifty cents for that."

But Georgine, leaning in between them, said, "Can I see it?"

Doris handed it to her, and Phil held out the rings, which Georgine, after a glance, took as well.

"Hmm," said Georgine. "I wish I had my loupe with me." She held the silver-colored ring close to one eye. "I can't tell for sure, but I think this stone is a real sapphire."

"What, that's *real*?" asked Godwin, wriggling his way close to her and peering around her arm.

"If I'm right, yes, and the ring itself is platinum."

"Oh, come on!" said Phil. "Tom Take owns a sapphire and platinum ring?"

"And a black opal and a ruby, both with real diamonds." Georgine was looking all three pieces over. "I'm pretty sure."

"Where do you suppose these came from?" asked Emily.

There was a thoughtful silence. Then Connor suggested, "The metal detector."

"Why, I bet you're right!" said Valentina.

Phil said, "You read about people finding great stuff with them."

"How much are they worth—if they're real?" asked Valentina.

"Hard to say, exactly."

"Well then, tell us inexactly," said Godwin.

"Okay. The platinum and sapphire, around ten to fifteen thousand; the black opal and diamonds ten to fifteen thousand; the ruby brooch—I'm not really up to date on rubies, so much depends on the color as well as the cut. I'd guess that ruby is three and a half or even four carats, and they're going for between seven and twelve thousand a carat. Plus the diamonds, plus the gold in the brooch itself."

"Jeee-zuz!" said Phil. He added to Doris, "Sorry, sweetheart."

Jill said, "That's something else to take to the bank."

"What's the other?" asked Georgine.

"The Morgan dollars."

"How many Morgan dollars?" asked Georgine.

Jill said, "We stopped at sixty-five; probably close to a hundred."

She stared at her. "Oh my, that's a lot!"

Phil reached for the brooch. "Meanwhile, can I hold on to these for a while? It'll make me feel rich, at least temporarily."

Valentina said, "Yes, you may."

Georgine said, "But have you got something to wrap them in? Don't leave them loose in your pocket."

Doris went into her own pocket and came up with a little packet of tissues. Phil wrapped each piece in a sheet then wrapped a fourth around the lot before putting it into his shirt pocket. With a solemn expression, he patted the pocket tenderly to settle them deep in there.

"Anything else?" asked Valentina.

Connor said, "Nothing—except for all the soft drink cans." He gestured at a cluster of gray plastic leaf bags that were leaning against one wall. "Hundreds of them. I wonder why he didn't cash them in?"

"God knows," sighed Valentina. "All right, everyone, back to work."

"Hold on a minute," said Jill. "I think Connor should take that mailbag over to the post office now. Get it out of our hair."

"Fine with me," said Connor. He checked his watch. "It's quarter to twelve, so how about, since I'm going out, I bring lunch back with me? Betsy said her contribution to today's cause will be to buy it. Do you want pizza or burgers?"

"Not pizza!" declared Emily. "Without access to hot water and a nail brush, these hands are not going to touch something I put in my mouth! At least I can hold a sandwich by the wrapper."

That made the others look at their hands—Georgine hastily stuffed hers in her pockets—and agree, except Valentina, smug in her white cotton work gloves.

Connor found a scrap of paper, borrowed a pen from Jill, and took everyone's order. Then he shouldered the mailbag and left the house.

The others went out to the backyard and used the outdoor faucet to wash up as best they could. Jill brought out a dirty old bottle of Palmolive she'd found in the kitchen, which helped a little, though they had to dry their hands on whatever clean spots they could find on their clothing.

Then they sat down on the overgrown lawn—it was a warm, sunny day—to wait for Connor and exchanged stories about the things they'd found.

Emily described the goose-egg object with its collection of tiny needlework aids. "Georgine says it's not a chatelaine, but she couldn't remember the proper name for it."

"Wait a minute, wait a minute," said Godwin. "I know! It's a . . . an etty. Or etu. Something like that."

"Maybe you're thinking of an emu," said Phil, mock-serious.

"No, that's a bird," said Doris, laughing.

"There's a bird sitting on top of it," Phil pointed out, although he was smiling as he said it.

"It's a pelican," said Emily.

"Why a pelican?" Valentina wondered aloud.

Jill burst out, "'A wonderful bird is the pelican. His beak can hold more than his belly can. He can hold in his beak enough food for a week, but I'm darned if I know how the hellican!'"

"Nice, nice, nice!" said Phil, laughing.

"One of the few good limericks that aren't naughty," observed Doris with a wry smile.

"What do you know about naughty limericks?" asked Godwin slyly.

"Not much," acknowledged Doris. "But, 'The limerick packs laughs anatomical, into space that is quite economical; but the good ones I've seen, so seldom are clean, and the clean ones so seldom are comical.'"

"And I think we'd better stop right there," said Jill, with an amused hint of her cop's voice, casting a sideways glance at Emily.

Emily saw the look and laughed aloud. "But there are plenty of 'clean' limericks!" she pointed out. "And they are too funny! I recite them to my children all the time!"

"Good for you, child," said Godwin with a sage nod that included the others. Then he kindly changed the subject. "Does anyone here present think the house is salvageable?" he asked.

"If it were completely rewired, maybe," said Jill. "And replumbed. Property in Excelsior is high-end, so it would probably be worth the expense to upgrade it."

Valentina said, "Why don't you go to the corner of the house and look down along the length of the sill?"

Jill looked at Valentina for a long moment, then got up and went to peer down one side of the house. She stood there for a while, frowning, then went to the other side for a look. "I see what you mean," she said as she came back to join the group on the lawn.

"What does she mean?" asked Godwin. He leaned sideways but couldn't see far enough to look down the line of the house.

"Go see for yourself."

Godwin rose and went to look. The group could hear his proclaimed, "Uh-oh!" He came back and said, "The walls are going crooked at the bottom."

Alarmed, Emily said, "Is it safe to go back in?"

"Sure it is," said Valentina.

Phil got up and went for a look, too. He came back shaking his head. "It's safe enough for the moment, I agree, but I don't think the house can be saved. Oh, and look, Connor's just pulling up out front."

In another minute Connor came into the backyard. He was laden with white paper bags marked with golden arches, a heavenly odor wafting in his wake.

The burgers and chicken sandwiches were distributed, along with plastic forks that Connor had thoughtfully supplied so that the fries could be eaten without anyone's fingers touching them.

"So, what are we talking about?" asked Connor as he sat down with his own sandwich.

"Did you notice the crooked walls as you passed by the house?" asked Phil.

"I noticed some bricks moved out of place, but not that the walls were crooked," Connor replied, glancing over at the house. "Are they actually leaning?"

"More like bulging at the bottom," said Valentina.

"So what does that mean?" asked Georgine.

"I'm pretty sure it means it would cost a whole lot of money to fix."

"Are you prepared to do that?" asked Connor.

"I can't afford to do that."

"Maybe we'll find more treasure inside another cookie jar," said Godwin, "and then you will be able to afford it."

"You mean treasure like the jewelry Phil found?" asked Connor.

"That, and the Morgan dollars," said Godwin, nodding. "I called Rafael and he says there's a wide range of values on Morgan dollars. Some are worth a lot—a *lot*—of money, depending on condition, date, and where they were minted. The price for an ordinary one is around forty dollars."

Jill said, "So if there are a hundred ordinary ones, the least they're worth is four thousand dollars. That's pretty nice."

Godwin said, "Rafael says we should take them to a coin dealer for evaluation, because in a collection that large, there are likely to be one or two worth a lot more."

"How can you tell where a coin was minted?" asked Emily. "I thought they were all made in Washington."

"Oh no," said Godwin, "there are mints all over the country: Denver has one, San Francisco has another. There are little initials on coins that indicate where they were made."

"Which Morgan dollar is the most valuable?" Doris asked Godwin.

"I don't know. Rafael knows. But please don't ask him, or he'll talk your ear off about things like condition and a rainbow patina."

Emily said, "Connor, maybe you can help us remember the name of this kind of chatelaine or sewing kit. It's shaped like an egg. It opens when you press down on a stem sticking out of it. It's even got a tiny pair of scissors, and needles, and spools for holding thread."

Godwin said, "What makes you think Connor would know? You'd think I'd be the one who knows, since I work in a needlework shop." But he looked at Connor and said, "It's a word that sounds something like *etty*."

"An *etui*?" suggested Connor.

"That's it!"

"How in the world do you know that?" demanded Phil.

"It's a word that shows up in crossword puzzles," explained Connor. He shrugged. "I guess all those crossword books I filled while at sea weren't entirely a waste of time."

"An etui," said Emily. "I never heard that word before. But then, I never saw anything like that thing before, either. Maybe . . ." She looked at Valentina. "Are you going to hold a garage sale? Maybe I could buy it then."

"A garage sale sounds like a really good idea," said Valentina.

Connor pointed to Georgine. "I think you should let your expert here take the measure of what we've got worthy of sale, and what prices we—that is, you—should set."

Georgine said, "You should get a professional to do the estimate of what I might think is valuable. Maybe, after all, there *is* enough treasure in the house to pay for its repair."

Emily said, "I found something else, a little red box carved with fish and flowers. You should look at it, Georgie. It was pretty, but inside was this little ball and when I looked again I could see it was like a ball of mice, ish!"

"A *ball* of mice? What do you mean? A nest of them? Were they alive?"

"No, it was like a carving or something, but they looked real," Emily said. "They were so icky that I almost dropped the box!" She shuddered.

"Ick is right!" said Georgine, climbing to her feet with a groan. "Are we all done here? There's lots more to do."

Valentina sprang to her feet with surprising ease, looking at her watch. "Everyone's finished with lunch, I think. So let's get back to work. You be careful with that box," she said to Emily, teasing. "Those mice might still be in there."

"But—" started Emily.

"Come on, honey," said Georgine. "Let's have a look at that box." As they filed back into the house, Emily said to Georgine, "It's pretty, it's got Chinese carving all over it."

Back in the dining room, Georgine looked around. "Where is it?" she asked.

"Here, on the table. I put a magazine over it." Emily lifted the old *Look* magazine to reveal the table's scarred surface. "Hey, it's gone!"


"WHEN did you last see it?" asked Jill.

"The last time was also the first time. It was when Connor found the mailbag and everyone was heading upstairs to see it," replied Emily. "I accidentally kicked the box. It was on the floor, under some magazines. I moved them and found it." She was shifting her hands around, palms inward, to indicate the size of the thing, about nine or ten inches by seven or eight inches, and perhaps three or four inches deep.

The volunteers had gone back out into the yard, where there was enough space for them all to look into one another's faces without stepping on one another's toes. The sky was clouding over and a wind had sprung up; they could hear the flapping of the thick blue plastic sheet laid over the roof of Riordan's bedroom. The temperature was falling even as they stood there, and the women tucked their hands into their armpits.

"And you didn't see this red box?" Jill asked Georgine.

"No, I must have left before she found it, going to see what Connor was shouting about. I don't remember seeing it at all."

"Anyone else see it? Maybe move it?"

But the others all shook their heads.

Jill asked Georgine, "Any idea how much that box might be worth? I mean, could it be really valuable?"

Georgine shook her head. "I'd have to see it. Was it painted wood? Maybe even plastic?"

Emily said, "I'm not sure. It wasn't very heavy. Maybe it was some kind of plastic." Her expression was doubtful. "Though it didn't exactly feel like plastic . . ." She shrugged. "I don't know."

Georgine made a disparaging face. "But it could have been plastic."

Emily said, "Yes, it could. But it was beautiful! It had flowers and curved Chinese fish with big tails! And inside it were three needle cases, you know, like tubes, very delicate and pretty. I opened one and there were three needles in it, wooden needles."

"Sounds like a toy sewing box," said Jill.

"Maybe," said Emily. "Or maybe the cases and needles were real ivory."

"What color were they?" asked Georgine.

"Sort of almost white—well, you know, ivory colored. And there was this ball, it was wrapped in a gray rag, and when I pulled the cloth away, I saw it was a curled bundle of white mice. So I put the rag back fast—I mean, they looked like real mice at first glance, crawling all over it, with red eyes and those naked tails, ish!—and then I saw they weren't real, but still—you know, mice! So I closed the box and went upstairs to see what Connor had found."

"I don't think someone would sneak into the house to take just that, when there were other things, obviously more valuable," said Connor.

"Especially since I put a magazine over it."

"Why did you do that?" asked Jill.

"Because seeing that mouse ball made me feel all tingly in my fingers. It wasn't very big. The mice were like baby mice." She made a circle with the fingers of both hands, not so big as a tennis ball.

"That sounds like a Halloween trick," remarked Doris. "Something you put in a teacher's desk drawer."

"So see?" said Georgine. "A child's toy box."

Phil said, "You know, there could be other things missing. We've been sorting through things in a big hurry—I for one couldn't make a complete list of everything I've set aside, much less what I've thrown away. A thief could have taken something from my saved stack, a few teacups—heck, even one of those rusty bicycles, and I wouldn't know it."

"That's true," several of the other volunteers murmured, nodding.

"We should have locked the door when we all went out back to wash up," said Godwin.

"Yeah, well, hindsight is pretty generally twenty-twenty," said Phil.

"I don't know why we're so fussed about this," said Valentina. "An old toy box with some little thingies—yes, all right, needle cases—in it, and a Halloween toy. How much could it be worth?"

Georgine said, "It doesn't sound like they were real ivory, because if they were real, they'd be old and turning brown. It's illegal to import things made out of new ivory, so they're probably plastic, like the box. The whole thing is probably worth six dollars."

Valentina said, "See? I bet some kid snuck in on a dare, grabbed something handy, and left. Big whoop!"

"*I* think it's scary that there's a thief in the neighborhood," said Emily. "And he walked right into the house while we were just outside the back door—that's *real* scary. This is a safe town. Things like that don't happen in Excelsior."

"Well . . ." began Connor, but then he changed his mind. "You're right, of course." Because she was, mostly. Especially now that Tom Take was in the hospital.

# Chapter Twelve

❖ ❖ ❖

BETSY went down the hospital corridor, looking at room numbers. The one she was after was easy to remember—321—and the door was open when she came to it.

She rapped once on the door frame. "Mr. Riordan?" she called.

"Who is it?" came a slow answer.

"Betsy Devonshire, from Excelsior."

"Come on in." The voice sounded a little brighter. When she entered the room, he asked, "Did you bring me something?" He laughed, not with his usual guffaw but weakly, and his dulled eyes were focused on her hands, which indeed held a shallow white box.

Betsy knew his begging ways and had brought a box of chocolates from Truffle Hill—their handmade candy was marvelous. Tom might be poor as a church mouse, but his taste in chocolate was epicurean.

She put the box on the one-legged metal table beside his bed, and he opened it. "These're real nice!" he said. Then, remembering his manners, he added, "Thank you very much—can I have a piece right now?"

Betsy laughed. "Of course."

His eyes ran swiftly over the choices. He picked up a milk chocolate caramel, put it in his mouth, and said, before he'd even finished eating it, "'Ould you lye a peesch?"

Betsy didn't have to be a mind reader to know the answer he wanted. "No, thank you."

Duty done, he relaxed back against his pillows. He looked worn down, his dark eyes sleepy and the skin around them shadowed, his graying hair ruffled. He needed a shave. But he wasn't hooked up to any IV lines. Betsy could see just the big bandaged brace on his leg, uncovered for viewing.

"If I ask you something, will you tell me?" he said, swallowing the last of the chocolate.

"If I can. What is it?"

"Them people in my house. Are they taking my things for their selves?"

"Good heavens, no!" said Betsy. "They're being very careful as they sort things out. It's a huge task, and very complicated, as you must know."

A complacent smile formed, and he nodded. "I got a whole lot of stuff."

"You must have been collecting for a long time."

"Sure I have," he said, nodding again. "Since I was six years old. Used to go out with my grandad, hunting for stuff. And I know where I got ever' single thing, and when I got holt of it."

Betsy doubted that. "Really?"

"But I do," he insisted. "They're my things, and I love them, every one. Ask me about one of them."

Betsy said, "I haven't been in your house, so how could I do that?"

"I have a birdcage made of wicker. It's in fine shape 'cept the door is broke out of it. I mean to get a new door an' then it'll be worth something. I got it from beside ol' Doc Menderson's house, after he died back in ninety-nine, and his fam'ly cleaned out the place. It was on the ground, outside the back door. It was about this time of year—no, more like a little while b'fore Thanksgiving." He smiled proudly at her. "See? Ever'thing. Ask me somethin' else."

"But—" Betsy broke off before she could tell him again that she hadn't been to his house. The Monday Bunch crew had brought stories to her. "Tell me about the mailbag."

Tom looked out the window for a few moments, though the view was of a brick wall. Without looking back he said, "It was back in ninety-six. I saw it on the ground, in the rain, all by itself. I didn't want the mail to get spoiled, so I brought it home. I meant to bring it back, but . . ." He looked at Betsy, his expression troubled. "After I kep' it awhile, I thought they wouldn't care anymore. I didn't look inside it," he added piously.

Betsy doubted that but said only, "Connor took it to the post office."

He looked away again. "Are they mad?"

"I don't think so. Surprised, though."

He chuckled and wriggled his shoulders, relieved. "I guess they would be."

"Can I ask where you got the etui?"

"I don't got a— What's a etui?"

"It's a holder for needlework supplies. Shaped like an egg with a stem on top of it, and when you press the stem, it opens and there's scissors and needles and spools inside it. Emily told me about it, said it was on the dining room table."

"Is that what that's called? I looked inside it but there wasn't no thread on the spools. I was gonna get some thread and keep it like a sewing kit, except the scissors was too small for my fingers. I got it at a yard sale in Shorewood just this past summer. It was real dirty and nobody knew it would open up, but I washed it careful, an' put a little three-in-one aroun' the bottom of it, an' in about a minute it opened just as pretty as could be. Cost me two dollars, which I never woulda paid, but I picked it up and it rattled and I thought maybe there was money inside it."

"Would you consider selling it?"

"What? Oh no, ma'am, uh-uh; I never would part with any of my things. Neither would my dad, nor grandad, too. We none of us ever threw anything away. Every last thing in that house has a story, an' I know the stories. Havin' all those stories in my head makes me feel good."

# Chapter Thirteen

❖ ❖ ❖

IT was raining the next afternoon, and at the store, Betsy was restoring order to a spinner rack after a customer had dropped nearly a third of the scissors and knitting needles on the floor searching for an item that was, as it turned out, on a different spinner rack.

She looked around as someone entered wearing a voluminous raincoat with its hood pulled up. "Hi, Gracie," she said brightly. "What brings you in today?"

"Actually, Betsy, I'm Gracie's sister, Georgie," said the customer, who'd pulled her raincoat hood back to reveal her cropped blond curls.

"Gosh, I'm sorry!" said Betsy. "It's just that you two look so much alike. Except for your hair, of course."

"It happens sometimes." Georgine turned and said, "Gracie and Valentina are right behind me."

And they were. They all stood there for a few moments

to let the rainwater drip from their coats and from Valentina's old umbrella onto the square of carpet remnant put there for that purpose.

"Betsy," Valentina said, "I asked these two to look over the things we're setting aside in Tommy's house to see if they're worth trying to sell. They picked out a few things, then told me I should hire someone more expert than them to look at what we found."

Georgine said, "Gracie and I have some expertise, but we don't know everything, and I'm afraid we might've misjudged some things."

Valentina said, "I thought about seeking out an antiques dealer—this town has a lot of antiques stores. But suppose some of the valuable stuff in there isn't actually antique? Georgie gave us information about some of the things, like that awful Black Mammy cookie jar, but she says to get someone else to offer us appraisals, too."

"We thought you might know someone," Grace added.

Betsy said, "I think Leipold's does that sort of thing."

"Who're they?" asked Valentina.

"Are they that strange shop on Water Street?" said Georgine.

"Yes," said Betsy, nodding.

Leipold's was an Excelsior institution. It had begun as a gift shop, then expanded into the sale of lampshades and the restoration of old lamps. Then it started carrying souvenirs of Lake Minnetonka, and then collectibles and antiques, later adding old books, T-shirts, vintage postcards, rag dolls, old coaster wagons, milk cans, comic greeting cards, and just about anything that caught its owners' eyes as interesting or peculiar or nostalgic.

"How's everything coming along in Tom's house?" Betsy asked.

"It's coming, it's coming," said Valentina. "Tommy got mad at me when I told him I had people helping me clear things out, told me not to visit him again. Mr. Penberthy said that might happen and told me not to worry about it, because when Tommy sees how nice the place looks . . . he'll forgive me." She did not seem very sure about that, though.

"I've been to see him," said Betsy.

"Really? What did he say during your visit?" asked Valentina.

"I'm afraid he is really attached to the things he's stored in that house. He claims he knows every object in his possession: where he got it, when, and from whom. He proved it by describing that etui, which he got at a yard sale in Shorewood for two dollars, and a wicker birdcage he found outside Dr. Menderson's house after the family closed it up."

"The etui we're keeping, but I'm afraid all the birdcages are gone," said Valentina.

"Have you told him that?" asked Betsy.

"No, like I said, he told me not to come back to see him anymore."

"Did you ask him about the mailbag?" asked Georgine.

"Yes, I did. He said he found it sitting alone in the rain and brought it home with him for safekeeping. I didn't press him, but I could see he wasn't telling the whole truth. The postman probably left it unguarded for a minute and he took it. That's his pattern, stealing opportunistically. I once had a notion that he does that sort of thing absent-mindedly, even unconsciously, but now I think it's deliberate, since his remarkable memory extends even to his thefts."

GEORGINE went with Valentina to Leipold's. Mrs. Leipold was behind the counter at the back of the thickly cluttered store. Georgine nudged Valentina when they saw the iconic flying red horse on the back wall. The horse was life-size, startling to the eye, but this one appeared to be modern fiberglass, while the one in Riordan's house was vintage enameled steel, with the rust and chipping that were common to old metal.

"Mrs. Leipold?" asked Valentina.

"Yes, that's me." Mrs. Leipold was a medium-size woman with short white hair and gentle blue eyes. "May I help you?" she asked.

"Is that fiberglass Mobil sign for sale?" Georgine asked, gesturing at the horse.

"No, we've decided to keep it. And it's not fiberglass but enameled metal."

"Really? It's in remarkable shape," Georgine said, and persisted. "If you did sell it, what would you ask?"

"Probably three thousand."

Georgine nodded appreciatively. Considering its condition, the price was probably in range—but high enough to keep idle bids away.

Valentina said, "I'm in town to clear out Tommy Riordan's house. Ms. Pickering, here, and her sister know quite a lot about collectibles, but I've decided I'd like a second opinion about some of the objects in the house. I understand you and Mr. Leipold are willing to go through a house and price its contents. Is that so?"

"Yes, we do that."

"How much do you charge?"

"That would depend on the size of the house, how much property is in it, and whether or not you need a written report."

"It's not a big house, two bedrooms, but it's got a lot of stuff. And I think a written report might be a good idea."

"Well . . ." Mrs. Leipold hesitated, then said boldly, "How bad is it?"

"Pretty bad," acknowledged Valentina.

"In that case, the cost will be about three hundred dollars."

When she heard the cost estimate, Valentina's soft whistle sounded like an old-fashioned bomb coming down out of the sky.

Mrs. Leipold shrugged and waited.

Georgine turned to Valentina. "That's not a lot," she whispered. "Say yes, then get the estate to pay for it."

So Valentina, blinking as if in pain, said, "Okay. When can you do it?"

"How soon would you want us to start?"

"As soon as possible."

Mrs. Leipold opened a big spiral-bound appointment calendar. "How about the day after tomorrow, starting at 9:30 a.m., sharp? We'll estimate two days; I'll take the first day, Darel will take the second. If it takes longer than that, we'll both come, and we won't charge more for the extra day."

"All right," said Valentina, and they shook hands to seal the deal.

M RS. Leipold was prompt. When she came to the Riordan door, with her yellow notepad in hand, Valentina was there to meet her.

"Welcome to our mess, Mrs. Leipold," she said.

"Please, call me LaVerna."

"All right—LaVerna. I was going to ask if I could come with you into the house, but I have a couple of errands to run, so I think I'll leave you to it. But I would like to come back around noon to see how you're doing. And I can bring you lunch, if you like."

"Why, that's very kind of you. Soup and a sandwich would be wonderful."

"All right. See you in a few hours."

Valentina stepped aside to allow LaVerna to enter before going out herself. As she hurried down the walk to her old car, she heard LaVerna say, as she closed the door, "Oh my!"

B ETSY came back from lunch to find Godwin waiting eagerly for her return.

"What?" she asked.

"The mail's on the desk," he said, looking at it significantly.

She shrugged and, without taking off her coat, went to see what had him so excited.

Godwin came close behind her, peering around her

shoulder as she picked up the stack of white envelopes, the kind with glassine windows. Under the bills was a fat brown envelope, the six-by-nine size. The return address bore a name she didn't recognize, from Atlanta, Georgia. The envelope was faintly stained, as if it had been left out in the rain and then set aside long enough to dry.

"Open it first, open it first," said Godwin, fairly hopping up and down.

She turned on him with a frown. "Is this a prank?"

He took a step back, surprised. "Oh, it's no prank! This is an envelope from that mailbag they found in Tom Take's house."

"Oh?" She turned the envelope over in her hands. "That's different. Connor told me about this. He should be down here to see it opened." She reached for the phone.

But when he answered his cell, he wasn't upstairs. "I'm on my way to East Saint Paul," he said. "There's a Luther Auctions preview going on to give prospective bidders an advance look. Go ahead and open it. Tell me about it later."

"All right. Bye."

"You didn't say, 'I love you,'" Godwin pointed out when she put the phone down.

"So?" she said and picked up a letter opener. "Neither did he."

"Never mind, never mind, open the envelope," said Godwin, moving around to the other side of the desk for a better view.

Inside the envelope was a folded piece of cardboard, the kind that came from the back of a notepad. With the cardboard was a small, square, pale blue envelope, the kind that holds nice notepaper.

Impatient now, Betsy dropped the envelope onto the desk and opened the flap of cardboard. A snow-white handkerchief with a deep froth of lace edging tumbled to the desk.

"Gosh!" said Betsy.

"Wow!" said Godwin.

She picked it up. The handkerchief was an eight-inch square of delicate linen, and the lace was crocheted, done several inches deep with very fine thread, dropping into five long points along the sides, and even longer points at the corners, edged with tiny scallops. She drew it slowly across the back of her hand. It was a lovely, frivolous thing, evoking a long-gone past.

"What do you suppose it is, something for a bride?" asked Betsy.

"It's kind of large for a bridal accessory. Maybe it's an antique. Whatever, I'd simply love to flaunt it at a party." Godwin took it from her. "Oh, my *deah*!" he said, fluttering it at eye level. "Just too, too sweet!"

Betsy let him examine it more closely while she picked up the little square envelope and opened it. Inside was a folded notepaper featuring a bouquet of tulips. The handwriting was beautiful, just short of calligraphy. It began, *Dear Mrs. Berglund—*

Betsy gave a startled cry.

"What? What?" asked Godwin, dropping the handkerchief.

"This is addressed to Margot!"

"Well, of course it is. In 1996, Margot was alive and in charge here."

"Well, of course you're right. But still, it's so strange to see her name."

"What does the letter say?"

Betsy read it aloud:

*Dear Mrs. Berglund, I am enclosing a handkerchief with a lace edging that I designed myself. It is a simple pattern, but I think it has a very nice appearance.*

*I have been doing crochet since I was six years old and have taught classes in it. I am no longer able to teach a class, but I would like to know if you would be interested in carrying this pattern in your store.*

*I look forward to hearing from you.*

*Sincerely,*
*Mrs. Viola van Hollen*

"Why, the poor woman!" said Godwin. "Probably thought Margot was dishonest enough to keep the hanky and never cared to answer her letter!"

"How sad," said Betsy. "Because I think Margot would have liked to carry the pattern. I know I would." She looked inside both envelopes but found nothing resembling a pattern. "But it isn't here."

Godwin picked up the envelopes and looked for himself. "Well, isn't that too bad!"

"Well, I suppose it's better, in a way. If she didn't include a pattern, then at least she knew Margot hadn't misappropriated it. But here, her address is at the bottom. I wonder if she'd still be interested after all this time. I mean, look at this gorgeous thing! Of course I'm interested!"

The door opened just then, and Betsy lifted her gaze to

see a young man looking very eagerly at her. "Have you opened it yet?" he asked.

"Opened what?"

"Did I forget to mention that this fellow came by earlier?" said Godwin. "Betsy, this is Phillip Maxwell, from the *Sun Sailor*." Which was a free weekly newspaper, published in Excelsior.

Phillip was a slender young man wearing a dark gray suit, blue shirt, and bright yellow tie under an unbuttoned trench coat. He came forward to look at the beautiful handkerchief on the desk. "Is that what came to you from 1996?" he asked.

Godwin said, "He wants to interview some of the people who got mail from that old mailbag we found in Tom Riordan's house. I said okay—is it okay?"

"Yes," said Betsy, after an instant's thought. She was not averse to free publicity.

"Who's it from?" asked the reporter.

"A woman in Atlanta, Georgia. She wanted my sister, Margot, who first opened Crewel World, to carry the pattern for it in the shop."

"Is it an antique?" he asked.

"No, it's something she crocheted herself."

"Are you going to carry it?"

"I'll have to contact her to see if she's still interested."

"How did she find out about Crewel World from so far away?" He answered his own question. "Oh, on the Internet, I guess. Did you—or your sister, that's right—have a web site back then?"

"I don't think there were such things as web sites in

1996," said Godwin. "I know Crewel World didn't have one, since I helped Betsy build one in 2001."

"So how did she find you?"

"I have no idea."

"I don't suppose it matters. This is an interesting story. Thanks for talking with me. I'm sure this will be a great story for the *Sun Sailor*." The young man asked a few more questions, took a photograph of the handkerchief with his cell phone, and went away.

# Chapter Fourteen

### ❖ ❖ ❖

"Bᴜᴛ she didn't include the pattern," Betsy said the next morning over breakfast with Connor.

"Very wise of her," he said. "Margot might have reproduced it and sold copies to customers without offering Mrs. van Hollen a penny."

"Margot would never have done such a thing!"

"And Mrs. van Hollen knew this . . . how?"

"Well, yes, of course you're right. I wonder how she came to send that handkerchief all the way from Atlanta? I searched on Google for her name and didn't find anything, so I scribbled a note to her and drove by the post office after work. I put the shop's phone number and e-mail address on the note. Figure two or three days to get there, so maybe we'll hear from her in a week or less. Unless she's no longer at this address. Or"—Betsy shuddered—"I suppose it's possible that she's no longer alive. Well, I hope that's not the case. Anyway, this is kind of exciting, I hope she's still very much with us, and that she wants to sell the pattern."

"Very likely when she didn't hear from Margot, she tried somewhere else."

"Oh rats, you're probably right. What a shame! But still, it's been going on twenty years. Maybe she'd be willing to let us offer it a second time around. I don't crochet so I don't look at the details of crochet patterns. But even so, I'd say I haven't seen that pattern anywhere."


WHEN Betsy came down to open up the shop the next morning, she saw Alice Skoglund waiting for her outside the front door. Betsy hastened to unlock it, though it was ten minutes before opening time.

A loyal member of the Monday Bunch, Alice was a Lutheran minister's elderly widow. She had gained the habit of good deeds so long ago that even with failing eyes, she still crocheted and knit tiny hats for newborn and preemie babies, and afghans for impoverished people in Africa and the Middle East. Lately she'd taken up knitting prayer shawls for her church, which were presented as the outward form of blessings to members who were seriously ill or newly bereft.

She was a tall woman with broad shoulders and big hands, homely and kind. This morning she was looking as if she'd received a shock. In one gloved hand she held an envelope.

*Uh-oh*, thought Betsy, using a key to unlock the dead bolt on the door.

"Good morning, Alice, come on in. The pot's just heating but there will be hot water for tea in another minute."

Godwin came out from the back. "What, a customer already?" he said in good humor. "Hi, Alice, how's my favorite girl?" Then he saw the look on her face and paused. "Oh my, has something happened? Here, come over here, you look as if you need to sit down." He showed her to the library table and pulled a chair out for her.

"Thank you, Goddy, I have had a great surprise come in the mail, and I don't know if I'm on my head or my heels."

"Oh, Alice," said Betsy, "did you get one of those letters from eighteen years ago?"

Alice nodded. She fumbled in her overcoat pocket for a tissue and used it to rub her shapeless nose, which was already pink.

"Was it bad news?" asked Godwin.

"I—I'm not sure what to think about it," said Alice, putting the tissue back in her pocket.

Betsy came to sit beside her. "Do you want to tell us what it is?"

"It's a proposal of marriage!" cried Alice, tossing the envelope onto the table. "Come eighteen years too late, a proposal of marriage." She sobbed once, then took fierce control of herself. "I just couldn't believe it. I thought—I thought we'd broken off. We had a terrible quarrel—over nothing! Nothing at all, and then I didn't hear from him again, and I thought—I thought it was over and I was so sad for a long time, and all this while . . ." She did break down then.

Godwin and Betsy looked at each other in dismay.

Godwin said then, "I don't understand. You didn't see

119

the gentleman again? You didn't call him or write your own letter?"

"I was too proud, too proud! I wanted him to come to me, to take the first step—and he did! And I never knew, oh, I never knew!"

Godwin reached out for the envelope but changed his mind before his fingers touched it. "What happened to him? Did he move away?"

"He went to Mexico to do missionary work. He was gone for five years. When he came back, he had a wife—another American; he'd met her down there. He sold his house and they moved away, to Texas, I think, or Arizona . . ." Her voice trailed away, and her eyes looked distant.

Then she suddenly came back to herself. "But I mustn't burden you with this. This has nothing to do with you. I don't even know why I came here!" She started to get up.

Betsy put a hand on her shoulder. "You were right to come here," she said firmly. "We're your good friends, and we're going to ply you with tea and cookies, and, if necessary, take you out to dinner."

"Absolutely!" said Godwin. "I'm all yours—well, until seven this evening, when Rafael and I are going to a Northest Coin meeting." He leaned in and said in a confidential murmur, "You know those coins we found in Tom Take's house? I'm going to ask Valentina if Rafael and I can take them to a coin club meeting next month to see what they're worth."

"Goddy . . ." warned Betsy.

"Why can't I tell her? She's one of us! She won't go running to tell on us! Will you, dear, sweet, kind, *understanding* Alice?"

Despite herself, Alice smiled. "Oh, *you*—!" she said.

"See?" Godwin said to Betsy. "Now you just sit tight and I'll get you a nice cup of tea. And over it you can tell us all about this very intriguing romance of yours."

Alice did draw comfort and courage from the tea. Paul Engstrom, Alice said, was a member of Mount Calvary Lutheran Church back when Alice's husband was pastor. He was an active member, even serving a term on the vestry, though his main interest was outreach. He was firm in his faith, but charming and funny—the Bible stories he told in Sunday school were related in a hilarious Bill Cosby style. He was always respectful and courteous to Alice and made no approach to her for the first year of her widowhood. Then he began a courtship so understated it took her several months before she finally understood what he was doing.

But when they got serious, they discovered their differences. He wanted to go to Mexico to do missionary work, and she thought there was plenty of work to do right here in Minnesota. He began taking classes to improve his Spanish and one evening, probably in an attempt to tease her, insisted on speaking only Spanish to her. She lost her temper and told him to go home and not come back until he gave up trying to persuade her to go live in some filthy hovel in Mexico. She never heard from him again.

"And now this!" she said, and pulled the letter from its envelope. "Read it, read it!"

The letter was handwritten and began with an apology:

*My dearest Alice, You know I would not for the world distress you. If I didn't feel God's own voice calling me to work in Mexico on His behalf, I would not argue so strongly in favor of going. I was blinded by my desire to answer the call, and did not realize the strength of your resistance, or your fear of travel to a place so strange and, in your mind, dangerous. I apologize from the depths of my being for distressing you.*

*I propose the following: Allow me to go alone, with your blessing, for one year. On my return, I will hang up my foreign missionary shoes and devote my life to making you happy. If necessary, by marrying you—joke, joke, joke, my dearest one. I would marry you tomorrow if I could, but hope you will agree to this compromise.*

*Say yes, please say yes, please, please, please say yes.*

*Your madly devoted—Paul.*

"Oh my God," said Godwin, awed. "And you never got the letter, so he thought you said no, and he went away brokenhearted. Oh, this is the saddest thing I've ever heard!"

"He probably thought I was insulted by the way he proposed—'if necessary, by marrying you'—and when he got no reply . . ." She sighed. "Oh, what a fool I was! When I didn't hear from him, I should have called or written myself. But I was too proud, too proud!" She broke down again.

Betsy put an arm around Alice's shoulders. "Not at all. It was his fault for trying to make you go with him to a place you thought of as dangerous, where you didn't speak the language or understand the customs. It was wrong of him to try to force you."

"But he offered a perfect compromise! If I'd gotten this letter, I would have gladly agreed! Oh, that dreadful man!"

"Wait, I thought you just said Paul wasn't being dreadful," said Godwin.

"I mean Tom Riordan! It's a good thing I'm a Christian, or I might go pay him a visit and tell him what a wicked thief he is, he who made my life sadder than it might have been!"


W HEN the next edition of the *Sun Sailor* came out, there was an immediate grab for copies. The paper was a weekly that paid for itself with advertising and normally there were numerous copies left over by the time the next edition appeared. But not this time. People sat in restaurants, in the new library, in the Barleywine microbrewery; they stood outside in the freezing rain, hunched under whatever meager shelter they could find—a young tree, a narrow overhang; they huddled in groups or sat alone at home, reading the story of the late-delivered mail.

THE MAIL MUST GO THROUGH read the headline, EVEN EIGHTEEN YEARS LATE. The article told of an old mailbag found in a hoarder's house, half full of undelivered mail postmarked 1996.

Betsy searched for and found the paragraph about her own experience with a long-delayed package.

"Small business owner Bessy Devonshire received a beautiful lace-edged handkerchief from a woman in Atlanta, Georgia, and a request that she sell the handkerchief in her store," read the article.

Betsy sighed. In her whole life, no matter where she lived, every single time she knew something about an event, the media report got at least some of the details wrong. This was no exception, beginning with getting her name wrong.

The article continued, "Devonshire has written to the handkerchief maker. 'It's sad that I didn't get this right away,' Devonshire said. 'I really would have liked to carry her handkerchiefs in my shop.'"

This after the reporter had talked with her for half an hour!

Well at least the subject was handkerchiefs, not overshoes. Or cotton candy.

Betsy went back to the start of the article to read it in its entirety. The article's author said there were fifty-six first-class pieces of mail in the bag. Twenty-seven of them were bills, long out of date. Sixteen of the remaining were undeliverable, either because the recipients had moved and the forwarding information was long expired, or the recipients were deceased.

That left thirteen. Betsy knew one was her own. Another was Alice's—but there was no mention in the article of Alice Skoglund, or even of a woman who received a proposal of marriage too late.

The article did mention Mr. and Mrs. Lundquist, who received a letter about Joey, their high school graduate son, offering him a scholarship to a fine university to study political science. Since the letter did not arrive on time, the boy had instead gone to a vocational school and now owned a very successful plumbing company. "I think I do cleaner work as a plumber than I would have as a politician," he was quoted as saying.

Betsy happened to know the plumber in question, and the quote was a highly bowdlerized version of something he frequently said. Which was all right; the *Sun Sailor* was a family newspaper.

She also knew that Joey had flunked out of the University of Minnesota before going to vocational school—from which he did not graduate, but he was apprenticed to a licensed plumber who owed his father a significant favor. Joey was very bright, but also very dyslexic.

The next story was about Dee Dee Millwright, who had a favorite nephew, Aaron Monroe. He was described by Ms. Millwright as a solemn little fellow, bright in his studies— he was in third grade—who, when he stayed with her, played placidly with her little dog, slept long and deep, and cried when the visit was over. He loved her cooking, and she sent him cookies every few months.

Aaron died after falling out of the big tree in his front yard, where he'd climbed after a quarrel with his father. Dee Dee was devastated. Aaron's parents sold their home and moved away, and Dee Dee lost touch with them.

Then came a last letter from Aaron, like a voice from the grave. Dee Dee did not wish to share its contents except to say his last wish was to come live with her permanently so he could play some more with the dog.

"Dee Dee's eyes filled with tears as she told the story," wrote the reporter.

But she did not share even a brief quote from the letter, Betsy noted. Was that important? Perhaps not. Perhaps Dee Dee shared Betsy's skepticism about a reporter's ability to get the facts right.

Which of course made Betsy wonder what about that story had the reporter gotten wrong.

# Chapter Fifteen

◈ ◈ ◈

NURSE Crowley opened the door to Riordan's room. "Good afternoon, Mr. Riordan," she called out cheerily. "Today we—Mr. Riordan? Oh my God!"

She pressed the alarm button on the wall that signaled Code Blue, and a very loud clanging began outside the room. In seconds two nurses came in, and within two minutes the crash cart rolled in.

A lengthy struggle began, but twenty minutes later a perspiring doctor sighed and said, "Let's call it."

Nurse Crowley checked her watch. "Three fourteen," she said aloud and wrote that down as the time of death.

As the adrenaline began to recede, the doctor asked, "How the hell did this happen?"

VALENTINA was sitting with Godwin at the library table in Crewel World. It was near closing time, and there were no other customers present. Godwin had a big crochet hook and a ball of thick yarn so Valentina could more easily see what he was doing. Valentina had the yellow yarn she'd bought and one of the hooks; the book *Simple Crocheting* was open in front of her. Both were making a chain; both stopped when it was about thirty stitches long.

"Next," said Godwin, "triple crochet. You've got one loop on the hook, so wrap the yarn around twice ahead of that loop to make three." He did so, and she followed suit. "Push the hook through the chain two stitches back, grab the yarn, and pull it through. Now you have four loops on your hook." He paused while she followed suit, using the same back-facing movement of the hook as he did, like putting on your shoes heel first.

"Good, now go through again and pick up the yarn with your hook and pull it through two loops. See? You now have five loops. Grab more yarn and pull it through two loops. You've reduced the loops by two but gained an additional one with the one you pulled through. Then grab it again and pull it through two loops. Finally, grab it one more time and pull it through the last two loops."

"Well, that's not so hard," she said, as she followed his instructions. "I don't know why I can't learn how to do these things by reading a book. That book on crochet you sold me is really good—but I can only see that now, after I sit down and watch someone actually doing the stitch I'm trying to learn. Once I've learned it from an actual live person, then I can more clearly understand the instructions. But I need to see it demonstrated first in person."

"Lots of people are like that," he said. "Do you have Internet access?"

"Dial-up," she said, "but yes."

"You can find short tutorials on any crochet stitch on the Net," he said. "They shoot close-ups of the stitcher's fingers doing the stitch. Easy peasy. I happen to know Betsy uses the video tutorials when she's attempting a knitting stitch she hasn't done in a while." He leaned in to confide, "People of her age—"

He was interrupted by the ringing of a cell phone not his own. Valentina's cell phone. Her ring tone was the sound of a phone ringing, which amused Godwin.

Valentine said, "Leona loaned me one of hers." She pulled it from her purse. "Hello?" she said into it. She listened to the caller, and the expression on her face changed from friendly interest to shock and dismay. She dropped her yarn and hook on the table to take hold of her phone with both hands. "Lord have mercy! When did this happen? Was it some kind of—" She listened. "Oh no, are they sure? But— No, I guess not." She listened some more, eyes closed. "This is so awful! I don't know what—What? I don't understand—really? Yes, yes. All right." She was crying now. "No, no, I'll be all right. Yes, I'm with someone." She glanced over at Godwin, whose expression showed the concern he was feeling for her. "Yes, yes, yes, all right. I'm sorry, I can't talk anymore right now." She broke the connection and dropped the little phone onto the table. "Oh God, oh God!"

"What is it? What's the matter?"

"It's Tommy, he's dead!"

"Dead? But he was getting better!"

"It's not because of the accident. They think . . . they think someone came into his room and, and killed him!"

"*Killed* him? But how? And why?"

"I don't know!" wailed Valentina. She slammed her fist down, sending her ball of yarn skittering across the table and onto the floor. It rolled away, unspooling in a thin yellow line across the carpet.

"But that doesn't make any sense," said Godwin, puzzled, trying to sound reasonable. "Tom never hurt anybody."

"She told me to, to expect a v-visit from a police detective," said Valentina, making hiccup sounds as she tried to stop crying.

"I think what they want is for you to tell them who might have had a motive to hurt Tom," said Godwin.

"But I can't tell them anything about him!" Valentina wailed, wiping her eyes with the tissue Godwin handed to her. "I'm practically a stranger in town. *And* a stranger to him." She looked over the tissue at Godwin. "But you aren't. You could tell them things. Who do you think would like to see my cousin dead?"

Taken aback, Godwin said, "Nobody. He was a good guy in a lot of ways, like his volunteer work with Art in the Park and Apple Days. He was kind of strange, it's true—but who isn't? I mean, look at me. I'm strange."

"Not as strange as Tommy," said Valentina, almost laughing. "Look at you? No, look at Tommy's house! My God, look at his house!" A huge sob escaped her. "Oh, this is so awful!"

"I know, my heart is aching for you. Would a cup of tea be useful?"

At first she shook her head no, but then nodded. "Yes, and another tissue, please; this one is all soaked."

Godwin pulled the cardboard cube of tissues out from behind the big bin that held needlework tools and set it in front of her. "Help yourself, we've got plenty. As for tea, would you like regular? Herbal? There's coffee, too."

"Anything, I don't care." Valentina pulled two tissues from the box and blew her nose. "Thangs," she said moistly.

In the back, Godwin picked a tea bag that featured soothing chamomile in its herb mix, put in a teaspoon of real sugar, and poured water from the simmering electric kettle into the pretty porcelain cup. For good measure he added a couple of shortbread cookies to the saucer before bringing the treat back to the table.

"Th-thank you," said Valentina in a shaky voice. She picked up the cup, which rattled against the saucer, spilling a little. She hesitated long enough to steady her hand and inhale its steam, then tasted the brew. "Ummmm," she said, nodding. "Thank you," she said again.

She sat for a full minute, not looking at Godwin, not drinking any more of the tea. The fingers of her right hand, trembling, fumbled over one of the cookies, but she did not pick it up or even seem aware that she was touching it.

Godwin, at a loss, finally said, "What can I do to help you?"

"Hmm?" She glanced at him, then away. "I don't know. I can't think straight. I don't know what to do next. I think I'm getting scared. Maybe I should just quit this project and go home."

Godwin said gently, "I don't think the police would like that."

Her eyes widened as she looked at him. "What do you mean?"

"Maybe you can tell a police investigator something useful. Maybe not—but they'll want to talk to you to find out what you know."

"I don't like cops, never have." Her tone was defensive.

"I agree that the safest position to—to aspire to, is to never draw their notice. It can be hard to find yourself the center of their attention."

"What do you know about it?" she asked angrily.

"Oh, my dear, a few years ago I was arrested on suspicion of murder. I wasn't guilty, but it took a lot of effort to prove that. Betsy . . ." He had to pause and draw a ragged breath. "Betsy went to bat for me, worked like a demon, and found out who really killed John. I will never, ever, ever stop being grateful to her. Ever."

She was staring at him, shocked. "Wow! I had no idea— Wait, Betsy? You mean the Betsy who owns this store?"

"Yes, that Betsy. She's done it for other people, too. If it looks like the police are seriously thinking of blaming you for this, you should ask Betsy for help."

The tears overflowed again. "How can you think I did this? How can you?"

He blinked, surprised at the intensity in her voice. "Why, hey, I don't think any such thing!"

She studied his face, her own expression gone quiet, then said, "Thank you." She pulled a tissue from the box. "God bless you."

# Chapter Sixteen

♦ ♦ ♦

POLICE detectives Mike Malloy and Sid Halloran were questioning the floor nurse at HCMC who was on duty when Tom Riordan's death was discovered.

Malloy was slim, with red hair gone tan, a freckled lipless face, and cool blue eyes. He was wearing his second-best dark gray suit and carried a fat notebook.

Halloran was more strongly built, of medium height, with keen hazel eyes, wearing a gray suit and perhaps a little too much jewelry.

The nurse was a dark-haired woman with deep brown eyes, long, narrow nose, wide mouth, and a complexion pale from years of working nights. She said, "I suppose I do see a fair amount of dying in this job. But murder, right here at the hospital? Never on my watch!"

"Who visited Mr. Riordan the day he died, Ms. Crowley?" asked Malloy. His blue eyes were chilly, his thin mouth a straight line, but his tone was courteous. They were in a small meeting room on the hospital's top floor.

"I don't know, we don't keep a log." Sunlight poured through a window over the table they were sitting at, getting into the nurse's eyes, making her squint. He rose, went to the window, and twisted a thin, clear rod, closing the narrow blinds.

"Thank you," she said.

"No problem."

Halloran asked, "Did you recognize any visitors as having come more than once?"

"Oh," she said, "well, yes. His cousin came at least three times, but then they had a quarrel and he told her not to come back."

"Was that quarrel on the day he died?"

"No, it was a few days before."

"And she did stay away?"

"I didn't see her again, but I'm not on the nurse's station twenty-four-seven."

Malloy and Halloran collected the names of all those on the desk within twenty-four hours prior to Riordan's body being discovered. Malloy asked, "Who else came to see him while you were on duty?"

"I'm sorry, I couldn't tell you. I mean, I don't know their names."

Halloran, writing, said, "Describe them for me."

"Well, there was an older woman—not an old woman, but about middle-aged, not tall, blond hair cut short and curly, wears a blue trench coat. She was carrying a box of candy."

Malloy wrote *Betsy Devonshire* in his notebook. "Who else?" he asked.

"A tall woman, maybe thirty or a little older, ash-blond, her face was beautiful in an old-fashioned way, you know? She stopped to ask me what room Mr. Riordan was in."

*Jill Larson?* He wrote.

"Who come to see him on the day he died?"

"Well, there was this one woman, very slim and good-looking, nice hair, about shoulder length, that color that looks dark brown until you see it's really dark red. She was dressed very nicely, I remember. I didn't see her go in, but I saw her come out. She stopped in the doorway to say to him, 'You take care now, hear?' kind of Southern, which I thought was sweet. And she stopped by my station to ask how he was doing. I wondered who she was, I mean Mr. Riordan wasn't the kind to have a high-end friend like her. She was his last visitor, that I saw."

Malloy, nodding, wrote down the description—he didn't recognize the woman, but the description was vivid—and said, "So she was the last person to see Riordan before the nurse found his body?"

"No, Bobby Boo went in to clean up his room, and I heard him laughing at something Mr. Riordan said as he came out."

Halloran's pen came to an abrupt stop on the page. "Bobby who?"

"He's an orderly, Robert Booth. We call him Bobby Boo. He's a student at the U, very bright, but has a strange sense of humor—he and Riordan were kind of a match in that regard."

"Is he here today?"

She looked at her watch. "He's due in about half an hour."

Malloy asked, "Is he usually on time?"

"Yes, he's very reliable. Do you want to talk to him?"

"Oh yes."

"I'll tell him. Are we finished?" She started to get up.

"Not yet."

She sat back down, amusement twitching her mouth. "What now?"

Halloran asked, "Did anyone go in to see Riordan after Bobby Boo left?"

"Nnnno, I don't think so."

"You don't sound sure."

"That's because I'm not. The station gets busy, so I'm not always paying attention to who's going past it on their way to visit someone."

Malloy said, "So for all you know, Bobby Boo was the last person to see Tom Riordan alive."

The implications of that took about three seconds to sink in.

"Oh, no! Oh, no, no! Not for one second! Not Bobby Boo!"

Malloy persisted, "Mr. Riordan can be touchy. Maybe he blew up at this Bobby Boo. Did he ever complain about something Bobby Boo said or did?"

"No, not once."

"How long had those two known one another?" asked Malloy.

"I'm sure they had never met before Mr. Riordan came here as a patient."

"How sure?"

"Well, the way Bobby talked about him, I'm very sure. He'd come out and tell me the funny thing Mr. Riordan told him just now—you know, like he never heard anyone say that kind of thing before. And Mr. Riordan said nice things about Bobby, like you do when you're making a new friend."

Halloran got the names and contact information of the other nurses assigned to the station on Riordan's floor. The two detectives split the list and spent the next several hours interviewing them.

ROBERT "Boo" Booth was a big, fair, solidly built, corn-fed farmer's son, genial, soft-spoken, with a glint of humor in his pale gray eyes. Born and raised near Mankato, he was the middle boy of three, probably the brightest, definitely the most ambitious.

"I thought large-animal veterinary, but my girlfriend wanted to be a nurse and said I should at least take premed at college. And she was right, I think I do better when the patient can tell me where it hurts."

Malloy obediently smiled and asked, "Tell me about Tom Riordan."

Booth reared back slightly, smiling, twisted his head a little, and said, "Now, he was a character, a real character. Had a sideways way of looking at the world."

"What do you mean, sideways?"

"You know, a little off-kilter, from an unusual angle. Smart, yes, but in an unusual way."

"Like how?"

"Like he knew a lot about collectibles and antiques, but he talked about them like you or I would talk about friends. Like how they smile when he comes into the room and surround him with love when he's down. And he told me when the country collapsed he would survive by selling food from this big stash he had in his basement."

"So he didn't say that perhaps he had more stuff than he actually needed, or that at least some of it was junk?"

"No, no, no, of course not. Anyway, nobody thinks his possessions are 'junk.' He said he had a lot of 'things.' Used that word a lot. Said his house was full of three generations' worth of valuable things." Booth shrugged his broad shoulders. "Maybe some of it's junk; I know my folks have a house full of things they treasure but other people might think is junk."

Accepting the rebuke placidly, Malloy shifted gears and asked, "Did Riordan mention anyone who was angry with him, or he was angry with?"

"His cousin, what's-her-name, Val. I think it went both ways, he was mad at her and she was mad at him."

"Do you know why?"

Booth thought briefly. "As I understood it, she was supposed to go into his house and clean it up, make some repairs to the plumbing, but instead she got a crew together and was throwing out all his things. He said she was mad because he was trying to stop her from selling his things and pocketing the money. She said she wasn't going to report to him anymore about what she was doing. He said if he ever got out of the hospital he was going to shoot her dead."

\*    \*    \*

FROM that start, it only took a few days for Malloy and Halloran to circle in on Valentina Shipp as their best suspect, mostly because there didn't seem to be any other suspects. Malloy got the address of the motel she was staying at. Halloran met Malloy at Excelsior's police building one midmorning, and the two drove over to Shorewood to see her. They prepared for the interview on the way by going over what they had already discovered.

They agreed that Shipp's motive was apparent and strong: money. She was not a wealthy person; in fact, she was probably perilously close to the poverty line—Halloran thought she was probably on the wrong side of it—despite having no dependents and owning her own home.

Being Tom Riordan's only living relative put her in line to inherit his home and property. The house was probably not much of an asset, but Malloy pointed out that the lot on which it stood was very valuable. And there were apparently many things of considerable value inside it. He'd had a talk with the Leipolds, who said their estimate of the contents of the house amounted to something above twenty-five thousand dollars.

"Holy buckets!" exclaimed Halloran.

"Yeah, and that doesn't include the hoard of Morgan dollars or the three pieces of high-quality jewelry currently residing in a safe deposit box at First Bank of Excelsior."

"How did you find out about them?"

"Had a little talk with a couple of people who were helping Shipp clear out the house. One of them told me—I promised not to mention the name."

Halloran nodded, then asked, "What's a Morgan dollar?"

"It's a silver dollar minted between the late 1870s and early 1900s, named after the man who designed it for the U.S. Mint. It's got a woman's head on one side and a spread eagle on the other. They're about ninety percent silver and weigh a tad over an ounce, so there's value to be had in just melting them down. They're also very collectible, some are much more valuable than the others."

"How many in the hoard?"

"My informant isn't sure, a couple-three dozen—and I don't know if any of them are the high-end kind."

"Have you already talked to Ms. Shipp?"

"No, but I've talked to someone who knows her, and he said she's a lot like her cousin, an outlier, well out on the fringes of normal behavior."

"Was it your informant who told you that?"

"No, I called her hometown and got hold of a sergeant on the Muncie PD, and got an earful. Years back, before people started keeping chickens for pets, she had her own little flock in her backyard. They laid eggs and when they didn't she'd whack off their heads and make chicken dinner."

Halloran snorted.

"Also, she'd been cited repeatedly for not cutting the grass in her front yard, but then she came up with a plan to 'restore' her property to 'natural prairie' status. Granted, she did her research, testified before the city government to get a special permit—and won. But the result was all weeds all the time, because she couldn't afford the seeds of native prairie plants, and she didn't have the knowledge or skill it took to do it right."

"Hmmmm," said Halloran. "Anything else?"

"I saved the best for last. She's got the kind of funny-looking house and she looks just odd enough to start rumors that she had a stash of gold coins in her basement. After a couple of burglaries and some vandalism, she got a concealed carry permit. She nailed an announcement to that effect on her front door, and beside it a target from a visit to a shooting range with six holes in a tight little cluster in the center."

Halloran laughed and Malloy smiled; after all, what she did was legal, and she didn't live in their jurisdictions.

Halloran said, "But still, I see how it might indicate a problematic personality."

"Yeah, like that of the late Tom Riordan."

"He's in your neck of the woods, how well did you know him?"

"Back when I was on patrol, I had had a few meet-ups with Tom, mostly on complaints that he was loitering or begging outside a store or restaurant, or nude bathing—seriously, he'd take a bar of soap and a washcloth and go down to our beach—did it about once a summer. But he didn't mouth off; when I called him in, he'd smile and apologize, come on out of the water to towel off, at least most of the time."

"And other times?"

"Aw, he'd get a little mouthy. But not often. He'd see it was me, and get friendly again, because he considered us buds. Once in a great while, he'd seem confused. There was something wrong in the man's head, that was obvious. But I never saw him offer to strike anyone. Ever."

"But nobody thought to arrest the fellow and get him the help he so obviously needed?"

"Well, I'm not sure that was a mistake. You know the kind of help most of those impoverished hopeless cases get: none. I think he was better off being a public nuisance than serving as prey to thugs incarcerated with him. People liked him, or at least put up with him. The worst thing about him was, he was an incorrigible thief. But what he took were little things, an orange pop at the gas station, an old magazine at Leipold's, a couple pieces of candy from the bowl at a restaurant checkout register without first buying a meal. Sometimes he'd look up, see the owner looking back, and take the item anyway. He'd grin and walk out with it. Other times, he'd look ashamed and put it back. If you stood in his way and asked him what the hell he thought he was doing, he'd give it back—but if he got as far as his house with it, he would deny he knew anything about it."

"And no one filed an official complaint?" Halloran's scorn was clear.

"Aw, Excelsior was used to him and his ways, no one had cared to press charges. Oh, now and again some one of us would haul him in, tell him he was banned from someplace, and have the chief give him a lecture, but he never appeared in court charged with a crime. He was mostly harmless."

"Yeah, a harmless jerk who made a threat of violence against someone he thought was taking serious advantage of him. And now he's dead."

*Yes,* thought Malloy, *someone came into his hospital room and leaned on his face with a spare pillow taken from the room's closet. And now we're going to talk with someone who just might be the someone we're looking for.*

They parked in front of Valentina Shipp's motel room, beside the shabby old car that belonged to her, and went to rap on the door. She answered it promptly, but said nothing, eyeing them with suspicion, a tall, thin woman somewhere in her early fifties, with dark, intense eyes and dark graying hair pulled back and fastened with a rubber band. She was wearing faded jeans, green sneakers that had a hole in one toe, and a tan sweater a size too big that looked hand-knit.

She was younger than Tom, less strange-eyed, but obviously cut from the same genetic cloth. Like him she was bony and narrow, with that same beaky nose, wide mouth, and lots of oddly dark freckles. But the thing that sent Malloy's cop-alarm ringing was how sharply defensive she turned as soon as he showed her his ID and asked if she would speak with them.

"Why? What about?" she asked, eyes widening, and one arm lifting as if to close the door on them—a gesture she quickly halted half made.

"About Thomas Riordan. He's your cousin, right?"

"Yes?" She made it a request for more information.

Halloran spoke up. "And you have an emergency conservatorship over him, is that correct?"

"Well, I did, but now he's dead, it's ended, according to my attorney, Mr. James Penberthy." There was noticeable emphasis on the phrase "my attorney."

Mike knew Jim Penberthy, knew he wasn't a criminal defense attorney and therefore only a little better than useless in the predicament Ms. Shipp was about to find herself in.

"So the work on sorting out the material in the Riordan house is ended?"

"Yes, for now. The conservatorship ended when Tommy

died. But I'm going to be appointed a—" She hesitated, looking for the right legal term. "Ah, yes, personal representative. My attorney says it takes about five days or a week. Then I get to go back to work." She frowned and took several deep breaths through that prominent nose before bursting out, "This delay is *outrageous*! No one really cared about Tommy while he was alive! I cared, I drove hundreds of miles to help and people like you think I came here on purpose to kill him!"

Halloran said, "We're not here to blame you, we're here to find out what happened to him."

"So why aren't you doing that, instead of picking on me?"

"We have to go where the case leads me. You profit by his death, so here we are to ask you about that. Would you be willing to come with me downtown?"

"No . . ." She wasn't sure she was entitled to refuse.

Malloy said, "Or you can meet us at the Excelsior police building."

"Am I under arrest?" She was becoming belligerent.

Halloran said in a surprisingly conciliatory tone, "No, of course not. But we're conducting an investigation, and you may be able to help us go forward with that. You do want whoever murdered your cousin found, right?"

Sudden tears in Shipp's eyes were quickly blinked away. "Of course I do! But you can ask me anything you like right here."

Halloran gave a big, exasperated sigh. There was no way they could tell her they wanted her in a law enforcement environment, where her growing impudence would be cowed and therefore she'd be more likely to cooperate, less likely to shout and throw things. Drawing from experience with other citizens, Malloy was sure Shipp was a shouter.

Still . . . she was right, she was not under arrest. They did not have the evidence—yet—to arrest her.

As lead investigator, it was Halloran's decision. "Fine, let's sit down and talk right here."

Shipp stared at Halloran for several seconds, her face a careful blank, then she stepped back and let them come inside.

The room was small but clean. The carpet was thin and worn, a sad shade of brown. The blackout curtains on the window were also brown. The cushion on the only chair in the room was a dusty maroon, pulled up to a table with a scarred veneer surface. She gestured at Halloran to take the chair, and Malloy went to stand against the wall next to the door. She sat on the bottom edge of the bed, which had a red and brown paisley coverlet slightly disordered, as if she'd been lying on it.

A radio in the next unit could be heard broadcasting a news program, the words unintelligible but the urgent voice of the reporter and the bumper music that marked a segment were unmistakable.

Mike got out his fat notebook and wrote down the date, time, location, and Valentina's name.

"Have you been able to make final arrangements for the burial of your cousin?" he asked.

He made the query in a quiet voice, but the words made her flinch. "Not yet. I don't know . . ." She hesitated. "I'm not sure what I'm going to do about Tommy. The medical examiner is supposed to call me, and then . . . I don't know."

"There's an excellent funeral home in Excelsior, Huber's

is the name. They can help with arrangements, even if it's to send his body somewhere else for burial."

She was surprised at this offer of assistance. She asked, half serious, "It's not owned by your brother-in-law, is it?"

He smiled. "No, they're no relation. I understand you've hooked up with the owner of Crewel World, Betsy Devonshire. You can ask her about them, they buried her sister."

"Thanks, I'll do that."

The tension in the room had eased.

Halloran took over. "Now I want to talk to you about your cousin. How well did you know him? Did you grow up together?"

"Not well at all. For one thing, I'm ten years younger than he is, and for another, I grew up in Indiana and he grew up here. That house he lived in was bought by his grandparents and left to his parents, who left it to him, along with some kind of legal setup, a trust I think, because he can't earn his own living. I saw him maybe three or four times when he was growing up; once when we came up there for a week and twice when he came to stay with us for a summer."

"Are there any other cousins?"

"No."

"So he was an only child and you are an only child."

"Yes. Well, that is, we didn't start out to be that way. Tommy had a younger brother, or maybe it was a sister, who died right after she was born. My mother had two still-births."

Definitely something awry in the genes of these people, thought Malloy, taking notes as Halloran asked the questions.

"How did you two stay in touch? Phone calls, e-mail, Christmas letters?"

"We mostly didn't. He didn't have a computer and neither of us likes writing letters. I used to send him birthday cards, when I remembered to, and I almost always sent him a Christmas card. He sent me a Christmas card sometimes, and twice he sent me a postcard with a picture of a flying pig on it—same postcard, three or four years apart. No message, just his name. I don't know what that was about, maybe he thought it was funny and forgot the second time he already sent it to me the first time. The only reason they contacted me was I'm about his only next of kin."

Malloy spoke up. "So you are the sole heir?"

She stared at him for several seconds while a puzzled frown formed. "Heir? You mean like in a will? I didn't know he wrote a will."

"As far as I know, he never wrote a will."

"Then what's this heir stuff?"

"I mean, who gets his house and anything else he owned?"

"How should I know?" She was sounding belligerent again, and a little frightened.

Halloran gave Malloy a quelling look and said to Valentina, "Well, let's take another approach. You said you're his only next of kin?"

"Oh, that. Yes, I am. Is that what he means? Next of kin gets his stuff?" Her eyes shifted to a corner of the room and she said, "I hadn't thought of that."

Malloy nearly smiled at this lie and said, "Really?"

She looked uncomfortable, then her chin came up. She looked him in the eye but said nothing.

He said, "So, if there are no other relatives still alive, that would make you his sole heir."

She still said nothing, though she was breathing so hard the air whistled in her nose. "So what?" she finally asked.

Halloran said, almost gently, "That means that because he's dead, you get all his property: the house and its contents."

"I already got a house, and his house is full of crap."

Malloy said impatiently, "According to the Leipolds, there is more than twenty-five thousand dollars' worth of not-crap in the house."

"They said that? They haven't said that to me!" said Valentina.

"They will, they're making up a report for you right now. And there's no law that says you can't sell the property and take the money home with you."

She drew a breath to argue with him, then let it out. "So what?" she asked again, this time without the fangs.

"So who else had a motive as strong as that to kill Mr. Riordan?"

She blinked away sudden tears of fright almost before he noticed them, but said bravely, "It's not my job to find that out. It's yours."


"WELL, what do you think?" asked Halloran as the two rode in Malloy's car back to Excelsior.

"Apart from the fact that she's about as hinky as she could be? I think she's almost as scared as she's angry. I think she came up here thinking she could tuck poor Cousin Tom into some kind of locked ward, sell his house the following weekend, and go home on Monday with a purse full of money."

"I don't know," said Halloran slowly. "I think she's behaving—for her—normally."

"Normally? Seriously?"

"I don't think she told us a single lie."

# Chapter Seventeen

❖ ❖ ❖

I T was a little past noon the next day when Valentina came into Crewel World. She found Betsy and Godwin sitting at the library table in the middle of the room having lunch, each with a cup of soup and half a sandwich, a complex scatter of papers and catalogs between them.

The merry notes of a sort-of-familiar tune on the toy organ announced her arrival. Was it a different tune than last time? She wasn't sure.

Godwin and Betsy looked up as she came in. "How may we help you?" asked Betsy, starting to get up.

"No, stay there," said Valentina. "I want to talk to you."

"All right. Won't you sit down?"

"Thank you." Valentina came to the table and sat down in a chair one space away from the two of them. But then her nerves failed her. She clasped her hands on the table and looked at the pegs holding needlepoint yarn in thin skeins on the far wall.

After a bit, Godwin asked, "How's the work going on Tom's house?"

"I've stopped it for now. The conservatorship died with Tommy, so I'm not in charge anymore."

"Who is?"

"I don't know. I think a judge has to decide."

"Did the Leipolds finish their inspection?" asked Betsy.

"Yes, I'm supposed to go pick it up this afternoon." She was still not looking at them, and so didn't see Godwin and Betsy exchange puzzled glances.

Another silence fell, then Valentina took a deep breath. "Two police detectives came to talk to me yesterday. They think I murdered Tommy."

"Strewth!" exclaimed Godwin.

"Police detectives from where?" asked Betsy.

"One from Minneapolis and the other from here in Excelsior."

"Mike Malloy is *such* a jerk!" said Godwin. "It was Mike, wasn't it?"

"Yes."

"Did he threaten to arrest you?" asked Betsy.

"No. But he said he doesn't know anyone else with a motive as strong as mine."

Then she looked at the two of them. "I don't know what to do. Godwin, you said . . . you said Betsy helps people . . . with this kind of trouble."

"Yes, I did," said Godwin, looking significantly at Betsy.

"What is Mike doing investigating this in the first place?" asked Betsy, sounding defensive. "The murder happened in Minneapolis, and you're living right now in Shorewood."

"Betsy," Godwin began.

"Plus, I'm very busy right now. We're shorthanded and we're at the start of our busy season." She gestured at the papers on the table.

"Well, then, I'm sorry I bothered you," said Valentina stiffly. "I'll just go, okay?"

"No, you won't!" said Godwin fiercely. "Sit still! Betsy, she came hundreds of miles to help her last living relative, and now she's going to be charged with his murder if we don't do something!"

"'We'?"

"You know perfectly well my workload about doubles when you get started on these things. I'm willing to do my part, so you should be, too. Anyway, now we've got Connor to help out."

"Connor has nothing to do with the shop."

Godwin stared at her. "Oh, my dear, dear boss. Of course he does. He's *essential*. He can work here when I can't, and he can help you in your investigations."

"I *said*—" Betsy halted.

Valentina listened to them argue and stood up. "Please, never mind," she said. "I've taken care of myself most of my life, and I'll get through this. Forget I was even here."

Godwin got to his feet, too. "Oh, Valentina, this is bigger trouble than you think. You can't do this alone, you have to have help—you have to *demand* that someone help you."

Betsy stood and held out her hand to Valentina. "Godwin's right, you are in very serious trouble. I'm sorry I was reluctant to say right away I'd help you. All this—" She gestured at the table. "This can wait. Now, sit down and let's talk."

Monica Ferris

One thing they talked about was Tom Riordan's remains.

"The medical examiner still has Tom's body," said Valentina. "I don't know when he's going to release it. I also don't know what to do about Tom when he does."

"Call Huber's right here in Excelsior," said Betsy at once. "They were wonderful to me when my sister, Margot, died."

"And talk to Jim Penberthy," added Godwin. "Surely Tom's estate can pay for his funeral."


BETSY went with Valentina to the Leipolds' store on Water Street to pick up their report on Riordan's house.

Darel was behind the desk today. He was a stocky man with heavy features. He had sharp dark eyes behind glasses and a cheerful smile. He handed Valentina a plain white envelope, and Valentina handed him a long blue check.

Darel said, "I'm glad you asked us. I've wondered what was in that house for a long time—Tom was very defensive about the place, so I suppose we should have guessed he was a junker. It was an interesting job; more difficult than the usual, but I think you'll like the results."

Valentina ripped open the envelope eagerly and found two sheets of paper numbering, describing, and valuing nearly thirty items. The dollar values ranged from eighty to—shockingly—five thousand dollars. That last was for an autographed first edition of Zane Grey's first novel, *Betty Zane*. Valentina had heard of Zane Grey—he was her father's favorite author—but thought the books were cheap potboiler westerns. "Oh, no," said Darel, "he was a millionaire writer, back when a million dollars was serious money."

There was not a total at the bottom, and Valentina was too innumerate, and too anxious, to estimate what that might be.

Darel said, "We only listed items worth eighty dollars or more. You should be aware that we went into the Dumpster and found some items of value. We left them in the living room."

"What were they?" asked Valentina, looking at the list.

"I think we pulled six out in total and listed four of them on that report. I put a red check by them. One is a Victorian wicker birdcage—it's worth ninety-five dollars. More if you clean it up and get the missing door replaced. Another is a brown pottery vase. It's a North Dakota School of Mines piece, signed. If it didn't have that chip on the lip it would be worth several thousand; even with the chip, it's worth five hundred. The third is a Walt Disney Donald Duck comic book that has 'Christmas on Bear Mountain' in it— the first appearance of Uncle Scrooge. It's worth about two hundred dollars, maybe more."

"Wow, really?" said Valentina. "I thought the only comic books worth anything were *Superman* or *Batman*."

"No, sometimes the lighter comics are worth money, too. If that Disney one were in mint condition, it would be worth over three thousand dollars."

"Wow," said Valentina.

"The fourth is a pair of cowboy boots," said Darel. "They're probably from the fifties, and handmade out of croc belly by a company called Lucchese. They need to be cleaned by a professional—it looks and smells as if the previous owner walked in something nasty while wearing them and tossed them. And Tom probably found them in the trash. But they're worth about seven hundred dollars restored."

"Oh my God, *I* threw those boots away!" said Valentina. "I found them at the bottom of a box. They stank so much I didn't even look at them. I took them right out to the Dumpster, I couldn't wait to get them out of the house!" She laughed, embarrassed at herself. "But—*seven hundred dollars*? Really? For that old pair of boots? Wasn't the heel coming off one of them?"

"That's right," said Darel, with a smile. "Don't lose that heel, it can be put back on. I put them in a Ziploc bag so they won't stink up the room. Bad as they are, you could sell them right now for a couple hundred. It's going to cost you something to get them restored, but you'll be glad you did. If you do and then put them up for auction, you might get as much as a thousand."

"Holy Shinola!" said Valentina. "That right there makes the price you charged for the survey worth it. I never would've thought that pair of boots was worth a nickel. Thank you!" She turned to Betsy. "This is so wonderful!" Then back to Darel. "Sergeant Malloy said you told him there was twenty-five thousand dollars' worth of things in the house, but I didn't know whether to believe him!" And again she turned back to Betsy. "I'm so glad you suggested the Leipolds. And God bless Tommy for saving all this stuff!" Then she pressed the estimate and her other hand to her face. "Oh, Tommy, Tommy, you stupid, silly man! You could've sold some of this stuff and saved your house!" She burst into tears.

"Here, now!" said Darel, alarmed. "What's the matter?"

"She's just upset over her cousin, that's all," said Betsy,

embracing Valentina with one arm, patting her on the far shoulder. "He died, you know. She's taking his death pretty hard."

"Well, I'm sorry," said Darel.

Valentina managed to control her tears long enough to say, "I've got an appointment with Mr. Penberthy, so I'd better get over there. See you later. Thanks, Betsy. Thanks, Mr. Leipold." She fled up an aisle and out the door.

After she was gone, Betsy said, "Darel, did Tom Riordan ever steal anything from you?"

He laughed, his face scrunching up like a big-nosed Santa. "Oh yes. Once he found a *Life* magazine that was published on the day he was born and stuck it up inside his shirt. It was an old T-shirt, and I could see the cover through the fabric. I suppose I should have stopped him, but heck, it was probably worth three dollars. He never stole anything we couldn't afford to lose. Or if he did, and I caught him, he'd give it back. He liked magazines, especially the kind with photographs of foreign places. That reminds me, tell Ms. Shipp that we'll buy some of those magazines in her house, will you?"

"Yes, I'll tell her. But about Tom, what was he like?"

Darel thought briefly. "He was a man baffled by reality. For example, he didn't steal out of meanness. I think he thought it was clever of him to walk off with something he didn't have to pay for."

"Do you know anyone who was seriously angry with him for stealing something?"

"I'd want to ask LaVerna about that, but I don't think so. I'm sure nobody ever said anything to me like that." And

Darel was known for talking to everyone on any occasion, so he, more than LaVerna, would know.

"Who actively hated him?"

"Oh, nobody hated him! He could be aggravating, of course, especially when it was near time for his next check and he was out of money. He'd come around talking about how he was kind of hungry and hoped somebody would give him a quarter for a candy bar, as if you could buy a candy bar for a quarter anymore. What he wanted was a dollar." He smiled, remembering. "I'm going to miss him and his thieving ways. Odd, isn't it? But he was a real character. He added spark to the community."

"You say you and LaVerna were surprised by how many valuable things there were in Tom's house. That Zane Grey book, for example. Where could he have gotten such a thing? Could it be that he didn't always steal token items?"

"Oh, I suspect that came from a garage sale, or an estate sale. Families come from out of town to close up Grandmother's place after she dies, and they're in a hurry or they're ignorant or both. Maybe Grandmother got a little foolish toward the end and mixed her good jewelry with her costume jewelry and a real diamond ring or ruby brooch gets put out on a tray at the yard sale and someone buys it for fifty cents. Happens more often than you think. Suppose your great-uncle had a thousand books in his house when he died; nobody's going to look at every single volume, so a rarity or a first edition goes for a dollar." He shrugged and said again, "Happens all the time."

"So you think Tom Riordan had a good eye for a bargain?"

"Oh heck no! He was like a crow that picks up anything

shiny. A chewing gum wrapper, a twenty-dollar gold piece, all the same to the crow. Tom just did so much collecting that no wonder he got lucky once in a while. They will undoubtedly throw a ton of useless, smelly, worthless junk out of that house."

# Chapter Eighteen

❖ ❖ ❖

Friday morning Betsy went to talk to Mike Malloy, to see if he'd found something helpful about the Riordan case. She brought him four fresh doughnuts from a shop on Water Street as the price of an audience. But at first he said he hadn't got anything useful he cared to share with her.

Betsy knew Malloy didn't trust her, because she had no official role in this case. He liked rules and clearly marked boundaries, not surprising since his job was to deal with people who didn't honor them.

She said, "So do you have time for me to tell you my own ideas and conclusions about how this is unfolding?"

"Start in, I'll tell you when we're out of time."

So Betsy set off telling the story of a woman who had compassion for her sole living relative who had been injured in an accident. She told Mike about her own efforts to organize a volunteer crew among Crewel World's customers to help Valentina Shipp begin the gargantuan task of cleaning out Tom's house.

"They did an orientation walk-through one day and started work the next day. Emily Hame was in the dining room and found a small red box containing three carved ivory needle cases and an ivory ball carved to look like it was covered with little white mice with red eyes. She left the room to go upstairs when Connor Sullivan called every-one to come look at the mailbag he'd found. Then every-one went out into the backyard to eat lunch, and when they went back in, Emily discovered the red box had gone missing."

Malloy didn't seem very interested in any of this. "So the red box was taken by one of the people working in the house?"

"That sounds extremely likely—except that I don't see how it was done."

"You should maybe expand on that a little bit." He got out his fat notebook.

"Emily was working in the dining room with Georgine Pickering. Jill Larson and Valentina Shipp were in the kitchen, Godwin DuLac and Doris Galvin in the living room, Phil Galvin in the upstairs front bedroom. Connor Sullivan, also working alone, was in the back bedroom. When Connor shouted out, they all came to see what Con-nor had found. Emily says she was the last to arrive because she was dealing with the box, and saw them all up there, and they all went down the back stairs to the backyard—except Connor, who took the mailbag to the post office and then went to McDonald's to buy everyone lunch. They ate together and went back into the house to get back to work together. And when they went back in, Emily went to show Georgine the box she'd found, and it was gone."

Mike thought about it. "Looks to me like the only person who could have taken it is Connor. If they all came down the back stairs to the backyard, and Connor came down the front stairs with the mailbag, he could have ducked back into the dining room and taken the box. Hidden it in the mailbag until he got away from the house."

Betsy nodded. "I'd entertain that solution if Connor were a dishonest person and came home that night with a Chinese-style red box, but he isn't and he didn't. And anyway, Emily hid the box under a big old magazine, so Connor would have had to go on a search for an item he didn't know was there. If he was a thief, he'd more likely have continued into the kitchen and taken the cookie jar full of Morgan silver dollars. Which he and everyone else knew about."

"Why did Emily hide the box?"

"It was less an attempt to hide it than an attempt to weigh it down. That ball of mice spooked her, so she put the lid back on the box and added the magazine for good measure."

Malloy chuckled. "That sounds just goofy enough to be the truth."

"Believe me, it sounds very much like her."

"So who took it, do you think?"

"I don't know. The theory of the volunteers at the house is that some kid on a dare slipped into the house while they were at lunch and grabbed the first thing he saw."

"Which was hidden under a magazine."

"Yes, that rather dashes that theory, doesn't it? If he went in there on a dare, surely he'd be nervous and just grab the first portable object he saw, not go pawing around in the debris looking for something pretty."

Malloy sighed and tossed his pen onto the notebook in which he'd been writing. "Have you been in the house?" asked Betsy.

"Yeah, I went in there right after we got the news about Riordan's death. I was looking for something, anything, that might tell me who the hell wanted him dead."

"What did you see?"

"Trash, trash piled to the ceiling. In the house, in the basement, out in the garage. He must've started bringing home stuff as soon as his mama let him go out of the yard."

"He said his father and his grandfather were also collectors," noted Betsy. "I wonder if it doesn't go back further than that. I mean, those Morgan dollars date to the late 1800s."

"The house was built around 1927 or 1928."

"Ah well," Betsy sighed. "You didn't see anything that stuck out?"

"Not that would catch the eye of an amateur thief."

"What about the rifle?"

"What rifle?"

Betsy stared at him. "You're a police officer and you didn't see the rifle? A rusty old thirty ought six. Connor says they found it when they were cleaning out the living room the first day. Now that I think about it, it seems to me a teen burglar would never walk past that to go burrowing under old magazines in the next room!"

Malloy looked at her. "There was no rifle in the living room," he said. "Not in plain sight, anyway."

Betsy got out her cell phone and punched Connor's number. "Connor," she said when he picked up, "what happened to the rifle you found in Riordan's house?"

"Nothing, *machree*. It's still there."

"Where, in the living room?"

"Yes. We put it on the couch where you can't see it from a window. No need to tempt thieves."

"Thanks, hon." She broke the connection. "You're sure there wasn't a rifle in the living room?" she asked Malloy.

"No—and believe me, cops have an eye trained to see things like that."

Betsy sat back in the hard wooden chair beside Malloy's desk. "It seems that red box *wasn't* the only thing taken after all."

"So what does that mean?" asked Malloy.

"I don't know. Mike, have you looked at anyone else but Valentina?"

"Like who?"

"Did you see that article in the *Sun Sailor* about the long-delayed mail finally being delivered?"

Malloy nodded. "So?"

"So did you go talk to any of those people?"

"You think I should? Who? And why?"

"Because some of them were extremely angry with Tom Riordan for keeping vital information from them all these years."

"Like who? Joe the Plumber?"

Betsy smiled. "No, not him. But I have a feeling there's someone in that story with a motive."

"You amateurs are always getting 'feelings,'" Mike said.

\*　　\*　　\*

BETSY went back to Crewel World to find Godwin deeply immersed in teaching a young woman to darn a hand-knit sock. It looked like a sock from one of his knitting classes—bright orange, with small black diamonds. Something inside it was pushing the heel into a smooth bulge. The heel had a small hole in it.

Ah, he's using a darning egg, thought Betsy. The smooth wooden implements came in various sizes and shapes—some looked more like a computer mouse than an egg. They slipped inside socks or in the arms and even the backs of sweaters that had worn or torn a hole in themselves. The darning eggs made mending easier by freeing both hands for the work and also by preventing the stitcher from accidentally stitching the front of a garment onto the back.

*There's something satisfying about mending a handmade garment*, she thought, approaching Godwin as the door chime finished playing "The Cuckoo Song" theme from old Laurel and Hardy movies. *Ours is a throwaway society; it's good to push back against that once in a while.*

Godwin did not glance up. He had a small ball of orange yarn in one hand and a set of four thin, double-ended knitting needles in the other. The yarn was a bright orange that matched the area where a hole had worn through.

"And now I take some of the leftover yarn from your stocking, which you wisely kept per my advice, and note I am not cutting off a length of it, because it's ever so much easier to cut the extra off than try to pick up and continue with a new length."

Monica Ferris

"Okay," the customer said, nodding.

Without changing tone or looking around, Godwin said, "Hello, Betsy. Valentina called. She's going to stop by in a little while." He continued to the young woman, "Now, have you darned anything before?"

She said, doubtfully, "I've looked at duplicate stitch darning on the Internet, and so I understand the *theory* of it, but I've never tried it. Is it as easy as it looks?"

"Nothing is as easy as it looks. But this mending I'm going to show you is not duplicate stitch because there's an actual hole, not just a spot worn thin. And it's not *really* difficult. What you need is four double-ended knitting needles, which you used to knit this sock in my class, so you already know something about them. We'll use a littler quartet, size double zero, okay?"

"Fine." She turned to Betsy. "I'll take a set of double zeros, please."

"That's great, Molly." Betsy brought a packaged set of four to the desk.

Godwin put down the ball of yarn, opened the package of needles, and said, "First, find the first row below the hole that has no damage. You're looking for strong, solid stitching." He pointed the row out and, using a needle, began carefully working across the row, starting about half an inch to one side of it, lifting a single stitch and running the needle through it, then the next, then the next. He continued across the row to half an inch beyond the hole. "See?" he said.

"Gotcha," Molly replied.

"Now, from the farthest left-hand picked-up stitch, run up that column with another needle, picking up each stitch,

164

past the hole to a solid row above it." He did so, his fingers moving nimbly, while she watched.

"You do that so smoothly," she said admiringly.

"Lots of experience," he said. "I'm always wearing a hole in my socks, though it's usually at the toe." He leaned a little sideways and murmured, "I have *such* sharp toenails."

Molly giggled.

"Now, run the other needle up the right side, same as you did on the left. At this point you've got that ole hole practically surrounded."

"Except at the top," Molly pointed out.

"Yes, well, we'll take care of that as we approach. So, you take your fourth needle, and the yarn left over from the sock lesson, and you verrrry carefully pick up that first stitch on the bottom row *and* the first stitch on the right vertical row, and you knit the two of them together with the strand of yarn. Like so."

He deftly picked up the stitches onto the free needle and knit them into the strand of yarn.

"Now, continue across that row to the other side."

In a few minutes he said, "And now we turn and knit our way back, picking up that first stitch from the vertical needles, so we're tacking it down on either side. You see? We're knitting a patch over the hole."

"Well, isn't that clever?"

"Yes, it is." Godwin handed over the sock with its needles. "Here, you do a row while I watch."

Molly set out, moving slowly as she felt her way into the knitting. "I'm not used to such tiny needles," she said. "But look, it's coming along."

She did another row, this time without her tongue sticking out of the corner of her mouth, her movements quicker and smoother. "Say," she said, "this isn't very hard at all!"

"Tol'ja," said Godwin. "When you reach the top, thread the empty needle across as you did at the bottom, then knit the last row onto it."

"Yeah, yeah, that makes sense."

"So now you know you don't have to throw away a pair of socks you worked so hard making just because you blew a hole in one of them. Come back later in the fall. I'm teaching a class on duplicate stitching, which you can use to prevent a weak spot in a sock or sweater or hat from turning into a hole in the first place."

"All right, I will. Thanks, Goddy!"

All confident smiles, the young woman paid for her set of needles, and left the shop, her knitting stowed in the high-priced bag Godwin had sold her the first time she came in.

"Alone at last," Betsy said, smiling. "What did Valentina want?"

"She didn't say. But she sounded . . . upset."

"Upset how? Sad or angry?"

"I'd say angry, definitely angry. I wonder if Mike's been at her again."

But Valentina, who in fact came in half an hour later hot with anger, had had a quarrel not with the police investigator but with Minnesota law. "Thirty days!" she shouted. "I can't do a thing about that house for thirty days! I don't have thirty days to spend hanging around here. I can't afford to eat and drink and sit useless in a motel room for thirty days—and *then* spend another couple of weeks finishing up in there! It's not fair, it's not rational! I just can't do it!"

"Who says you have to wait thirty days?" asked Betsy when she could get a word in edgewise.

"That fool Penberthy! He says it's the law, there's nothing he can do! He must be wrong—there has to be a way! I think I'm just gonna leave. I've got things to do back home. I can't lollygag around here! As it is, I'm already near my limit on my one good credit card. I got to pay for my room, I've got laundry, I don't know how I'll buy the gas it will take to get home! What kind of a state are you people running here?"

"Hey, there are people living here permanently who ask that question all the time," said Godwin, trying to lighten the atmosphere.

But Valentina was having none of it. "So why don't they *do* something?" she shouted. "Have a revolution! Bring out the guns and pitchforks! Tar and feather a few people!" She threw her hands into the air and whirled around twice, in a dance of fury. "What the dickens am I supposed to *do*?"

Betsy said, "I really don't know. And you're too angry to be able to think calmly—not that I blame you, I completely understand. But here, come and sit down, have a cup of tea. Maybe if we all put our thinking caps on, we can come up with something."

Valentina's wrath blew wide open. "Argh, you're treating me like a *child*! *Thinking* caps! Cups of *tea*! This is *serious*! Can't you see that? Oh, you're no use, no use at all! As usual, I'm going to have to take care of this all by myself!"

And she stormed out of the shop.

"Wow," Godwin said, awed. "I had no idea she could get like that! Did you?"

Betsy, looking thoughtfully at the closed door, said, "I sure didn't."

# Chapter Nineteen

✦ ✦ ✦

Betsy gave Valentina an hour to calm down, then called her at her motel. There was no answer. The owner picked up and said she wasn't there.

"Where could she be?" she asked Godwin.

"Maybe she's over yelling at Penberthy," he said.

Betsy called Penberthy. "Jim, has Valentina been to see you today?"

"Not today. I know she's upset because of the thirty-day hold on her work in Tom Riordan's house. Have you talked to her?"

"Yes, but she still went away angry."

Betsy thought and then called Connor. "Could you do me a really big favor?"

"Certainly."

"Go over to the Riordan house and see if Valentina's in there."

"And bring her away?"

"Ummm, no. For one thing, I don't think you could do that without resorting to violence."

He laughed. "Then why go looking for her there?"

"Because I want to know where that rifle got to. See if she tossed it or knows if someone did—or if it's still in the house somewhere."

"Ah, a clue, right?"

"Maybe."

CONNOR drove over to the Riordan house and parked behind Valentina's car. He went up onto the creaky porch and rapped on the door. "Valentina?" he called. "It's Connor Sullivan."

She opened the door. She was dusty and the white cotton work gloves she wore were dirty.

"What do you want?" she asked, frowning at him.

"Betsy sent me over to ask you if you know what happened to that rifle we found. Sergeant Malloy has been in the house, he came after Tom was murdered, and he didn't see it."

"Why was he looking for a rifle? Tommy wasn't shot."

"He wasn't looking for it, it's just that he didn't see it. And you know cops and weapons. If it was sitting on the couch where we left it, he would have seen it."

Valentina made an exasperated sound. "Well, I haven't seen it," she said.

"May I come in and help you look for it?"

She studied him for an insultingly long moment. He bore it patiently. "All right," she said grudgingly.

Together they searched the living room, which by now

was nearly clear of trash and junk, though a corner was piled with things thought to have some value. But they couldn't find it anywhere in the room.

"You know, that is odd," said Valentina, closing the closet door.

"When did you last see it?" asked Connor.

"I think it was the third or fourth time a crew came to work in here. Somebody pointed it out, like it bothered her it was there."

"Was it on the couch then?"

"Yes."

"Well, just in case, let's look around. Maybe somebody didn't like it sitting out in the open and stuck it away somewhere."

But still they couldn't find it.

"Are you by chance keeping track of who is on these crews?" asked Connor.

"Of course."

"Could you get Betsy a copy of the list, please?"

"All right, it'll just take a minute, the list is in my purse. That *is* bothersome, isn't it? That someone took the rifle. Dammit, I hate that people who are supposed to be helping me are helping themselves to Tom's things!"

# Chapter Twenty

### ◆ ◆ ◆

THOMAS Riordan's funeral finally took place that Sunday, in the afternoon. Riordan's body had been released by the medical examiner earlier—much earlier—and Huber's Funeral Home had arranged to pick it up. But it took longer for funds to be released to Huber's. They had had him cremated per Valentina's instructions, but the ashes were held pending payment.

There was a general stir of interest in town when the funeral was announced. Lots of people attended. Tom had no close friends, but he was a well-known figure in Excelsior, and his murder was a shock. The story of his house, packed with both junk and treasures, was a source of gossip and speculation, which meant many attendees were there out of curiosity. Valentina, of course, was the only family member Riordan had.

The service was held at Huber's, as Riordan was not a churchgoer. His ashes had been placed in a gleaming brass urn, which sat resplendent on a small, long-legged, sturdy table covered with a dark green velvet cloth.

Valentina, wearing black slacks, a dark purple blouse with long sleeves, and a silver and lapis necklace and earring set so exotic it had to have been borrowed from Leona, stood at the door to the large room, greeting people as they came in and thanking them for coming.

She spoke softly, and her eyes, while shadowed, weren't red from weeping.

Betsy and Connor came together, accompanied by Rafael and Godwin. Jill came alone—Lars was on duty, and Jill could not think of a reason to bring the children. The mayor came, but not the chief of police. Mike Malloy came. Members of the Monday Bunch came, including Grace, who brought her sister, Georgine. The Leipolds came. The owners and waitstaff of Antiquity Rose Antiques and Tea Room and Sol's Deli came, and some McDonald's employees were there, too, because Tom had eaten often in their places of business. In the end, about thirty-five people attended.

The service was short. The senior Mr. Huber offered a generic set of remarks regarding the value of modern funeral practices in marking the passage of a neighbor, and then Valentina went to the lectern.

"Thank you all for being here," she began, her voice a little husky, as if she was moved by the turnout. "My cousin, Tommy—Thomas Riordan—was a sweet, kind, and . . . unusual person. He lived all his life in the house his grandfather built, and never married. He was a—an ardent collector with a wide range of interests. He truly loved his 'things.' He wasn't religious—I don't think any of our family was religious—but he was very spiritual. He did a lot of volunteer work and he had a great sense of humor. It seems to me, a stranger here, that everybody in Excelsior knew him, and he had lots of friends. But there's a big, black, friendly dog named Bjorn here in town who is going to miss him probably more than any of us. God bless you, Tommy, and I hope wherever you are, you can forgive the person who took you from us." She stopped short, leaving unsaid what her expression stated firmly: *Because I won't.*

The weather had turned blustery and the air smelled of snow. Not many who came to the service continued on to the cemetery for the interment. Valentina, with Mr. Penberthy's assistance, had obtained permission from the City of Excelsior to open Tom's father's grave and put the shining brass urn in on top of it.

Betsy went to the cemetery with Connor, but Godwin and Rafael went home. Malloy came, too, but that was part of the police routine in homicide cases. Alice and Cherie came, because their strict code of manners demanded it. Leona came and stood shoulder to shoulder beside a solemn, silent Valentina while the urn was set in place. It didn't take long, and the diminished gathering broke up quickly.

Betsy shook hands with Valentina, who then left with Leona. She took Malloy aside to ask him if he found significant any of the stories about the people who got delayed mail. "They're interesting," he said, "but none of them amounts to a real motive, in my opinion."

"You don't think it's significant that now two items have been discovered missing from the Riordan house?"

"Ms. Devonshire, I wouldn't be surprised to learn that three hundred and six items have gone missing from that house." He turned away and walked off down the hill.

As long as they were there, Betsy decided she wanted to visit her sister's grave, a little farther up the hill. Oak Hill Cemetery was on the highest hill in the area.

Connor came with her. She left a pebble on Margot's gravestone to mark her visit and was making her way down by a different route when she thought she saw something lying on a grave.

Was it—? She went for a closer look. Yes, it was a rifle, an old rusty thing, half covered with leaves, looking as if it had been there all summer.

Connor made an exclamation and went for a closer look. "Hello," he said, "I think I've seen you before."

"Is it the rifle missing from Tom Riordan's house?"

"I think so." He reached for it.

"Wait, don't touch it," said Betsy. She went into her purse for her cell phone and called Malloy.

"Mike, that rifle that was taken from Tom Riordan's house? I think we've found it."

She described their location, and in a very few minutes, Malloy came swiftly up the hill to squat and look at the weapon.

"Are you certain this is the gun you saw in Riordan's house?" he asked Connor.

"It's a thirty ought six bolt action, which is what Riordan had," Connor replied. "And it looks to be in the same bad condition. I didn't look closely at it in the house, so I'm not positive."

Malloy used his cell phone to take several pictures of the rifle in place, stooping to get a clear photo of the modest tombstone.

"Chester A. Teesdale," said Betsy, also stooping to read

the name. The date of death was August 14 of last year, and a little math indicated he was sixty-two. "That name sounds familiar."

"He died young. I wonder of what?" said Connor. "And, did he know Riordan?"

"I don't know."

Betsy thought but couldn't come up with where she'd heard the name.

Malloy took the rifle with him when he left, and Connor and Betsy went home. All evening she mused off and on, "Chester, Chester Teesdale, Chet Teesdale," but it rang nothing but the faintest bell.

Preparing for bed that night, she found a book on her pillow. "What's this?" she asked Connor.

"I believe it's called a 'book,'" he replied.

The book was called *Art Crime*, by John E. Conklin.

"Have you read it?" she asked.

"Parts of it, the parts about auctions. You wonder what I'm doing, going to auctions. This book tells the dark side of them."

She shrugged, but she did read parts of it before putting it down and turning off the reading lamp on her side of the bed.

But a little later, on the verge of sleep, she had a sudden notion so strong she climbed out of bed to check it out. Sophie the cat barely moved, but Thai, always up for action, accompanied her into the back bedroom she used as an office.

She closed the door so as not to disturb Connor—or Sophie—and went into the file pocket where she kept her notes on whatever case she was working on. In it she found the list of names Valentina had given to Connor to give her, of the people who had worked in Tom Riordan's house.

And there, with a check beside it, was the name C. Teesdale.

"I *knew* it!" Betsy was so excited she nearly went to wake up Connor, but thought better of it.

"Mau!" said Thai in his deep-for-a-cat voice. She turned to look at him and saw he'd brought her his favorite toy, a pair of shoelaces tied into one length.

"No, it's too late for games," she told him and carried him back to bed.

S HE called Valentina the next morning to ask her about the C. Teesdale who helped clear out Tom's house.

"Oh, him," said Valentina. "He only worked that one morning. I think he volunteered because he was curious about what was in the house—which is fine; that's probably why most people volunteered."

"How did he find out about the need for volunteers?"

"He didn't say. But I know lots of places in Excelsior were talking it up and giving people my phone number. I'm still getting calls, even though I'm trying to put out the word that it's all over, at least for now. He called at a time I was at the motel, so I took his name and gave him a day to come, and he did."

"Was he a young man?"

"Hard to say. Maybe late twenties or early thirties. A tough-looking fellow."

"Was he a good worker?"

"Yeah, he was, pretty much. Kind of a gawker, but they

generally were, at first—even your Monday Bunch crew. He was working in the living room—there's a coat closet there we were just getting started on—and then suddenly, whoosh! He was gone. Didn't say boo to anyone. I kind of wonder if he found some treasure in that closet, tucked it under his jacket, and took off."

"Did anyone see him leave?"

"I don't think so; nobody said anything to me. I came to see how he was doing and there wasn't anybody there, so I figured he was working alone—which I'm trying not to let people do, for that very reason. Somebody could find a Ming vase, and if nobody's there to watch him, off he goes."

"I'm thinking he took the rifle."

"Really? Why?"

"I think to leave it on his father's grave."

There was a startled silence. Then Valentina said, "How do you figure that?"

"Because it was found on the grave of a man with the same name who was old enough to be his father."

"Why would he do that?"

"I don't know, but I'm going to find out."


A FEW days later, Betsy was sorting an order of the new Kreinik colors of metallic thread. She set aside a spool of 5835, Golden Olive, for herself. She would use touches of it on a little Christmas tree canvas she was stitching as a model for the shop—she liked using mixes of fibers in needlepoint.

She looked up to see her finisher, Heidi, come in with a big box of items for her customers. As she came through the door, she stopped to listen to the music playing: *Dee-doop, dee-doop, dee-doop, dee-doop, dee-diddle-dee-doople, dee-doop, dee-doop.*

"What is that?" asked Heidi, laughing.

"Something Godwin put up. It's 'The Cuckoo Song' that Laurel and Hardy used at the start of all their movies."

"Too rich!"

"Thank you." Godwin rose from the table, putting down his knitting, to help her carry the box to the library table in the middle of the room. The top was open, and there were so many pieces in the box that they threatened to spill out of it.

Most, if not all, independent needlework shops offer to arrange for pieces of stitchery to be "finished": washed if necessary, stretched or blocked, then framed or turned into pillows or have hangers attached in the case of bellpulls. Stitchers know a fine piece of needlework can be ruined by an amateur hand at finishing, so they pay willingly for this expensive professional service.

Betsy checked the contents of the box against her master list and wrote Heidi a substantial check, and Heidi left, laughing again when the door played its silly song.

The star of the finished pieces was a nice long piece of Ashley Dillon needlepoint featuring Santa leading a polar bear attached to a flatbed cart carrying a snowman and a small decorated Christmas tree. A crow was hitching a ride on the snowman's head. Unlike most Christmas pieces, it was done in muted colors. Santa was wearing brownish maroon, his beard was gray, the bear was shades of buff and ivory, the snowman was more gray than white, even the tree was a muted green and its ornaments were tiny beads in dim colors. Betsy held it up for Godwin to admire, then had him hold it while she backed away and studied it.

"You know, I only sort of liked it when I sold it to Dee Dee," she said, "but now I think it's gorgeous. I was a little concerned about that heavy dark frame, but it's perfect. And *such* a relief from the bright and twinkly Christmas stuff!"

"Not that you don't have an assortment of bright and twinkly projects you'll haul out to decorate your place in a few weeks," said Godwin drily.

"Guilty as charged!" said Betsy, laughing.

WHEN Dee Dee came in later to pick up the finished piece, Betsy agreed all over again that it was gorgeous and certainly qualified to be an heirloom. Then she protected it with bubble wrap and covered it again in heavy brown paper. When she had finished taping it closed, she said, "Dee Dee, may I talk to you about something?"

"What, you've got another Ashley Dillon piece you want me to look at?"

"No, this has nothing to do with needlework."

Her serious tone made Dee Dee frown. "Is something wrong?"

"I don't think so. But I don't know. I read that article in the *Sun Sailor* about the delayed mail delivery—you know, I got a surprise myself from that same mailbag."

"Yes, I saw the article. I don't think Margot ever thought seriously about carrying handkerchiefs in Crewel World."

Betsy smiled. "No, Mrs. van Hollen wanted me to carry the pattern. Which we're arranging to do. But I noticed that the reporter didn't quote anything from that delayed letter your nephew sent you. Didn't you read it to him?"

Dee Dee turned away for a few seconds, then said without turning back, "No, I didn't."

"May I ask why not? Was it true what the reporter said, that you were in tears over it?"

Dee Dee turned around then and nodded. Her face was red and she looked about to cry. "Because it broke my heart when I read it. There was no way I could share what he wrote with the world, because it showed me I failed that little boy."

"Oh, Dee Dee, I can't believe that!"

"But it's true, it's honestly true." She paused, and Betsy tried to look as friendly and sympathetic as she could. Dee Dee grimaced, shrugged, and said, "Aaron wrote that his father hit him and was angry all the time at him and his mother. And that he tore up Aaron's letters to me, so he was going to sneak this one out in a schoolbook. I remember now that when he'd arrive, he was very quiet. It would take a day or two for him to get happy. And when his visit was coming to an end, he'd get quiet again. But I didn't know— I had no idea—!"

"You think his father was abusing him."

"I think his father murdered him!"

"Oh, Dee, surely not!"

But Dee Dee nodded. "I should have stayed in touch, I should have called, or gone to their home. Maybe I would have realized . . ."

"Maybe it isn't what you're thinking. Maybe he did fall out of a tree. Little boys exaggerate, you know that."

"I don't think that was the case with Aaron. All I can

think of now is that I would have asked some hard questions. I could have saved his life, if only I'd known, if only I'd gotten that letter!" Dee Dee was weeping now. "I know that dreadful man had no idea the damage he was doing when he stole that mailbag, but oh, I'd *like to try to make him understand*!"

Dee Dee would not stay to be comforted—and what could Betsy have said to comfort her?

When Godwin came back from a late lunch a minute later, he said to Betsy, "I just saw Dee Dee going up the street with that framed Santa, and I think she was crying! Didn't she like it?"

"Oh yes, she loved it. There's another problem she told me about. It's got her all upset."

"You want to tell me about it?"

"Not right now. Look, here come Emily and Julie."

Emily came in with a damp-haired little girl by her side. Emily was carrying a large white plastic garbage can liner, its orange drawstring pulled tight shut.

"Hello, Ms. Devonshire. Hello, Mr. DuLac," said the child, who was being taught good manners.

"Hello, Julie-Poo," said Godwin. "Have you been out in the rain?"

Julie giggled. She knew as well as Godwin did that it was a sunny day. "No, I been swimming, at the Y!"

"You know how to *swim*?" Godwin's eyes grew big as he stared at her.

She grinned at him and struck a pose. "Yes, don't you?"

He pressed a splayed hand on his chest. "Me? Oh no, I never go in the water, I'm afraid I might *melt*!"

Her pose dissolved as she bent over laughing.

Betsy said to Emily, "What is it you've brought with you?"

"A piece of needlework. Valentina found it in the house. I think Tom dug it out of a garbage can, it's so nasty." She held up the bag. "It's in here."

"Let me see, too," said Godwin—but he drew back when Emily loosened the drawstrings. "Uff-*da*!" he said, wrinkling his nose and holding a hand up to his face. "What's *in* there, a dead cat?"

"Mommy, Mommy, is there a dead kitty in the bag?" cried Julie

"No, of course not, honey, Goddy's just teasing."

But Julie stood halfway behind her mother while Betsy opened the white bag. "Whuff!" exclaimed Betsy, as the odor made her eyes water. "Mercy!"

Then she looked at Emily and said, "When did Valentina find this?"

Emily winced and looked out the front window. "I don't know."

Betsy and Godwin exchanged a look. It seemed Valentina was making no secret of her continuing efforts in cleaning up her cousin's house.

Betsy picked up a catalog to use as a kind of pincers to pull the article out.

It was a tall sampler, done on light brown linen. It had been framed, and broken lengths of the light brown wood clung here and there to the needlework, making it hard to pull free. If there had been glass covering the work, it was gone without a trace.

"Why, it's an old sampler," said Godwin, coming close again, but keeping one hand vertical in front of his face.

"It's dated 1882," said Emily, "but is it real or a copy?"

"That frame is modern," Betsy said. "And it was stretched onto a thin piece of plywood." Which also was broken into fragments.

"Yes, but the linen is real, and it isn't evenweave," Emily pointed out. "Maybe someone reframed it recently." Modern needlework linen is evenweave, the same number of threads per inch in both warp and woof.

The pattern was period to the year stitched on it—two alphabets, birds, deer, dogs, and flowers, a house with evergreens bracing it, the words *Elizabeth Woodard* beside the date, and at the bottom a tree of life motif, with Adam and Eve standing on either side of a highly stylized tree with apples and birds on it.

"Okay, here's why Tom took it from wherever he found it," noted Godwin with a smile. He gestured at the two human figures. "They're naked, except for fig leaves."

"Oooooh, Mommy, he said *naked*!"

"So?" said Emily to her, then to Godwin, "You can hardly see anything with that funny old cross-stitch!"

"You can tell enough—especially . . ." He gestured at his chest, head cocked sideways. "Did you find any girlie magazines among the *Looks* and *Lifes* in his house?"

"No . . ." Emily choked back a laugh. "You mean this was his . . ." She gestured. "That, in *this* day and age?"

"You gotta go with what you got," said Godwin mock-sententiously.

"Oh, I give up! Betsy, what about the uneven weave linen?"

"We have natural linen right over there on the shelf," she said. "It isn't evenweave, and we stock it for our stitchers who duplicate old samplers," Betsy said. "Which reminds me, we need to order some more of it."

"Oh heck, that's right," said Emily, disappointed. "So this isn't real, is it?"

"No, sweetie," said Godwin. "It's a copy. See also the silk on the back is the same color as the silk on the front, but the front would be exposed to light for years and years, so it should be more faded. And look, down in the lower right corner, some initials that don't match the name of the original's stitcher." He held his breath while he took a close look. "RNJ," he read aloud.

"So it wouldn't be worth my while to try to clean it?"

Betsy said, "Perhaps if RNJ was someone you know, it would be."

"No. So I guess it'll go back in the garbage. Too bad."

She picked the sampler up using Betsy's catalog and put it back in its bag.

"So," asked Betsy, pushing the catalog into the bag, "have you talked to Valentina lately?"

"Just about this thing. I asked her if I could show it to you. She said okay. She sounded mad, but I think that's because she's supposed to stop work for thirty days."

"Yes, she told us that."

"It's a legal thing. Mr. Penberthy had to go to court to have her made the estate's personal representative, so that's been done. But for some reason there's a hold or a wait or something for thirty days. They have to make sure there are no . . ." Emily thought briefly. "I don't think they're looking for other heirs, but maybe they are. And they're looking for . . ." She thought some more. " 'Other claims against the estate.' Something about medical assistance."

Betsy groaned. "Tom's social worker—I wonder if Hennepin County is going to file a claim."

"I don't know." Emily lowered her voice. "And she's been going into the house anyway. She wants this over so she can go home."

"But she can't go home until the police have finished their investigation."

Speaking even more softly, Emily said, "She said she has things to do back in Muncie. I think when she's had enough of Mike Malloy, she's just going to leave town."

Godwin said, "I hope she doesn't do that. It would be a big mistake."

Emily nodded. "I think so, too. I'm hoping you will find out fast who really murdered Tom Take—I suppose I shouldn't call him that anymore—Tom Riordan."

Betsy said, "I'm working on it. Emily, I want to ask you about that red box you found. What happened?"

"Well, I was alone in the dining room and I stumbled on something on the floor and I picked it up and it was a red box, all carved, with Asian motifs."

"Was it plastic? Or wood?"

"If it was wood, it was some kind of very light wood. It kind of felt like plastic, but somehow not like plastic, too. It was a little heavier than plastic. The inside was black. The carving was flowers and those fish with the big tails."

"Koi," supplied Godwin.

"That's right, koi," said Emily. "Inside the box were three ivory needle cases, very beautiful, carved with flowers and a teeny little dragon, all narrow and long, wrapped around and around. I picked one up and I could see it pulled apart near the top, and inside were three ivory needles, that's how I knew they were needle cases.

"But also there was some little ball thing covered with a gray rag, and when I pulled the rag off, it was carved so it looked like the ball was made of lots of little white mice with red eyes, ish! I almost dropped the box. Instead I put the rag back on top of those mice, and closed the box, put it on the table, and put a magazine on top of it, and went upstairs to see what Connor was shouting about. He'd found that mailbag. Then we went out in the backyard and he went and bought us lunch—thank you, Betsy, for paying for it, that was very nice of you. And when we went back inside, I was going to show the box to Georgie, only it was gone."

"And nobody else said they noticed something had been taken?" asked Betsy.

"No, but they all said they couldn't remember every single thing they'd seen, so we don't know."

Betsy said, "It seems there is something else missing, too: that rifle that was in the living room."

"Really?" Emily drew up her shoulders. "It made me feel kind of shivery to think someone just walked in and took stuff. And now, the rifle was stolen, too? That's even worse!"

"Well, we got the rifle back, so that's something good. But I wish there was a way to know for sure if more things were taken, and from where. It would be nice if you weren't the only person there who has that gift of eidetic memory."

"What's eidetic memory?" asked Godwin, but then answered the question himself. "Oh, you mean photographic memory. That's right, you can do that, can't you?" He beamed at Emily.

"It's not something I learned," she said defensively. "It's

just something I can do. I've always been able to do that."
She looked around. "Julie, come back here."

The child was turning a spinner rack to look at the beautiful little scissors. "Yes, Mommy," she said, and obeyed.

Betsy said, "That's why your description of the box is so complete—and, I'm sure, so accurate. I wish Georgie had seen it. She might have some idea if it's rare or expensive."

"What's interesting," said Emily, "is that I hid it under a magazine, so whoever took it had to go looking for it."

"Was the rifle hidden under other things?" asked Betsy.

"No. It was kind of behind some books, but not covered up."

"So you could see it from outside, through a window?"

Emily shook her head. "No, the couch was turned away from the windows."

"What was the magazine?" asked Godwin. "Some magazines are collectible, you know."

Emily closed her eyes briefly. "It was a magazine called *Look*," she said. "It had a black-and-white photograph of President Kennedy on it." Her eyes opened. "But they didn't take the magazine; it was still on the table."

"Mommy—" Julie began.

"Hush, sweetie, Mommy's talking."

Betsy asked, "How sure are you that the needle cases were ivory?"

"They didn't feel like plastic, and they weren't pure white like plastic," Emily said. "They were kind of yellow-white. Georgie said they probably weren't ivory because old ivory turns brown and new ivory is illegal in America."

"Could they have been bone?" asked Betsy.

"Ick, bone? Like a chicken leg?"

"A chicken leg!" said Julie. "Yum!"

"There are some very beautiful bone needle cases, elaborately carved," said Betsy. "I've sold some here in Crewel World."

"Really? Could I see one? Do you have any for sale right now?"

"No. They're expensive and some people"—she rolled her eyes at Emily—"are repulsed when they learn they're made of bone."

Godwin had been fussing with his phone, which was equipped with many features. He said, "Here, look at this," and held it so its screen was facing Emily.

Emily took it and saw a narrow cylindrical object, white, deeply carved with flowers. A ruler next to it showed that it was a little less than six inches long. "That kind of looks like the needle case I saw," she said. "I mean, it's the same shape."

"Let me see," ordered Julie, and Emily showed her the picture.

"That's not a chicken leg," said the child.

"No, it's chicken bone," said Godwin, reaching for the phone.

"Let me see an ivory one," said Emily.

It took a couple of minutes before Godwin could find one close to Emily's description—the first one he found was shaped like a fish and the next was tubular, but English with modest carvings on it. But at last he handed the phone over to her, saying, "Here, is this what yours looked like?"

"Well, kind of. The one I saw wasn't brown at the edges like this one. But the shape is right. Mine had this little bitty dragon going around it, so pretty. This one doesn't. Is this one you found expensive?"

Godwin took the phone back and clicked back a screen. "Three hundred dollars, to buy it now—it's an auction. Current bid is a hundred fifty."

"Ohhhh, that's a lot of money. I was hoping the needle cases in the box I found would be in the yard sale Valentina is going to hold, so maybe I could buy one. I have a silver needle my grandmother gave me back when she was teaching me to cross-stitch. The eye is worn through, but I just can't throw it away. I could keep it in the needle case—if I could buy it. If they ever find it." She sighed.

"Mommy, can we go home now?" asked Julie. "I'm hungry."

"Yes, darling, we can go home." Emily smiled at Godwin and Betsy. "She gets so hungry after swimming. Good luck with your investigation, Betsy. Do you think what happened to Tom is connected to that missing box?"

"I don't know. I don't think so. There doesn't seem to be anything about it that would cause someone to murder Tom. A ball carved to look like mice, three needle cases, all in a lightweight red box. Besides, someone stole it from him, not the other way around."

"Why, yes, that's true."

Godwin said, "Suppose Tom stole it to begin with?"

Betsy said, "Okay, suppose. The box has been taken again—perhaps by the person it was taken from. No reason there to kill Tom over it."

Julie began tugging at her mother's hand, and Emily, compliant, began walking toward the door. "Still, I hope there's some way to find out who took that box—and get it back. Bye-bye."

# Chapter Twenty-one

❖ ❖ ❖

OVER dinner that evening, Connor said to Betsy, "What if there aren't two Pickering sisters?"

She paused, fork halfway to her mouth. "What?"

"What if there's only one of them and she has this auburn wig? They look awfully alike, you know."

"They don't look *that* much alike when you see them side by side. One's taller than the other, and about ten pounds heavier. I've seen them together—there are two of them, all right. You get the nuttiest notions."

"They are extraordinarily alike," Connor insisted. "Their features are virtually identical, they are the same height and weight. One wears higher heels than the other, and one wears fat clothes."

"'Fat clothes'?"

"You do it, too. You have a really nice figure, you know, but sometimes you wear clothes that disguise that lovely fact."

"I used to weigh more than I do now, and haven't had the heart to give away some good clothes I really like. Besides, I'm not advertising for a replacement for you."

"I'm glad to hear that. Anyway, I suppose my original point is moot, since you've seen the two of them together."

She shook her head at him. "What a strange idea, that Georgie and Gracie are the same person. Why would someone want to do something like that, pretend to be two different people?"

"I don't know. I hadn't gotten beyond my original thought that Georgine and Grace look very alike, that their differences appear to be mostly in hairstyle and dress. Why do people do anything? And speaking of people, did you see the dinner invitation from Jill and Lars after the Halloween Parade tomorrow?"

"Yes, I think we should go, of course. And to the parade, too. I simply adore Emma Beth and Erik, and little Einar seems to be settling in at last." The last few months of Jill's pregnancy with their third child had been difficult, and newborn Einar was a fussy, colicky mite. Born a month early, at three months he was still frail but starting to gain ground, his dark gray eyes no longer scarily huge in his little white face.

Amazingly, his favorite toy in all the world was the family's enormous black Newfoundland, Bjorn. The first time Einar smiled, it was when his father laid the infant against the dog's side and the huge head came around and whuffled at him. It was love at first sniff.

Bjorn, a model of his breed, was as gentle and protective of Einar as he was of Emma Beth and Erik. The baby smiled and cooed whenever he was with the dog, and clutched happily at his shaggy black coat.

This year the dog was hitched to a specially built wagon that Einar, Emma Beth, and Erik rode in the parade. The two older children wore costumes from the late nineteenth century and pretended to be fishing over opposite sides of the wagon. Their mother, walking alongside, wore a traditional Norwegian costume and a clown nose. She and the children had worn the same costumes—without the clown nose—in the Fourth of July Parade. This Halloween, as on the Fourth, their father drove the family's Stanley Steamer, a perennial favorite, elsewhere in the parade.

When Connor and Betsy arrived at the Larson house, they were not surprised to find Einar snuggled against the animal on the floor, watching the goings-on from that safe place.

Dinner was childproof salmon loaf with creamed peas, then a noisy and hilarious game of Chutes and Ladders—Connor was winning when he remembered his manners and allowed Erik to edge him out—and then the children were put to bed. The grown-ups sat down in the living room. Two minutes of blissful silence fell.

Then, "Have you discovered anything helpful on the Riordan case?" asked Lars.

"No," said Betsy in a low, discouraged voice. "I never paid much attention to Tom when he was alive, so I don't really know how to explore his life now that he's gone."

Lars said, "I can tell you about his police record."

"He had a record?"

"An informal one. He was 'known to the police' as a nuisance, not a criminal. Nor a drunk. I saw him drink half a glass of beer at a Fourth of July picnic once, and he made a face that lasted an hour. Said it tasted like goat piss— though how he knew that, I don't want to know."

"So what kind of record did he have?" asked Connor.

"Trespass—he was banned from several stores because he'd go in and walk around fingering the merchandise. Probably waiting for someone to not pay attention so he could steal something. Begging. He was on a monthly allowance and was generally broke the week before a new check arrived, so he'd stand outside restaurants and ask people to give him their doggie bags, or he'd rummage through the garbage outside McDonald's—well, that is, until they moved the cans inside. At last Attorney Penberthy took mercy on him and started giving him an allowance every week instead of monthly. That schedule made it easier for him to manage the money he was given."

"Good for Mr. Penberthy," said Betsy, "but I don't see how any of that could lead to someone needing to kill Tom."

Jill said gently, "That's why Mike is looking so hard at Valentina Shipp. She's the only one who profits by his death."

Betsy looked down at her stocking feet—her shoes were over by the door, as were Connor's. "I don't think she's a murderer."

"Not all murderers look the part," said Jill.

"I know, I know," said Betsy. "And it's true that anyone can be goaded into killing another human being if the circumstances come around just right—or do I mean wrong? But Valentina was living her own life in faraway Indiana and not involved in Tom's life at all. When the county called to ask if she would come and help Tom, she could have said no. They didn't make her come. And they didn't tell her Tom owned anything of value."

Lars said, "Those three pieces of jewelry they found in Riordan's house are worth over seventy thousand dollars. The house and lot are worth at least two hundred thousand dollars. The Leipolds' estimate of items found in the house—not counting the coins or jewelry—is around twenty-five thousand dollars. That's a whole lot of money that comes to her because someone leaned hard on a pillow over Tom's face for a few minutes. You're right that she wasn't involved in his life, but that actually counts against her, don't you see? It wasn't like she was killing someone she knew."

The silence that fell this time was darker.

"Well, I still don't think she did it," said Betsy, setting a stubborn chin. "Come on, now, help me here. Who else should we be looking at?"

"Who's this 'we,' woman?" asked Lars. "I think she did it. Tom Take was living just fine here in town until she arrived. He was obstinate and sometimes a pain in the neck. But he was also helpful, cheerful, funny, and kind. He was the small-town eccentric, and I think we're worse off without him. The only person I know of who might be glad he's gone, because she profits by his death, is Valentina Shipp."

Betsy looked at Jill, who sighed and said, "I don't have any ideas. The person here who knew him best is Lars, and you just heard his thoughts."

"Yes, but Lars knew him from a law enforcement angle. Did you know him from a personal angle? Was he a friend?"

"No, the person in this family who thought of him as a friend is asleep."

"You mean Emma Beth? Or Airy?" (Erik's nickname was Airy, given to him by Emma Beth.)

"No, I mean Bjorn. Bjorn's tail would start wagging as soon as he saw Tom on the street."

"Why? I suppose Tom sometimes gave him a treat?"

"No, all he did was stoop down and stroke him on the head and chest. Bjorn would stand there as long as I'd let him, grinning like a fool, soaking in the strokes."

"Awwwww," said Betsy. "I guess Bjorn knew a sweet soul when he met one."

"Bjorn thinks everyone has a sweet soul," said Lars. "No, it's because Tom would stoop. It's intimidating to a dog when someone looms over him. Tom would reduce his size so he was face-to-face with Bjorn, which Bjorn found friendly."

"How did he know to do that?" asked Connor. "Did Tom ever have a pet?"

"Not that I'm aware of," said Lars. "Of course, God knows what he kept in that house."

Jill said, "I didn't see any sign of pet ownership, apart from the old birdcages, and they were just stacked in the upstairs hallway. No sign they were ever used."

"Connor," Betsy said, "did you notice anything missing after you broke for lunch and came back into the house that first day?"

"No." He thought briefly. "No, I didn't. After Emily told us about the missing red box, I did look around—but there was so damn much stuff in such a mind-boggling variety, it was impossible to keep a running inventory in my head. Now I know Emily has that trick memory, but she said the only thing missing from the dining room was the box.

Nobody else noticed anything missing that same day, which makes me think it likely that nothing else went astray. Though now, of course, there's that damn rifle."

"Yeah, what about that rifle?" asked Lars.

"It was found on the grave of one Chester Teesdale," said Betsy. "And someone with the same name, presumably his son, worked half a day in Tom's house. Lars, has Mike talked to him?"

Lars shrugged. "If he has, he didn't tell me about it."

Betsy asked, "Can any of you think of a link that might exist between the red box and that rusty rifle?"

No one could.

Betsy said, "I can see someone taking a rifle, even a rusty one. But what was so special about the box that someone would take it?"

Jill shrugged. "Nobody knows, not even Emily. Nobody else saw it but Emily. Georgie was working with her in the dining room but says she didn't see it. Emily only found it because she literally stumbled over it, and that was after Georgie, Valentina, and I went upstairs to see what Connor was shouting about."

Betsy said, "Emily says she left it on the table under a magazine."

"So not only was it the sole item taken, it was actually searched for and taken?" asked Lars.

"Looks that way," said Connor. "Which would mean the person who took it was after that specific object."

"But why? It didn't have anything particularly valuable in it," said Jill. "Three plastic needle cases and a Halloween trick."

Betsy said, "Emily thinks the objects were made of carved ivory but describes them as light colored. If they are ivory, they are illegal ivory, because antique ivory—legal ivory—is deep yellow, even brown."

"So where did Tom get it?" asked Connor.

"Does it matter?" asked Jill.

"Maybe he stole it, and the person he stole it from stole it back," said Lars with a grin.

"That's been suggested," said Betsy, "but how does that lead to murdering Tom? Once you've got it back, that should be the end of it. And on that note, I think we should start for home. I've got a busy day tomorrow."

"YOU aren't going to look!" said Godwin.

"Of course I am going to look," said Rafael serenely in his lovely Spanish accent, pulling open the heavy canvas bag.

"But there's a thirty-day hold on working through the contents of the house," said Godwin.

"The coins were not kept in the house, *mi gorrión*, but in a bank, a what do you call it, safe box, in her name."

"No, she was supposed to stop working on the whole estate for thirty days."

"Yes, that would likely be the case," said Rafael, preparing to gently empty the bag.

Godwin said nothing, and Rafael paused to see what he would say next.

Godwin looked at the bag. "Oh, all right, let's take a look."

Rafael smiled. Now that the objection had been made and acknowledged, Godwin was willing to take part in the illicit sorting.

Carefully, Rafael spilled out a lively hoard of silver coins onto the dining room table. Several rolled across the linen tablecloth nearly to the edge; one made it all the way and dropped onto the floor. "Catch it, catch it!" said Rafael.

Godwin stooped and picked up the coin. "Oh, wow, look at the face of that woman on the front."

"Obverse," said Rafael.

"What? Oh, that's right, it's obverse and reverse, I keep forgetting. Anyway, she looks like the teacher who made me tremble in fourth grade."

"I don't know, she reminds me of my great-aunt, who was very kind to me. But I much prefer the face on the Peace dollar, so young and fresh."

"Do you see a Peace dollar here?"

"No, but I have three in my collection."

"Oh. So how do we begin?"

"Sorting them by year, I believe, is the most efficient way. I have my new copy of *The Official Red Book*, so we can see if any of them are especially valuable."

The room fell silent except for the quiet clink of coins being arranged into a long row down the table. Morgan dollars were minted between 1878 and 1904, so they quickly formed twenty-seven places, though there weren't coins from all the years. Then Rafael said, "Hold on, hold on, here's one dated 1921."

He consulted the book. "No, here it is, there's a gap after 1904, then they minted it just that one additional year." He began a twenty-eighth stack, set a little apart from the others.

Silence fell again. There were more minted in the later than earlier years. Now and again, Rafael would give a little grunt when he found one the *Red Book* said was more valuable—though he was not a good judge of condition, which was terrifically important. He set the more valuable coins a little to the front of the rest of the stack.

It was getting late, and they were near the last when Godwin said, "Hey, here's one that's not a Morgan."

"Is that so? What is it?"

"You're asking *me*? It's completely different, a whole woman instead of just the head."

"What year is it?" Rafael asked.

Godwin held the coin up. "Ummmmm . . . 1838."

"You are sure?" Rafael said sharply. "Give it here."

Godwin passed it to him and watched as Rafael looked closely at the coin with a lighted magnifier. *"Madre de Dios!"* he muttered.

"What? What?" said Godwin.

"Do you know what you have found, *mi gorrión*?" Rafael held the coin out as if accusing Godwin of something.

"What? It's not a Morgan, but it's a silver dollar, right? A woman wearing a whole lot of flowing robes, sitting down, looking over her shoulder at something. What's she looking at?"

"Her nation's illustrious past, of course." There was a shield resting against her leg, with the word *Liberty* on it. "It's called the Seated Liberty dollar."

Godwin smiled. "Imaginative names you fellows give these coins."

"The 1838 Seated Liberty silver dollar is worth a great deal of money."

"How much? I mean it's not what you'd call Brilliant Uncirculated, right? And that affects the value, right?"

Rafael turned back a few pages in the *Red Book*. "Here, look at this." But he didn't hand the book over, so Godwin rose and went to stand behind him.

On the page were two photographs of the obverse and reverse of coins that looked very much alike, featuring a seated woman on the obverse, a flying eagle on the reverse. The eagle side of one coin had a ground spangled with stars, and on the other the eagle had none. On the obverse of the second there was a semicircle of stars above the seated woman that was not there on the first.

The coin Godwin had found had the half circle of stars. "You mean, we have a VF-20 coin?" he asked, touching a line in the book. "Heavenly days! Fifteen thousand dollars!"

"No, *mi gorrión*, I think this is better than that; a very, very rare coin, one of a few 'sample coins' struck while they were preparing to do a regular minting. See how sharp the stars are, how delicately the details on the eagle's wings show."

Godwin looked but shrugged. "Looks kind of—what's the word you guys use? Circulated."

Rafael nodded. "Indeed, this coin has led a harder life than its very few mates. So we must take it to an expert who will tell us what we have here. But if I am right, *if* I am right, we have an extraordinary prize right here in my hands."

Godwin moved his finger up a line. "You mean this one?

Wow, it says it's worth seventy thousand dollars! Do you really think we have a coin worth seventy thousand dollars?"

Rafael shook his head. "Condition is almost everything—but the extreme rarity of this coin carries great weight. It is going to take an expert to tell us how much this coin is worth."

"So what do you think?"

"I don't know what to think. I cannot believe we have this coin here in my hand." It wasn't in his hand, though; he was holding it carefully around the edges with just his forefinger and thumb.

"Well, we need to write something down. Let's write that it's worth fifty thousand, just so we have a number."

"All right," said Rafael, nodding.

"And I think we need to call Valentina and tell her what we've found."

"No, not yet. Let's finish sorting the Morgans and see if there are any more rarities."

In the end, they had two 1903S coins (the S meaning it was minted in San Francisco) that Rafael said might be considered Extra Fine in grade and therefore worth close to three hundred dollars apiece. They found an 1881CC (Carson City Mint) of perhaps the same grade, which made it worth a little over two hundred. But the prize for most valuable of the Morgans went to two 1893S coins, one of which was rather worn—"Maybe a Good grade," said Rafael, which still made it worth sixteen hundred dollars; and one Extra Fine "or better," said Rafael, which made it worth fifty-eight hundred dollars.

The rest were worth perhaps thirty or forty dollars each.

Which, with the remarkable Seated Liberty, brought the total to something under sixty thousand dollars.

"Strewth!" exclaimed Godwin, exultant, staring at the calculator results.

"This may well be a high estimate," warned Rafael. "We are being very optimistic."

They decided to wait until they had shared the find with a member of the Northwest Coin Club and gotten a better estimate. Rafael was a member, and there were several professional numismatists in the club so he felt comfortable taking the collection to a meeting.

# Chapter Twenty-two

❖ ❖ ❖

BETSY came back from lunch on Saturday to find Connor and Godwin deep in plans to rearrange the knitting display on top of the long white counter that thrust out from a wall near the front.

"What's all this?" said Betsy, looking at the library table crowded with the rattan upper torso form that had held a magnificent shawl of knit lace, two careless stacks of expensive homespun and hand-dyed yarn, two costly books of knitting patterns she had bought from Irish and Scottish printers, and a little basket holding expensive rosewood knitting needles.

"We've got this great idea," began Godwin.

"Who's 'we'?" interrupted Betsy. Godwin had not said a word to her about a change to the knitting display.

"Connor and I. He came down and looked at it and said he had an idea to spark it up, and I thought it was great, so that's what we're doing. First of all, we're going to take that shawl away; it's been there for three months. Instead, we're putting a Sue Stratford sweater on display and her book on Christmas sweaters next to it. And a stack of the yarn it takes to make the sweater next to that."

"But you didn't talk to me about any of this," Betsy said, trying to keep her tone calm.

"You said you wanted to make some display changes," said Godwin, reading her negative reaction correctly, and seeming surprised by it.

"I wanted the two of us to decide on the changes," she said.

"But this is a good idea," argued Godwin.

"It may well be, but you should have run it by me first," she insisted.

"I think I should take the blame here," said Connor.

She turned on him. "That's true, you stepped in where you don't belong."

He raised both hands. "I apologize. I was only trying to help."

"I don't need your help." Betsy felt herself getting angry. "Why don't you go back upstairs?"

He looked about to say something but instead nodded at Godwin. "Sorry, fellow."

"It's all right," said Godwin, but it was to his back. Connor went through the twin set of box shelves that divided the front and back of the shop on his way to the back door.

"Now, what was that about?" Godwin asked Betsy.

"It's about his taking a role in this place. I don't like it. He's assertive, which is mostly all right, but he has a tendency to take over. If I don't nip this in the bud, next thing

I know, I'll be sitting upstairs stitching models while you and he run things down here."

"Well, if that's what you think, all right, I guess. Lesson learned. Meanwhile, do I continue with the new display or not?"

Angry as Betsy was, she wasn't about to cut off her nose to spite her face. "Is it a really good display?"

"*I* think so."

"Talk to me about it."

So he did, and in the end she said, "All right, go ahead with it." She helped him arrange the skeins of yarn, then made a few suggestions for the rest of the counter, which included keeping the shawl on display, laying it out so it just barely fell over the edge of the counter but didn't block the glass doors. She'd made some good sales to customers whose eyes had been caught by the lovely detail of the stitches. They also put up an easel and on it the booklet pattern for the shawl.

On the end closer to the wall they put up the Sue Stratford sweater knit in a tiny pattern designed for a baby. It had an arm-and-shoulder pattern of midnight blue scattered with stars over a white skirt lined with red reindeer. They hung it on a baby-size hanger suspended on a stand.

It was a cardigan, and the buttons were gold stars. Betsy had knit it for Einar, but it was too big; she was going to save it for next year. Betsy was torn between annoyance that Connor had gone into her stash without permission and pleasure that he and Godwin thought the sweater worthy to be a model for the shop. She quashed the pleasure firmly. Looking through her stash was marginal; taking something from it without asking was crossing a line.

What was the matter with Connor lately?

Or was it her, getting defensive over nothing?

He seemed fine at dinner that evening. He didn't mention the display change but talked with concern about the missing rifle.

"Stolen guns get used in crimes," he noted. "So it's a good thing this one turned up, and not at the scene of a crime. Speaking of opportunities missed, that is so sad about Alice not getting that letter from her would-be beau. Is she going to be all right?" he asked.

"I hope so. She's very upset. I don't know whether or not to share her story with the Monday Bunch. They're good at offering comfort and support, but this is a very private pain for her."

"I'd vote not to. Let her tell it to them in her own time. Or not, as she chooses."

"I think that's good advice."

After dinner, Connor helped with the dishes. "Now there's two of us, maybe we should get a dishwasher," he said.

"Maybe you'll find a nice one at the auction tonight," she replied, putting the last plate away.

"No, this one doesn't have any appliances. But why don't you come along? The Pickering sisters will be there."

"So now you agree there really are two of them?" she teased with a smile.

"Yes, I saw them together at the pre-auction on Saturday. I agree there are two of them, but I still think they're identical twins who no longer dress alike—if they ever did. I know parents are more likely nowadays to give them differentiated names and not make them dress alike if they don't want to."

"I know of a mom who had to put an indelible ink dot on the wrist of one of her twins because they were so alike. Even so, she was never sure that the names she gave them at the hospital were the names she assigned them after she got them home. Did you know that Dear Abby and Ann Landers were identical twins?"

"Yes. Do you want to come to the auction or not?"

Betsy looked toward the back bedroom, which she used as an office, and in which her computer and several hours of record keeping waited. But she wanted to spend time after work this evening with Connor to make sure they were not on the verge of a quarrel, and so she found it easy to say, "Sure. What time does it start?"

"Seven, but we should get there early to look around." She checked her watch. "So we'd better leave now."

"So let's buy a pair of Jimmy John's sandwiches to eat on our way."

Luther Auctions was a longish drive, located at the far east end of the greater Twin Cities, in the middle of a quiet street of shops and taverns. The entrance was in the center of what had once been three stores. They found a parking space down the way and walked back to the center store entrance.

A statue of a human-size frog stood upright inside the door, wearing a blue tailcoat and red vest, a salver in one hand—it had once been at the entrance to a grand house, collecting calling cards. Betsy paused to admire it, then saw the five-by-seven sign: NOT FOR SALE.

"What would you do with it, anyway?" Connor asked.

"I don't know. It's one of those things I sometimes see and have to tear myself away from before I buy it. Curious trait to have."

Connor chuckled. "I think you will see a great many people here tonight with that same trait."

She looked up at him questioningly. "Why do you come to these things? You're not forever coming home with tchotchkes."

"For all you know, there is a storage shed I've rented somewhere filling up with little precious things."

She cocked her head sideways. "Somehow I don't believe that."

He nodded. "Very intelligent of you."

They walked into the back of the place and found a large room with row upon row of unoccupied folding chairs. At the front of the room was a high stage about twenty feet long with a podium and lectern in the center. It was brilliantly lit. No one was on it.

Near the stage was a display case featuring pocket watches, with a pleasant-faced woman behind it. "Are you going to be bidding this evening?" she asked.

"If I see something I like," Connor said.

"In that case, you'll need to sign in and get a number," she said, and turned a notebook toward him.

Connor filled in his name and address, phone number and e-mail address, and was given a white square of cardboard with a three-digit number on it.

"Wow, a hundred and nineteen people here already," said Betsy, looking at it. "How many do they usually get?"

"It varies, from just under a hundred to sometimes close to three hundred if there are some hot items."

They were also handed four sheets of paper, printed front and back, stapled together. It was a list of everything going up for auction, with a one- or two-line description. There were over two hundred items listed. Betsy, looking down the list, saw that at least a third of them were "lots," meaning two or more related items grouped together.

Connor and Betsy walked around the rooms, looking at the articles to be auctioned that evening. The auction was to begin in about forty-five minutes. Betsy couldn't believe the variety, from early twentieth-century furniture to estate jewelry to baseball cards.

In one of the side rooms, full of old toys and sports equipment, they ran into Grace and Georgine.

"Hey!" said Grace, surprised. "What are you doing here? Are you after the spinning wheel?"

"No, I'm just curious," said Betsy. "Connor's the one who likes auctions. Are you after anything in particular?"

"Just smalls—things we can send through the mail," said Georgine. "For our mail-order business," she added.

"So you're not interested in that giant wardrobe in the other room," said Betsy, smiling.

"Definitely not."

A man's voice came through the sound system. "The auction begins in five minutes," he said. "Five minutes until the auction starts. Please take your seats."

The four of them went to find seats. There weren't four together, so they broke apart. The Pickerings sat near the front, Betsy and Connor near the aisle in the center.

A brawny man with a graying crew cut jumped up on the stage. He had a clipboard with a lot of paper on it in one hand. A young man, tall and thin, and a woman with Indian features, nearly as tall, and strongly built, joined him, and they had a quick conversation.

The two assistants left the stage, and a very young woman came to sit beside the lectern. She had ash-blond hair streaked with pink. After picking up a pencil, she looked at the man and nodded. He stepped up to the lectern and turned on the microphone, which gave a loud pop.

"Good evening, ladies and gentlemen. Welcome to Luther Auctions. We have a lot of items this evening, so we're going to move fast. If you see something you like, hold up your numbered card. We have spotters throughout the room to let me know when you are making a bid. A reminder: All items are cash-and-carry. We do not take checks but will take credit cards with proper ID. Everybody set? Good, let's get started."

He consulted his clipboard.

"First up, a bentwood rocking chair and footstool, fresh from your great-grandmother's house." The thin man and dark-haired woman came to the front of the stage, the man carrying the rocker and the woman holding up the footstool. "Do I hear fifty dollars?"

He didn't, so he immediately dropped back to thirty, and someone held up a card. Using a combination of fast talk and auctioneer's chant, in less than a minute he built the bidding to a hundred and twenty, then slammed down his gavel. "Sold, number fifty-six." The young woman made a note.

"Next, a smoked-oak matched set, dresser and chest of drawers, as is." Connor murmured in Betsy's ear that that meant there was some not-obvious damage to the pieces.

Betsy found the auction a strange combination of exciting and boring. She had no interest in the vast majority of things offered, and when a very fine nineteenth-century oil painting of an old woman darning a sock came up, it quickly rose to a price beyond her comfort level.

Connor occasionally bid on items—an early edition of Dickens's *Little Dorrit*, a sailor's peacoat that looked his size, a heavy gold ring with a ruby stone—and was outbid on all of them. The Pickerings, when Betsy managed to follow their participation in the swift action, did much better. They bought about a dozen "smalls": things like Hummel figurines, a box of baseball cards, a necklace and brooch set.

One item Betsy was interested in, a quartet of antique engraved steel needle cases—she had in mind buying them and selling at least one of them to Emily—was skipped over when their turn came. No explanation was given.

Betsy asked Connor, "Why aren't the needle cases being offered?"

"I don't know, but that sort of thing happens. Sometimes it's because someone got to the person offering them on consignment and bought them, sometimes it's discovered there's something wrong with them—"

"'Wrong'?"

"Yes, the description is faked somehow. Maybe those cases aren't for needles, or they aren't antique, or not even steel. Or, maybe they were stolen."

She stared at him. "Really?"

He nodded. "It happens."

"But—"

Betsy was interrupted by Connor's abrupt raising of his card. The auctioneer didn't see him, so Connor continued to hold it up, and his bid was taken on the next raise. But when the bid was raised again, he brought his hand down, shaking his head in the negative.

"Outbid again," he murmured.

"That seems to happen a lot."

"You have to stay cool at an auction," he said. "The auctioneer is an expert at getting people excited, and unless you're careful, you wind up bidding more than you meant to, and paying more for something than it's worth."

"You don't seem to have that problem—and I don't think the Pickerings do, either."

"No, they're a pair of very cool heads," he said.

"They've probably been at this a long time," said Betsy. "I know they are making a living at it. That's two reasons for them to be doing well."

"Mmm-hmm," he said. She thought he was being negative, then realized he was focused on the next item being brought forward, an antique rocking horse with real horsehair mane and tail.

"You don't want that," she said, surprised.

"No, but I want to see how much it goes for."


MUCH later, on the long drive home, she said, "That was interesting. But I think I'd be afraid to go to another auction. I kept catching myself wanting to bid on things that I now realize, in my cooler moments, I have no use for."

A little silence fell. It was a fine night, the temperature just chilly enough to make the car's heater a welcome presence.

Connor started to hum, and in another minute he broke

into an old English music hall song. "Two lovely black eyes," he sang. "Oh! What a surprise!"

Betsy joined in, "Only for telling a man he was wrong: Two lovely black eyes."

They wandered into other selections. God knew where Connor learned these old songs; Betsy had learned them at her father's knee. They wound up singing another favorite together. "With 'er 'ead tucked underneath 'er arm, she waaaallllks the bluddy tower!"

"Maybe we should listen to the radio some more," said Connor, "instead of singing this nonsense."

"No, please!" protested Betsy. "When you listen to the radio, they keep breaking in to tell you the news—and it's generally so awful, I don't listen more than once a day."

"As you wish," he said, and began singing about a fellow who wouldn't perform a number of deeds for his girlfriend because, "I'm shy, Mary Ellen, I'm shy."

Another little silence fell, then Connor said, "Something I wonder: You have been involved in a number of criminal investigations. Do you ever feel compassion for the people who end up in handcuffs?"

"Sometimes. Other times, my compassion goes to the victim, and the victim's family and friends."

"Are you forming a theory about Tom Riordan's murder?"

"I don't think so. It looks very much as if the only person with a motive to kill him is Valentina—which, if she had any intelligence at all, would keep her from murdering him. And while she's an odd person, she's not crazy or stupid."

"Still . . ."

"Yes, I know. People do the darndest things."

"Including me, right?"

"What makes you ask that?"

"I was surprised at how angry you were at me for partnering with Godwin to rearrange that display in the shop. I thought we were partners."

Betsy said, "In all but that, my darling. If anyone is my partner in that shop, it's Godwin, and he doesn't own a share of it."

"How did that come about?" Connor asked, diverted.

"I was almost totally ignorant about both needlework and owning my own small business when I came here, and content to remain so—until Margot was killed. Only hubris can explain why I didn't immediately sell out. Well, that and anger. I couldn't believe it was some random burglar who killed her. I was mad at the police for thinking so, mad at the town because they celebrated Margot's life instead of mourning her death, mad at Margot for abandoning me. All I had left of her was the shop, so I held on to it. The struggle to learn how to own that business was successful because I had Godwin and Jill and the Monday Bunch. And now you come along—and don't get me wrong, I'm very happy you did, because you have made my life so much better, and I love you with all my heart. But, you haven't earned a part of my continuing struggle, so you must stay out of it."

"But all I did was—"

"All you did was conspire with Godwin—at whom I am angry, too—to make a significant change in the shop's display, a change you have no authority to make. And, you went into my stash upstairs to pull out a sweater I have made for Einar's next Christmas. You didn't ask if I was willing to spoil Jill and Lars's surprise."

Betsy, to her surprise, found tears forming in her eyes. "I know you mean well, but it feels like you're taking over, and it's making me feel threatened."

His fingers tightened on the steering wheel, and he said nothing for about fifteen seconds. Then he said, "Do you want me to move out?"

Her heart felt a squeeze of alarm, instantly banishing the tears. "No!" She took a breath and forced a chuckle. "Where would you go? I rented your apartment."

He immediately fell in with the silliness. "I bet Annie Summerhill would let me sleep on her couch until I found a place." Annie was a formerly homeless woman who had shared an adventurous train ride to Fargo with Betsy and become a friend. Betsy had helped her get an apartment and then Connor had helped her with her ne'er-do-well son. Annie would doubtless be thrilled to do a favor for Connor.

Not that that was going to happen. Right?

They rode in silence the rest of the way home, and, alarmingly, Connor slept in the guest room that night. He said he wanted to stay up and read, but when she went to the bathroom an hour later, there was no light shining under the door.

Though feeling not at all up to it, Betsy went to the early service the next morning—she had long ago learned that she needed church most when she was least willing to go.

Father Rettger had retired to Florida, to Betsy's great sorrow, and Trinity was trying out some new priests. Today, they had Father Paul LeMain Wheat, who appeared to be in his late thirties, built kind of straight up and down, but nice looking, with straight black hair and brown eyes behind black-rimmed glasses. His moves around the altar were smooth and competent, unlike last Sunday's entry, who had nearly dropped the chalice and flicked water over the server while performing the ceremony of washing his fingers.

Father Paul's sermon was intelligent and direct, and included a spirited defense of the Book of Common Prayer. But one paragraph of it struck Betsy to the heart:

"One of my most vivid memories as a child was a children's sermon. My minister scattered salt on the carpet, and then urged us to pick it up. Of course, we couldn't. He said that the salt grains were like words, which, when they come out of our mouths, cannot be retrieved. It was the first time I remember knowing, really knowing, that some words, written and spoken, can hurt, and the damage done may be irreversible."

Betsy didn't stay for coffee and doughnuts after the service but went straight home and prepared a hearty breakfast of bacon, eggs, English muffins with butter and preserves, and coffee while Connor was in the shower. Over the meal, she confessed that she might have been too hasty in condemning his actions down in the shop.

He, buttering his third muffin, said that perhaps he'd been too hasty in assuming authority in matters that did not concern him.

Together, they agreed that when he had a good idea, the person to talk to about it was her.

Betsy, washing up after breakfast, felt the same shaky relief she suffered when, many years earlier, a huge truck came out of nowhere to slide across the road in front of her and her then boyfriend, very neatly amputating the passenger-side headlight off the tiny old MGB car they were riding in. It happened so fast and with such little consequence that they broke into laughter and continued on their way. It took an ambulance roaring up in the other lane toward the accident a few minutes later for the reality of the close call to sink in. Then they had to pull off the road for a few minutes to gasp and hug and worry about the ones who hadn't managed a mere close call.

And a sermon now to bring home the danger she had brought to her relationship with Connor.

She resolved to be more circumspect in her dealings with him. And maybe she needed to speak kindly to Godwin on Monday, too.

# Chapter Twenty-three

❖ ❖ ❖

ON Monday morning, right at ten, the shop's phone rang. Betsy, standing closer to the desk, swooped it up. "Good morning, Crewel World, this is Betsy, how may I help you?" she said cheerfully.

"Hello, I'm Ellen Jo Whitfield, calling from Atlanta. Viola van Hollen was my mother."

"The woman who sent me the handkerchief!" exclaimed Betsy, pleased.

"That's right. I'm sorry to tell you that she passed away five years ago."

"Oh, I'm so sorry to hear that."

"Well, yes, it is sad, but she was ninety-three, so she lived a good long time. I was surprised to get your note after so many years. It's fortunate that we're living in her house. The post office delivered it to the address rather than returning it as undeliverable."

"Well," Betsy said, "as I explained in the note, a bag half

full of undelivered mail was returned to our post office after nearly two decades, and it's being delivered in our town. Margot Berglund is my late sister. I have taken over her business, so that's how your mother's handkerchief got into my hands. Have you any idea how she found out about Crewel World?"

"Back in the nineties she and her best friend, Ida Mae Proudfoot, took a notion to travel all over the country. Every place they went, they visited needlework shops. I know they visited Minnesota, so it's possible they came through Excelsior and bought something in your shop."

"What a happy thought!" said Betsy. "And how awful to think she thought my sister wasn't interested in her lovely crochet pattern. It's too late to offer your mother a chance to sell the pattern in my shop, but would you be interested in doing so?"

"I would be, but I don't do crochet, and I'm afraid all my mother's papers are long gone, so I don't have the pattern anymore."

"Oh, what a shame," Betsy said. "Shall I send the handkerchief back to you?"

"No, you keep it. I've got three of them. My mama always said a proper lady will have a fancy handkerchief in her purse at all times and should arrange it so the lacy edge shows."

"Oh, what a charming old custom, and how sweet of her to continue it. And thank you for allowing me to keep the handkerchief. That's very kind of you."

"You're welcome. Good-bye."

"Good-bye," said Betsy, and broke the connection.

"That wasn't Mrs. van Hollen, was it?" asked Godwin.

"No, it was her daughter. Mrs. Van Hollen died years ago—and her daughter has gotten rid of all her papers, so the pattern for the handkerchief edging is gone."

"Oh, foop! So what are we going to do with the handkerchief?"

"She said we can keep it. It's such a pretty thing." Betsy opened a drawer and took it out. "I'd like to carry it myself."

"So would I," said Godwin. "I wonder . . ."

"What?"

"Maybe we could get one of our crochet mavens to look at this. She might be able to figure out the pattern." He took the handkerchief from Betsy and opened it out, then held up one edge toward a ceiling light. "It's not a complicated pattern, really," he said. "Mostly repeats of the same loop de loop de loop."

"Except in the corners," Betsy pointed out. "There's that row of tight stitches, like lily of the valley blooms."

"Well, yes, that's true." Godwin laid a corner on the palm of his hand, poking at it with his thumb. "Still, maybe it's one of those stitches that only looks hard."

"Perhaps you're right. So I tell you what, let's get back to"—she looked at the scrap of paper on which she had written the daughter's name—"Ellen Jo Whitfield, asking her how she'd feel if we try to re-create the pattern and call it Viola van Hollen's Lace Edging. We can carry it in the shop."

"I like it."

Betsy pressed redial on her phone—how amazing that phones these days could automatically place calls to the last incoming number!—and asked Ms. Whitfield how she'd feel to have her mother listed as the creator of the handker-chief pattern, assuming they could re-create it.

"Can you really figure out the pattern just by looking at it?" she asked.

"Yes. Well, I can't, personally—I'm afraid I'm not good enough at crochet work—but I know several women who are experienced with it, and I've been assured it can be done."

"I think that's wonderful! Mother would be so proud if she knew about this!"

"I'm pleased you think so. Now, let's talk about pricing. What do you think would be a fair dollar amount to buy the right to sell the pattern?"

"Oh dear, I don't have any idea. But since it's not my design, I don't think it's right to charge you anything for it. Certainly Mother is in no position to need the money." She chuckled just a little. "I think just using her name is suffi-cient. Perhaps you could send me a copy of the pattern when you are ready to sell it?"

"That's very kind of you, thank you!" said Betsy warmly. "And certainly I will send you a copy of the pattern."

A minute later, she was talking busily with Godwin. "Who do we know who can look at a piece of crochet and write out the pattern?" she asked.

"I don't know, offhand," he replied. "Pauline Morgen-stern, maybe . . . Hey, wait a minute! Gracie Pickering! Remember, we both saw her crocheting at a Monday Bunch meeting. She was working on something really tiny and detailed. Let's ask her!"

Just then, Valentina entered the store. She cocked her

head to listen as the door closed behind her. "That doesn't sound like the song I heard last time I came in," she said.

"It isn't," said Godwin. "It's so easy to change the tune that accompanies the door's opening and closing that I do it every time the mood strikes me. That's 'Funeral March of a Marionette,' also known as the Alfred Hitchcock theme. In honor of Halloween," he added.

"Huh," said Valentina. "Well, listen, Goddy, I want to buy another skein of yarn, something that contrasts with that yellow you sold me. And it better be from that sale basket."

Betsy said, "Let me give you a skein. Consider it a contribution to the 'keep Valentina sane' movement."

"Thank you," said Valentina, gratefully.

"No problem at all. May I ask where you are staying these days? I'm worried about you, I have to admit."

Valentina's face lit up. "Leona Cunningham is letting me use her spare bedroom. Her cats like me, so we're getting along fine."

Betsy smiled back at her. "Now that sounds like the perfect solution. I should have thought of that. I can see the two of you being very compatible."

After Valentina left with a skein of yellow-green wool, Godwin turned to Betsy. "The two of them might make a formidable pair," he said. "I think the rest of us should be relieved when she goes back to Muncie." And he made a few cabalistic signs with his fingers and pretend spit over his left shoulder. Leona was an accomplished practitioner of Wicca, and Godwin was obviously thinking Valentina was ripe for conversion.

Betsy laughed at him and went into the back room to make a fresh urn of coffee.

E MILY came into Crewel World about half an hour before the usual Monday Bunch meet time, responding to Betsy's earlier phone call to arrive before the others. She saw Jill sitting at the library table working on a counted cross-stitch Easter bunny pattern—stitchers only rarely work on patterns that match the actual season—so clearly she wasn't the only early arrival. "Hi, Jill," she said before turning to greet Betsy. "What did you want to talk to me about?" she asked.

"Connor?" Betsy called, and he came out from the back of the shop, where he'd been getting himself a cup of coffee.

"I want to talk to the three of you," said Betsy, "about the work you did in Tom Riordan's house."

"I want to talk to you, too," said Emily, and she went to sit at the table, putting the little valise with her needlework on the floor beside her.

Connor sat down beside her, and Betsy joined the trio, sitting next to Jill, and holding her long, narrow reporter's notebook, on which she had already written the date and the names of the assembled trio.

Emily spoke first. "I went searching on the Internet to try to find out more information about that red box I found at Tom's house, and I was able to find pictures of similar objects. I think the box is not wood or plastic, but cinnabar."

"What's cinnabar?" asked Jill.

"Well, to tell you the truth, I wanted to wait until I spoke to you to research it online. The pictures I found make me sure the box in Tom's house is cinnabar, however. Here, let me show you."

Emily went into her valise—it looked like an antique doctor's case, which, in fact, it was, and very handy with its little shelves and dividers—and came up with her iPad. She poked and swiped and poked again, and then used four fingers of her right hand to enlarge the picture that appeared on the device's screen. Then she handed the iPad to Betsy. "The pattern on the one I found is different, but it's about the same size, and that's the same color."

It was indeed a pure red box, the top deeply carved with exotically robed Asian figures and twisted trees. The sides were a diamond pattern interspersed with more dwarf trees.

"Why, it's beautiful!" said Betsy. "And expensive," she added, noting it was for sale for seven hundred dollars. She handed the iPad to Jill.

"I don't see how someone could miss something this color, even in a room as packed as that dining room," Jill said, and handed the iPad to Connor.

"You can buy these in Asia," he said, "although as I recall, the carvings on the ones I saw for sale over there weren't as nice, or as detailed, as this one."

"Did you buy one?" asked Betsy.

"No, I think it may kill people to make these—literally."

"What do you mean, kill people?" asked Emily, as Connor handed back her iPad.

"Cinnabar is made from mercury ore, and mercury is a dangerous element."

"But mercury is silver, not red," protested Emily.

"Yes, but the ore is a natural compound of mercury with sulfur, and it's red. To get mercury, the ore is heated in an oven. The mercury comes off as a vapor and is cooled into a liquid."

"Like a distillery," said Betsy.

"Yes, exactly. You can handle liquid mercury briefly without any problems, but as a vapor, it's deadly.

"Now to get a cinnabar lacquer, the Chinese grind the ore into a red powder and mix it with a lacquer derived from insects. It's painted onto a surface, allowed to dry, then another layer is painted on, allowed to dry, and so on, until it's built up thick enough to carve."

"Is cinnabar lacquer dangerous?" asked Betsy.

"I don't know. Probably not. But grinding the ore makes powder, and carving the dried lacquer makes powder, and I can't think it's healthy to breathe either form of it in. On the other hand, traditional Chinese medicine sometimes contains powdered cinnabar."

"How scary!" said Emily.

"Well, our old-fashioned medicines sometimes contained small amounts of arsenic or strychnine. Arsenic cleared up the complexion, and chocolate-coated strychnine was ingested to increase energy."

"The things you know!" exclaimed Emily.

"Sorry." But he was smiling, and he winked at Emily, who blushed and smiled back.

"But back to cinnabar," said Betsy. "It's lovely, but is it rare as well as expensive?"

"Not really rare. I saw quite a bit of it in the bazaars in Asia. And it wasn't very expensive. But then, I was told some of what was sold as cinnabar isn't actually cinnabar. Or else the objects I saw were constructed with just a thin layer of the lacquer over carved wood."

"So maybe what Emily found was not an expensive piece of art," said Jill. "But there's no way to tell without getting hold of the box."

"What about the needle cases it contained?" asked Betsy.

"Aha," said Emily, as she returned to the screen of her iPad. In short order she came up with another photograph, this time of a narrow cylinder, richly carved with lattice-work overlaid with flowers and an extremely narrow dragon wrapped around it. The cylinder lay on a gray surface beside a ruler that indicated it was not quite five inches long. "This looks *exactly* like the needle case I picked up out of the box," she said. "And it's from right around here." She handed the iPad to Betsy.

"Oh, Emily, how lovely! And you were right, it *is* ivory, and it's not darkened at all." A caption under the object said it was one of three, and that they were Chinese, made in the late 1800s.

"Maybe there's a way to restore old ivory's pale color," said Jill when she was handed the iPad.

"Where did you find this image?" asked Betsy.

"My friend Ellie found it and forwarded it to me. It's from an auction," said Emily. "The auction is over; it was over well before I found the box in Tom Riordan's house. So somebody bought it at the auction and . . . and then lost it, I guess."

"More likely Tom took it," said Connor drily.

"Was it part of a lot?" asked Jill.

"A lot of what?" asked Emily.

"Well, you found it inside a cinnabar box and there

226

was also that ball of mice, so I'm thinking it was sold as a lot—a set—the box, the ball, and three needle cases, sold together."

"Oh. I don't know."

"What's the name of the company that held the auction?" asked Betsy.

"I've forgotten. But I can ask Ellie and let you know."

"Okay, thank you. Now, all of you, is it possible that something else was found in that house that could provide a motive to murder Tom Riordan?"

"The coins?" suggested Jill. She turned in her chair. "Goddy, you're living with a coin expert. What does Rafael say about the coins?"

Godwin looked at Betsy, who nodded. "Valentina gave them to me to show to Rafael," he said. "We found some valuable Morgans among the rest, but also a Seated Liberty dollar all by itself, which was mixed in with the Morgans. And it's a very, very rare coin, worth tens of thousands of dollars."

There was a collective intake of breath around the table as everyone grasped the implications of the information Godwin had just shared.

"Are you sure?" asked Jill, after she'd recovered enough to speak. "I mean, you've told us that Rafael is an amateur collector."

Godwin said, "That's true. But we took it and some of the Morgans to a meeting of the Northwest Coin Club, and I think that several members—who are experts—almost had heart attacks when they saw that coin."

"So how much is it really worth?" asked Connor.

"One guy said probably sixty thousand, another said

forty-five or fifty. They insisted we put it in a coin holder to prevent any more scratches or wear." He shook his head at the memory. "I thought they were going to nominate Rafael for president of the club on the spot. We called Valentina as soon as we got home, and she was delighted."

"Where is the coin now?" asked Betsy.

"We gave all the coins back to Valentina. I assume she put them back in the safe deposit box at the bank." He looked around the table anxiously. "I hope none of you goes telling Mike Malloy or Jim Penberthy about this. She's not supposed to be messing with anything from the house until the thirty days are up."

They looked at one another, then all soberly nodded agreement.

"Not that Mike and Jim probably don't know already," said Jill. "She's not exactly being sneaky about it."

"One coin in the collection, different from the rest, and worth far more than the others," said Connor. "That's odd, don't you think?"

"It sure is," said Betsy. "And I'm not sure what to make of it."

"Maybe instead of things being taken, things are being added," suggested Jill. "Someone wanting to hide that silver coin put it in with all the other silver coins, thinking it wouldn't be noticed, at least not right away."

"But it would have to be somebody who (a) knew the value of the coin, and (b) knew he or she was going to own that hoard," said Betsy.

"Anyway, who had an opportunity to do that?" asked Connor. "I wasn't in the kitchen but once, when that cookie jar was found. I didn't touch the jar or handle any of the coins."

"Maybe when we all went upstairs to see that mailbag you found," said Godwin.

"Where was everyone between the time the Morgan dollars were found and when Valentina took the coins away from the house?"

Godwin said, "I was in the living room with Doris and we went up the front stairs."

Connor said, "And Phil was in the front bedroom and came down the hall to see me in the back bedroom."

Jill said, "Valentina and I were in the kitchen and went up the back stairs."

Emily said, "I was in the dining room. Georgie went through the kitchen ahead of me and up the back stairs. I was the last one to go up."

"Hold on," said Connor. "When I came down the front stairs with the mailbag, I saw Georgie going from the living room into the dining room."

Emily frowned at him. "No, you didn't. Georgie went into the kitchen to come up the back stairs, and then came down the back stairs again with the rest of us and out into the backyard. You must have seen her earlier, maybe coming back from dumping a wastebasket into the Dumpster."

Connor shook his head. "Once I was up there, I didn't come down even once. Besides, I remember having to be especially careful coming down the stairs with that bulky bag on my shoulder. That's when I saw her just going into the dining room."

"Did you see her go outdoors with the rest of the group, Emily?" asked Betsy.

Emily nodded, then frowned. "I think so. Anyway, she

was out there with us. Why would she go back into the dining room?"

"To steal the red box, of course," said Jill. "She stuck it up under her sweatshirt—didn't any of you see the bulge when she was in the backyard?" And they all laughed, except Connor. Betsy looked at him and was sure she knew what he was thinking. He knew what he saw, and making a joke of it didn't explain it away.

# Chapter Twenty-four

❖ ❖ ❖

BEFORE anything more could be said, Phil and Doris arrived, ready for the Monday Bunch meeting. Jill and Emily greeted them cheerfully. Connor said hello, then got up to leave.

"Why doesn't Connor join our group?" Phil asked the others, and Connor paused. He didn't look at Betsy.

"You mean you don't enjoy being the only rooster at the hen party?" teased Jill.

"I ain't afraid of a little competition," said Phil, then he offered a creditable crow.

Betsy said, "If you like, Connor, go get one of your projects and join us."

His smile told her he'd been hoping for that, and her expression turned apologetic for not having invited him sooner. How awful of her to be so thoughtless!

In a few minutes Cherie, Gracie, and Alice came in, and

they all cheered when they heard Connor was going to join the Bunch.

Though Betsy would have preferred the topic not come up, almost the first thing Phil said was, "So, what's going on with the Riordan house?"

They all looked at Betsy for an answer, so she told them, "The emergency conservatorship died with Tom Riordan, but Valentina is going to be named personal representative—if she hasn't been already—because she's Tom's sole heir."

"'Sole heir,'" said Phil. "Does that mean she gets everything?"

"I don't know. These things are always more complicated than we think. I hope Valentina is listening to her lawyer and doesn't end up in trouble because she forgot to dot an *i* or cross a *t*."

Cherie said, "Not that I'm a lawyer, but I think the county is going to have a claim on the estate for all the taxes due. Not to mention the medical expenses related to Mr. Riordan."

"No, no," said Doris, "he had health insurance, I know that for a fact. He was bragging about it the summer before last when he got walking pneumonia."

Doris said, "He got pneumonia in the *summer*?"

Jill said, "He always was a contrarian."

Phil laughed. "Maybe he stole the germs from somebody else."

Doris said, "Maybe the county will make a claim for the expenses they incurred by assigning a social worker to him."

Phil said, "I'd tell them they better not make a claim or Valentina will sue them for incompetence. They didn't realize he was filling his house with trash, or that the house was falling apart."

Alice spoke up then, more warmly than was customary for her. "He had a perfect right to buy anything he wanted and bring it home. Besides, not everything in that house is trash."

Phil said, "That's for damn sure! There's those two rings and the brooch I found. I thought they were—what's the term? Costume jewelry, right? Because the stones were so big. Of course I wasn't going to throw them away. I figured Valentina would get at least a quarter apiece for them at a yard sale." He shrugged, grinning. "I about fell over when Georgie said they were real."

"And there's those Morgan dollars," said Doris. "Does Valentina know yet how much they're worth?"

Betsy said, "She's not allowed to take them to a professional to be valued right now. She has to wait a month, remember?"

"I bet she's not happy about that," Phil ventured.

"I wouldn't be surprised," said Betsy with a nod. Valentina was angry, and at least in part she was ignoring the restriction; but there wasn't any need to make that common gossip.

"What's going on with the mailbag?" asked Cherie. "Does anyone know who else—besides the people listed in the *Sun Sailor*, I mean—got a blast from the past via the post office?"

Alice looked at Betsy with pleading in her eyes, so Betsy said, "I want to show you the handkerchief," and went to get it and hand it around.

When it got to Gracie, Betsy spoke up again. "Do you think you could figure out the pattern just from the hand-kerchief?" she asked. "The woman who made it has died, but we have permission from her daughter to publish it if we can re-create the pattern."

Gracie looked closely at the edge of the handkerchief, lifting one of the points of lace from the underside with a forefinger. "I think so. There's nothing unique about the stitches. Pretty pattern, however. The problem would be finding the linen. You want a very fine variety for the hand-kerchief, and it's not common anymore." She looked over at Betsy. "Could I take this with me?"

"Yes, of course. How long do you think it would take you to construct the pattern?"

"I'm not sure. I think the best way would be to just try copying the edging onto a square of linen, and write it down as I go along. It might take two or three weeks—maybe longer, if Georgie and I get busy."

"All right, no rush. And thank you very much."

"Another thing," Gracie added. "Since you already have this model"—she held up the handkerchief—"I can keep the sample that I make for myself?"

"Of course."

The group got out their projects at that point, and a silence fell as they found their places in the work and began stitching. By then Connor had come back to the table with a canvas bag, sat down, and taken out his knitting.

Betsy gave them a couple of minutes to settle in, then said, "I have a question to ask those of you who worked in the Riordan house."

"What is it?" asked Jill.

"How many of you saw the rifle that was found in the front room?"

Hands went up—including Cherie's.

"But you weren't there," protested Emily.

"Not the first day, that's true," said Cherie. "I came on the third day. And I remember seeing the rifle then. It was on that nasty green couch in the living room, half hidden behind some books. It didn't look usable. The barrel was rusty and there were scratches on the stock." Cherie was wearing a denim squared-off military-style hat called a "field cap" that Betsy secretly coveted.

Connor said, "I came over to work on the house that same afternoon—remember? And I can tell you that the rifle was not in the living room or anywhere else in the house."

"But I saw it," Cherie said.

"Yes, you did. But by the end of the day, it was gone. I was the last one out that day and I stayed behind for a look at it. I wanted to see how bad it was." He looked up at Betsy. "I was thinking of buying it, restoring it, and reselling it."

"Ah," said Grace with a broad smile. "Taking a page from our book, right?"

"Well, yes, actually," Connor admitted. "But the rifle wasn't there. I asked Valentina, who was waiting to lock up after me, and she said maybe someone had given it a second look, realized it wasn't worth keeping, and thrown it away. But you saw it?" he asked Cherie.

She nodded. "Yes, I did."

Betsy asked, "When? I mean, what time of day?"

"Midmorning, I think. Before lunch, anyway. I was

bringing some more books into the living room and dropped them on the couch with the others, and one of the volumes bumped up against the gun. Gave me a kind of start, frankly; I hadn't realized it was there."

"What make of gun was it?" asked Phil. "Something decent?"

"It started out decent, a Marlin. Bolt action. Not sure of the age or the model—that's why I wanted a closer look."

Emily said, "The thing that needs to get thrown away is that couch. It smells." She wrinkled her nose, remembering.

"Did you go looking for it?" Jill asked Connor. "The rifle, I mean."

"Just quickly, so not thoroughly; there are still places in that house where you could tuck a dead horse, much less a rifle." He shrugged. "In any case, I didn't find it. And didn't worry about it, either." He looked at Betsy. "But it's been found, thanks to our own private amateur sleuth."

"Where did it turn up?" asked Jill.

"On the grave of a man named Teesdale," said Betsy.

"Bum, bum, bum!" sang Godwin in dramatic voice.

Betsy continued, "It's the second thing we know of that's gone missing from the house. I have to wonder how secure that place is when no one's inside."

"The back door has a dead bolt," Cherie pointed out. "And the front door has that big padlock."

"The windows are painted shut, too," said Connor. "I tried to open a couple of them that afternoon. It was a warm day, as I remember."

Phil said, "I remember the weather that day, too. I was wearing an old sweater over a shirt over an undershirt, and I was down to the undershirt before we finished."

"Did you see the rifle?" asked Betsy.

"Nope. Wasn't looking for it, and anyway, I was working in the kitchen."

Betsy checked the list. "Alice, you were there that day, too."

"Yes, I was," said Alice in her deep voice. "I came right after lunch. But I didn't see any rifle. Nor did I see anyone walking out either door of the house holding it under his arm. Or her arm," she added.

Jill turned to Betsy. "Perhaps you should look at who was there the day the cinnabar box went missing, and also who was there the day the rifle went away."

"Hmm," said Betsy. "I am going to contact the other people on the list who were in the house the day Connor couldn't find the rifle and the day the cinnabar box disappeared."

"It's getting late," said Georgine to her sister. She was already in her nightgown.

"I know, but this is going to be interesting," said Gracie.

"We're not earning any money working on that handkerchief," said Georgine.

"Money isn't everything," said Grace.

"Ooooh, what you said!" Georgine said, pretending to be shocked. "All right, suit yourself, I'm turning in."

Grace was intrigued by the problem Betsy had offered her. She had gathered the tools she needed to work out the pattern: a fine linen hanky, a spool of tatting thread, a size ten crochet hook, and a notepad and pen.

She spread the handkerchief out on the middle of the

table beside her notepad and turned on the lamp she had moved there so that the light shone directly on her work area.

She'd found three linen handkerchiefs at Leipold's already edged with narrow crochet lace and carefully cut the lace off the largest one, making it the same size as the van Hollen handkerchief.

She looked carefully at the lace edging, then, beginning at the upper right corner of her blank handkerchief, she ran her thread through and crocheted a chain of four. Then she went back to the same place and single crocheted, making a loop on the corner. She did this twice more, making three loops in that one corner.

She wrote this down.

Then she picked up her hook and, making the stitches a quarter inch apart, made a series of loops across the edge, working from right to left.

She wrote this down, too.

She continued around the handkerchief to the starting place, making three loops at the corners—this reduced puckering—writing as she went, and thinking.

Excelsior was an interesting little town. Normally the sisters stayed in cities, which offered ready access to museums and art galleries, as well as to auction houses, which were the sources of their income. But once in a while they stayed in a little town, whose treasures were less well known and less picked over.

A shame there was this long delay between the discovery of the jam-packed Riordan house and the distribution of its contents. She was getting restless with all the waiting. To heck with the snow, to heck with the possibilities of that house; she wanted to move on. Georgie wanted to wait, of course. Her sister had more nerve than she did . . .

So until they made up their minds, she would work on this crochet pattern for Ms. Devonshire—who was turning out to be a surprise. Not just a small-town shop owner but a clever sleuth. She'd probably started that second career out of sheer nosiness. By the way, that was a damn attractive boyfriend she had in tow.

There, she was done with the first round. Satisfied she'd made a good beginning, Grace went to bed.

# Chapter Twenty-five

❖ ❖ ❖

As had become routine, when Betsy rose early on Wednesday morning for her thrice-weekly water aerobics class, Thai followed her around the apartment. He didn't ask for anything, or get underfoot. He was just there, like a loyal friend determined to be present. He watched her pull on her old swimsuit beneath jeans and a thick sweater. He balanced on the side of the tub and watched her brush her teeth, and then pluck her zippered bag off the hook on the back of the bathroom door, already stuffed with shampoo, deodorant, comb, and underwear. He followed her to the door, and after she left the apartment, he gave a little sigh and went to rejoin his fellow feline, Sophie, and Connor, who were still in bed.

It was a few minutes to six as Betsy rolled up Highway 7, heading east. It was dark out; the sun wouldn't rise until going on eight. Her class at the Courage Center started at six thirty. She stayed on 7 until it intersected with Highway 100 and headed north a couple of miles, then took the Duluth Street exit. And just about a mile later, she turned onto the road that led to the Center.

The two-story windows that fronted the pool glowed golden in the darkness. There were other cars in the parking lot. Sometimes it was hard to believe there were as many as a dozen other crazy people who came to exercise in warm, warm water at this hour of the morning.

What was perhaps more surprising was how many of the clients were retired seniors. Some had begun coming while they were still working, because they could get their hour of exercise in and still make it to their offices on time. Perhaps the early exercise had become enough of a routine that they found it easy to continue. Others had never had to beat the clock to exercise. It was just easier to get this part of their day done early enough that it didn't interfere with whatever else they had to do.

Betsy, of course, was one of two or three exceptions: She still had a job to get to. Would she continue to work out after she retired? She wasn't sure. Maybe she'd do it if she could persuade Connor to come with her.

She greeted her fellow water buffs in the women's locker room: Rita, Ingrid, Sarah, Gerry, Renee, Gloria, Diane, Cheryl, Barbara. They rinsed off in the showers and went out into the pool room. The water was perfectly still; it almost seemed a shame to break that calm surface. The men arrived then: Jim, Peter, Marty. The instructor stood on the far end of the pool, waiting for them all.

He was something of a novelty at the Courage Center. All the instructors heretofore had been women, so everyone was surprised the first time he showed up. He was slim but extremely fit; Betsy was a little surprised by her own reaction to that hard young body. Surprised or not, it was pleasant to watch him move.

He had them do warm-up stretches such as raising and lowering their arms while turning the hands over and breathing deeply in rhythm to the movements, and soon enough he'd upped the ante, getting them to "surprise their muscles" by mixing movements, such as cross-country ski legs and jumping-jack arms.

The class went fast, and by quarter to eight Betsy was on her way back home.

There, she found Connor up and making breakfast. This morning it was old-fashioned oatmeal with dried cranberries and chopped walnuts, sweetened with Splenda's version of brown sugar, augmented with a generous dollop of half-and-half. He'd also prepared some thick-sliced bacon. The teakettle was murmuring softly, keeping the water hot for black tea.

"You're too good to me," she said, coming to the table after changing into work clothes. Today she wore a sunny yellow sweater spattered with autumn-colored leaves and a brown wool skirt. Just for contrast, she wore bright blue lizard-hide shoes and matching sapphire earrings.

"Yes, I am," he admitted with a smile, in an unsuccessful effort to sound sheepish. He poured hot water into the teapot where the tea leaves had already been placed, covering it with an embroidered tea cozy while it brewed. "What's on your agenda today?"

"I want to contact Chester Teesdale," she replied, picking up a slice of bacon with her fingers.

"He's the one who took the rifle?"

"I believe so."

Betsy had looked for Mr. Teesdale on the Internet, but she'd found almost nothing except an e-mail address. And when she sent him a short message, it bounced. According to her online research, he lived in a part of Excelsior located on the other side of Highway 7, a place seldom visited by people who lived on this side of it.

So, around ten thirty she phoned him, dialing the number she'd found listed. No answer, no voice mail, not even an older message machine.

She tried again at noon. No answer.

At three, she tried once more.

"Yuh," he answered after four rings.

"Mr. Teesdale?"

"Who wants to know?" He sounded a little suspicious but mostly uninterested.

"My name is Betsy Devonshire, and I'm calling about the Marlin thirty ought six you took from Tom Riordan's house and left on your father's grave a couple of weeks ago."

"What makes you think that was me?" he said sullenly.

"Wasn't it you?"

"So if it is, what business is that of yours?"

"I'm not sure. Have you heard from Sergeant Mike Malloy of Excelsior PD?"

There was a startled pause. "No . . . But I been out most of the day."

"Is there someplace we can meet? I'd really like to talk to you."

"We're talking just fine right now. What do you want? Are you a cop, too?"

"No, but I am conducting a private investigation."

"What about?"

"First of all, about the disappearance of a bolt-action rifle from Tom Riordan's house. You were in the house the day it vanished."

"Suppose I tell you I don't know anything about it?"

"Then I would think you are lying to me. You gave your name to Ms. Shipp, who is in charge of the Riordan property, you were seen in the house, you were working in the living room where the rifle was located, and you abruptly left the house around noon with no warning. The rifle was there in the morning and gone in the afternoon. What was so remarkable about that rifle that you felt you had to take it away with you?"

After a pause, he spoke very quietly. "It was my dad's gun."

"I should have figured that, since it was found on his grave. So it was a sentimental gesture, giving it back to him after Tom stole it?"

Another pause. "Well, yes."

"I think you'd better be careful when Sergeant Malloy comes to talk to you, because he's quicker than I am at detecting falsehoods."

"What do you want?" Teesdale shouted over the phone, sounding oddly near tears.

"I've already gotten what I want," Betsy said. "I wanted to know why you took that rifle, and you just told me. What I want to know now, is why you put it on your father's grave."

"The rifle didn't belong to Mr. Tom Take, it belonged to my father! My father is dead. And the thief is dead now, too, which means no one should object if I take the rifle! So I short-circuited the legal process and took it back, so what?" He hung up the phone, hard.

Startled, Betsy paused to think. Okay, she could tell that last statement was true, or nearly so. But why did Teesdale put it on his father's grave? If the rifle now belonged to him, why not keep it? Perhaps it had been his father's favorite weapon—or even his grandfather's. There were some big emotions laid bare in that truncated conversation. Not just tears, but angry tears. There was something big, and important, that Teesdale hadn't said. But what was it?

Betsy needed to find someone who knew Teesdale, someone who might tell her about him. And not only him, but his father, too.

She decided to start with Mike Malloy.

"Who? What?" was Malloy's initial response. "Oh, him. Yeah, he's kind of a thorn in the constabulary's side."

"'Constabulary'?" queried Betsy.

"What, did I use the word incorrectly?" He didn't sound as if he thought his choice of word was wrong.

"No, I don't think so," she said. "I just didn't think . . . um . . ."

"You didn't think I was the sharpest hook in the tackle box, I know."

"Now, Mike, I don't think that of you."

"Damn right. Well, never mind. Tell me again what you want to know about Teesdale."

"Is he a drunk?" Betsy asked. "Or maybe a thief?"

"No and no. Marijuana's his brain-killer of choice. Actually, I wish he'd smoke more of it; the stuff makes you slow and lazy, and his favorite occupation on Saturday nights is getting into fistfights. One of these days he's going to seriously injure someone and do hard time."

"What's wrong with him?"

"What am I, a psychiatrist? I not only don't know, I don't care. He's a pestilent germ in the body of this city. I wish there were a vaccination that would cure him." And on that somewhat mixed metaphor, he ended the conversation.

Betsy thought hard about who she might approach next. Anyone who'd had numerous run-ins with the law over the years in Excelsior would have crossed swords with Sergeant Lars Larson. So Betsy called his cell and left a message.

About an hour later he called back. "Wassup?" he asked, his relaxed, genial tone making her smile.

"What can you tell me about Chester Teesdale?" she asked.

"Junior or senior?"

"Oooh, there's stories about both of them?"

"Sure—though the stories about the senior one usually also involve the junior one. Their hate-fest goes a long way back, and only ended when the old man died."

"What was the main problem between them?"

"Junior was a big disappointment to his dad. He was a bright kid, the only boy among three girls, and his dad had high hopes that the kid would make him proud. But the story, at least as it was told to me, was that the kid took his dad's rifle and sold it, and his dad beat him so badly that his mom had to take him to the emergency room."

"Merciful heavens!" exclaimed Betsy.

"Now I don't know if that story is true or not; you know how gossip is. But from that point on, the kid was in constant trouble, skipping class, smoking dope, and getting into fights. He finally dropped out of school, got kicked out of the parental home, and hasn't held a job longer than a few months ever since. I've broken up a few of his fights, and in some cases I think he's more sinned against than sinning. I also think the fact that the rifle ended up on the senior Teesdale's grave is significant. How is it significant? Who knows? Your guess is probably better than mine."

Indeed, thought Betsy on hanging up, who would know?

She asked Godwin, who was a notorious gossipmonger. "I want to find out more about Chester Teesdale. Who do I ask?"

"I don't know. Nobody in the Monday Bunch knows more than me about him—and I don't know much, except that he's a grouch and thinks everyone is telling lies about him."

Micki Paulson, Betsy's newest part-timer, asked in a reasonable tone, "Why don't you just ask him?"

"Ask who?" said Godwin.

"Chester Teesdale. He already told you the gun was his father's and now it's his. Why don't you go ask him nicely why he put it in the cemetery? Maybe he loves his father and feels bad his father didn't get the gun back before he died."

"That's a good idea," Godwin said. "Take Connor with you; Chet won't be as likely to poke you in the nose if there's two of you."

# Chapter Twenty-six

❖ ❖ ❖

CONNOR was pleased to come along; he'd been feeling bored and useless lately. The outdoor auctions had begun winding down as fall threatened to slide into winter, and the indoor auctions seemed stale and unprofitable. Besides, there was more to life than auctions.

Connor wanted to feel useful to Betsy in some new way following his faux pas down in the shop. The fact that he heedlessly interfered in her business probably indicated he was starting to get restless, a very bad sign. All those years at sea without a real home base had contributed to his wandering soul. So long denied a permanent home, it became unnecessary, even undesirable, to find one. But now he wanted to settle down, sink roots. He loved this woman, Betsy Devonshire. Surely that was enough to bring about the changes necessary to find himself finally home from the sea.

So when she asked him if he would care to come along on

a visit to a possibly volatile person of interest in this murder case, he quickly agreed.

"Has he agreed to talk to you?" Connor asked as they got into Betsy's Buick.

"No. He doesn't know we're coming."

Connor started to ask if that was a good idea then changed his mind. Once burnt, after all.

But while they waited for the light to change crossing Highway 7, she glanced at him and said, "Do you think this is a foolish thing I'm doing?"

"I don't know," Connor replied truthfully. "Have you done this sort of thing before?"

"Sort of. But I don't usually go up against someone I've been warned has a temper."

"Is that why you asked me along?"

"Frankly, yes. Do you mind?"

"If you hadn't asked me and got hurt, I would have been very upset about it. You've been doing this investigative thing for some while, however, so I must trust your instincts."

"Oh dear, you are being really careful around me, aren't you?"

"Yes, and that will continue until we regain the equilibrium we used to have."

A pause. Then she said in a very sarcastic voice, "Well, if you weren't so damn bossy—"

He smiled and replied in kind, "Well, if only you weren't so damn independent—"

They both chuckled, because each had warned the other of those exact failings just before they moved in together.

But the meager good mood faded as Betsy began to look

back and forth at the houses on the street they were on, trying to find the right house number. It was a quiet street in a modest neighborhood of mostly 1950s look-alike homes. One, set well back on its lot, had its big front yard filled with very young children playing on swings, a hard plastic toy house, and a slide.

"What's the number?" asked Connor.

"Twenty-seven fourteen."

Connor looked out the window. "Twenty-seven oh nine, twenty-seven eleven, twenty-seven thirteen—should be right across the street from here," he said, counting up.

Betsy pulled to the curb. The house was big and old, different from the rest. It had probably started life as a farmhouse, back when this was all countryside. A sign in the front window read, ROOM FOR RENT.

Betsy and Connor walked up the wooden steps and onto the big front porch. Up close, it was apparent that the house was getting shabby around the edges. The floor of the porch was scabby, and the screen door—which should have been switched with a storm door by now—was a little too big for the doorway.

Betsy pressed the doorbell and heard a loud *brrrring* from inside the house.

In about half a minute the door was opened by a tall, spare gentleman with sharp brown eyes, a smiling mouth, and a halo of white hair. He wore a blue chambray shirt under a knit black and blue argyle vest, and shapeless old corduroy trousers.

"Lookin' for a room?" he asked in a thin tenor voice.

"No, sir, we're looking for one of your tenants, Chester Teesdale."

"Come on in, go on through to the kitchen. I'll fetch him down. Who shall I tell him is calling?"

"Connor Sullivan," said Connor at once.

"All right. Have a seat at the table."

They sat down at the stainless-steel-legged Formica-topped table, its pattern of tiny brown leaves faded from much scrubbing. The room smelled of coffee. Betsy said, "Quick thinking, giving your name. If he recognized mine, he might not have come." They sat quietly for a few moments. Then Betsy reached for Connor's hands, and he took hers in his strong, reassuring grip.

"Yeah?" said a deep, sleepy voice, and both of them turned to look at the big man coming into the room. His eyes were dull and red rimmed, his mouth a little slack. He wore a thick red plaid flannel shirt, dirty khakis, and flip-flops. His dark hair looked as if he'd combed it with his fingers.

"Do I know you?" the man said to Connor, speaking slowly, puzzled.

"No, I don't think you do," Connor replied. "But you've spoken to this lady here. Her name is Betsy Devonshire, and she's investigating the strange appearance of a rifle on your father's grave."

"Oh." He hesitated for a moment. "Oh yeah."

"I'm glad to meet you, Mr. Teesdale," said Betsy.

"Uh-huh," he nodded.

"What you said to me was very interesting, but I'd like to hear more of the story, if you don't mind."

After another few moments he said softly, "Maybe I do mind." But he sounded as if he weren't quite sure.

"I hope you'll think about it for just a couple of minutes.

It's important, more important than you know. You see, that rifle isn't the only thing that's gone missing from the Riordan house."

"No?" Teesdale sighed gustily and scratched the top of his head as if trying to stir up some thoughts. "I only took the gun."

"Here, sit down," invited Connor. "Do you think we can get a cup of coffee?"

Teesdale let his eyes wander around the kitchen. "Uh-huh," he said again, and then, after a pause, "Sure." Another pause during which he visibly pulled himself together. "Oh, hey, yes. Mick keeps the coffee going all day long for us and our guests." He paused again. "Are you my guests?" he said as if in jest.

Betsy said, "Maybe just visitors. But I'm hoping that together we can solve a puzzle."

"Huh," he said. Obviously he was a man of few words. He walked to the wall cabinet beside the big white refrigerator and opened it to reveal about three dozen coffee mugs of varying sizes, colors, amusing or snarky or sexy mottos and sporting emblems.

He took out a Vikings-purple mug, a Twins red and white mug, and a blue-gray mug with a big marijuana leaf painted on it. He brought them to the table, then paused for a few moments, picked them up again and took them to the counter under the mug cabinet. A gallon-size coffee urn with its little red light gleaming stood there and he filled the mugs one at a time and brought them to the table.

Betsy took the one he brought first, the Twins mug, and

Connor the second, marijuana one, leaving Teesdale the Vikings one. He, noting this, said "huh" again and sat down.

Already on the table were two café-style containers of sugar and dry creamer, and a mug half full of teaspoons.

He lavishly sweetened and lightened his coffee, took a big, noisy slurp, and said, "Okay, now what?"

"I'd like you to tell me the story of the rifle," said Betsy. "Where it came from, how it ended up in Tom Riordan's house." She had reached into her purse for her notepad, but when she consulted Connor with a glance he shook his head no. She took a sip of the coffee, made a face, and added sugar and creamer.

Connor tasted his coffee. It was overcooked, strong, and bitter. But he'd had worse.

"Why do you want to know?" asked Teesdale.

"Because someone is telling a strange story about a small red box with three needle cases and a ball of carved mice inside it going missing, and I'm trying to figure out what happened to it."

He stared at her. "I never saw no red box in Tom Take's house."

"But you saw the rifle—and took it."

"Well, yeah. But like I already told you, it's my gun and I can do whatever I want with it."

"Tell me how it came to be in Tom Riordan's house."

"That's right, Riordan's his real name, I kind of keep forgetting that." He drank some more coffee and looked expectantly at the two of them.

Connor, inhaling lightly, was not surprised to smell marijuana on the man's clothing.

"Tell us about the rifle," coached Betsy.

"Oh, yeah." Teesdale sighed, "Well, Dad took me to go target practicing as soon as I could walk and started letting me shoot when I was eight. The first time I fired his old over-and-under shotgun, he'd put a full choke on it and the recoil knocked me over. He laughed at me, but bragged to his friends that I got right up and asked to try again."

He looked at Betsy, who nodded and looked interested. Connor wondered if she knew what a full choke was, or, for that matter, an over-and-under.

"Dad and me was real close. Mom was kind of a witch. She liked my two sisters okay, but she didn't like me. But Dad and me went hunting and fishing and he let me help work on his truck as soon as I got big enough to tell a hammer from a screwdriver." He drew himself up and nodded once. "We was tight, y'know?"

"That must have been great," said Betsy.

"Sure. So this one time Dad was gone somewhere and I wanted to do some shooting, so I sneaked his brand-new Marlin thirty ought six out of the closet, filled my jacket pockets with ammunition, and went out on my bike to a gravel pit down by Christmas Lake."

"How old were you?" asked Betsy.

He blinked three times. "Fifteen, old enough to know better." There was regret and shame in his voice.

"Go on," said Connor gently.

"As I was coming up the street, I saw Dad's truck in the driveway, and here I was with his brand-new rifle out in the rain."

"Uh-oh," said Betsy.

"You bet. So I hid it in a kind of lean-to that was a fire-wood box built against the garage, and went in the back door." Teesdale got up and poured himself another cup of coffee. He seemed more fully awake now, even restless. He came back to the table and sat down without looking at either Betsy or Connor. He reached for the sugar and creamer and doctored his drink heavily.

He took a big drink and continued, "Dad didn't notice the gun was missing, but he yelled at me for leaving my bike out in the rain instead of bringing it up on the porch. I had to go back out and get it. And rain? It rained like it was the last time it was gonna get the chance, rained and rained. I finally went to bed, but stayed awake. After a long while, the rain stopped. Everyone else was all asleep and I snuck out and went to the wood box, and the gun was gone. There were some old logs left over from last winter and I lifted them out but it wasn't there. I couldn't think what happened to it."

There was a long silence. Connor took a breath to say something encouraging, but Betsy shook her head very slightly at him.

At last Teesdale, his voice harshening, said, "The hardest thing I ever done in my life was tell Dad what I did. And he didn't believe me! He said I musta sold it and where was the money. I didn't have any money so he beat me half to death. Mom finally got scared and made him stop and took me to the emergency room. He broke my nose and two of my fingers and cracked a rib on my left side and I was all over bruises.

"And things was never the same between us. He called

me by a new nickname, Thief. He never forgave me, never, till the day he died. It was like he loved that gun more than me.

"And I said all right, if you think I'm a thief, then I'll be a thief. I made some new friends at school who showed me how to steal and smoke dope and I never looked back."

The room fell silent for a long minute. Betsy looked inexpressibly sad.

Connor said, "But you volunteered to help Valentina Shipp clear out Tom Riordan's house. That was a good deed."

"Hah, I volunteered because I thought maybe I could steal something. I was working on that closet, looking for something I could stick in a pocket. There was six golf clubs in there, and I went to put them on that old green couch and, swear to God, the second I saw that rifle I knew it was Dad's. I picked it up and it was all beat up, but it was the Marlin. I just walked out of the house with it and kept it under my bed for two days while I tried to think what to do. Tom musta seen me put it in that firewood box and took it. He was a great one for walking out in all kinds of weather." He shrugged and took a drink of coffee. "You know where it ended up. I hope Dad looks down from heaven—or up from hell—and sees it there."

After another wait, Betsy asked softly, "Did you go see Tom Riordan in the hospital?"

"No, huh-uh, no." But he didn't look at either of them.

"They have video cameras in hospitals nowadays," said Connor. "At every entrance."

They waited again. Teesdale said angrily, "All right, I went to the hospital, but I was so mad I changed my mind about going to his room."

"Too mad? I don't understand," said Betsy.

"I was so mad I might've killed him."

On the drive home, Connor said, "What do you think?"

"I think we finally have another suspect besides Valentina."

"My dear, I think you may be right."

# Chapter Twenty-seven

❖ ❖ ❖

JILL called Betsy the next morning. "Lars thinks Mike is going to arrest Valentina today or tomorrow."

"Now hold on! I called him yesterday and gave him a viable suspect besides Valentina. Chester Teesdale."

"I know. But Teesdale is shown on HCMC entrance videotapes walking in and walking back out two minutes later."

"Really?"

"Really."

Betsy snorted. "Seriously? Two minutes? That's an odd amount of time. If he changed his mind, it should have been thirty seconds."

"You're reaching, Betsy."

She sighed. "Yes, I know, I know. But I still really feel Valentina didn't do this. I *know* she didn't!"

"You're going to have to offer Mike more than your heartfelt belief. You need some E-V-I-D-E-N-C-E."

\*   \*   \*

THE next day, Emily called Betsy. "I'm sorry I didn't get back to you until now," she said. "I had to wait till I got hold of Ellie—she went to a wedding in Omaha—and ask her to find out that the name of the auction company is House of Schwales. They're based in Edina—lah de dah—somewhere around Fiftieth and France." Edina was to Minneapolis the equivalent of Saint Paul's White Bear Lake. Both were high-end neighborhoods.

Betsy got the phone number for House of Schwales from Emily, thanked her, and hung up.

"What kind of a name is House of Schwales?" asked Godwin, coming to look at what Betsy had written down.

"I can only surmise that someone with the surname Schwales founded it," said Betsy.

She dialed the number Emily had given her, and a very loud and jolly voice answered, "*House* of Schwales! Wally *him*self speaking! How can I be of service to *you*?"

"Good afternoon," Betsy replied. "May I speak with the owner of House of Schwales?"

"He's out of town. But this is the head auctioneer *in person*!"

"I'm doing some research into auctions, and I'd like to make an appointment to interview you."

"Are you a reporter?" The voice had dropped in volume while gaining in respect.

"No, sir, this is a private investigation."

"Investigation into what?" Now he sounded suspicious.

"A trio of carved ivory needle cases that seem to have gone missing."

Monica Ferris

There was a long silence on the other end. Betsy bit her tongue and waited.

"Who do you represent?" he asked at last, very quietly.

"A woman you have never met, and who has never been to your place of business, but who has seen and handled the needle cases. The cases were stolen, I believe from your auction rooms, then stolen again by another person. They have disappeared a third time, and the second thief has been murdered. I am trying to learn if there is a connection between the thefts and the murder."

"What kind of—? There's no connection, couldn't possibly be a connection!"

"How do you know that?"

He said very firmly, "Because we never brought any ivory needle cases to the auction floor at House of Schwales."

"It's true that you didn't auction them off. But they were on your list of items to be auctioned."

"That was an error we regret."

"You had them, though," Betsy insisted. "There's a photograph of them on your web site."

"No, there isn't."

"Not now. But there was."

"Ma'am, why are you bothering us about this? You said yourself the person you're representing has no connection whatsoever to our place of business."

"Because Schwales had the needle cases, I'm wondering if you also handled a box made of cinnabar and a small ball-shaped carving of white mice, both presumably of Chinese origin."

"And you think the whole lot has gone missing?"

*Bingo!* thought Betsy. "So your needle cases *were* part of a lot."

"I didn't say that!"

"Yes, you did. You knew they were in a single lot, and I believe they were stolen from Schwales before they could be auctioned."

"Who do you think you are, Mrs. Sherlock Holmes?"

"No, I'm the owner of a small business in Excelsior, with a part-time hobby of criminal investigations."

"Hey, we haven't done anything criminal!"

"No, you had something criminal done to you. Do you have any idea who stole the cinnabar box and its contents from you?"

". . . No."

"Was anything else stolen?"

"I'm not admitting anything at all was stolen, and I resent your implication that my company is part of a criminal conspiracy."

"I'm not—"

The man hung up.

Betsy logged on to the Internet and looked up the site for House of Schwales. She found their post-auction listing of items, with the prices they had sold for, but didn't find the cinnabar box lot. She logged off and phoned Connor. "Dear heart, do you know anything about House of Schwales?"

"Not much. They're a high-end outfit. They specialize in Asian and African art and collectibles, which I'm not much interested in."

"Have you ever gone to one of their auctions?"

"No. I'm on their mailing list," he admitted, "but I'm on a lot of auction mailing lists. Why are you asking?"

"Because the picture Emily showed us on Monday came from an auction list at House of Schwales. Only it didn't come up at the actual auction."

"Was it pre-sold?"

"Apparently not. I just talked with their head auctioneer, and he admitted—inadvertently—that the needle cases were indeed part of a group that included the cinnabar box and mice ball, and that they were stolen in advance of the auction."

"That's a lot to admit 'inadvertently.'"

"You had to be there," she said, then laughed at herself when she realized that her entire conversation with the auctioneer had been over the phone. She hadn't been there, either! "I'm satisfied that Schwales had them, that they disappeared, and I know they took them down from their post-auction list."

"Hmm. Interesting. I wonder if they're having a problem with items disappearing."

"Is that a common thing, that thieves will steal things at a pre-auction display?"

"I don't know if it's common, but it is an ongoing problem at some auction houses."

"I wonder who to ask if it's a problem at Schwales? Or Luther Auctions," added Betsy, remembering the steel needle cases that did not get auctioned there.

"I believe there is a chapter covering that subject in that book I offered you, *Art Crime*. Which you should get back to soon, or the library will get on our case. Meanwhile, perhaps Mr. Schwales will be more forthcoming."

"He's out of town, and the man I talked with denies that the needle cases were taken. But I'm sure he's lying. They were pictured on the pre-auction list, they weren't sold at the auction, and he didn't volunteer that they were pre-sold. I'm quite sure they were stolen, even though he denied it."

"What explanation did he offer?"

"None. He hung up on me."

"You seem to be having a problem with that lately. So what are you going to do?"

"I don't know—wait, yes I do. There's some big web site that lists stolen works of art. I remember coming across it some while back when I was looking up some Asian needlework. I'll see if these pieces are on it."

"Maybe you should also call the Minneapolis Police Department, see if Mr. Schwales reported the theft."

"Good idea."

The items were not on the international listing of stolen art—but Betsy quickly noticed that the items that were listed were extremely valuable and often famous, and the lot Emily had discovered in Tom Riordan's house was neither.

She next phoned the police department and was transferred to the records section. When she inquired into a report of the theft—she had the approximate date and the location—the woman who searched the files had no record of it.

So Betsy asked to be transferred to someone who investigated thefts. She waited patiently on the phone until she heard a gruff male voice say, "Kennedy."

"Mr. Kennedy, my name is Betsy Devonshire, and I'm looking into a theft from an auction house."

"What was taken?"

"A carved box made of cinnabar, three carved-ivory needle cases and a ball-shaped carving of white mice with red
eyes, all antique Chinese, all in one lot."

"What auction house?"

When Betsy gave him the name Schwales and its address,
he said, "Have you talked to the Edina police department?"

"No, because this is really about the murder of Thomas
Riordan, who was killed at HCMC."

"Maybe the person you should be talking to is the lead
investigator handling that case."

"You mean Mike Malloy?"

"No, I mean Sid Halloran. Like you said, Riordan was
murdered in Minneapolis, so it's our case. I can transfer you,
if you like."

"No, but give me the number. I'll talk to Edina first."

"Sure." He did, and she wrote it down, then looked up
the number for Edina's police department and dialed it.

But Edina didn't have a record of a theft from Schwales
Auction House, either. Evidently—no, obviously, Schwales
hadn't reported it. What did that mean? Why hadn't
Schwales reported it?

Betsy dialed Halloran's number.

"Halloran," said someone—a female someone.

"Oh!" said Betsy, startled.

"You were looking for someone else?" asked Halloran.

"No, I guess not. Mr. Kennedy said Sid Halloran in Homicide and I just assumed . . ."

"Incorrectly, as it happens," said Halloran, but she
sounded amused.

"Sometimes I forget this custom of giving girls boys'
names. I think I'm older than I think—I mean—"

"Let's just say you're having a hard day and try again."

"Thank you." Choosing her words carefully to allay any suspicion she was an idle rumormonger, Betsy went over the details of the missing Chinese box and its contents, giving the location and approximate date of the theft—and that the owner of the auction house denied anything was taken.

"So if he says nothing was taken, why do you think it was?"

"Because someone showed me a screen-save of one of the needle cases. The photograph was on the House of Schwales web site. Now it's been wiped completely. And this same person actually found the box and handled the needle cases and the white-mice ball while helping clear out a junker's house. Only they've disappeared again. And the junker has been murdered."

"Oh, you're talking about Thomas Riordan?"

"Yes. I understand you're the lead investigator."

"And you think this House of Schwales theft—alleged theft—is wound up in the Riordan homicide somehow."

"Yes."

"What's your role in all this?"

"I'm trying to help Valentina Shipp clear herself. I'm strictly an amateur—"

"Hold on, hold on," interrupted Halloran. "Do you own a needlework store?"

"Yes, I do."

"And does Sergeant Malloy know you?"

"Yes, he does."

Halloran began to laugh. "I might've known you'd turn up! Malloy mentioned your name!"

"I hope he wasn't too cruel about me."

"Not entirely. So you're the needleworking sleuth. It's nice to meet you."

"Thank you. About House of Schwales—"

"Yes, what you've told me is very interesting. But the fact that Mr. Riordan never visited the auction house would seem to indicate he is not the original thief."

"Oh, I agree. But I wonder if the thief didn't somehow wander into Riordan's sphere of activity and Tom took the cinnabar box from him. Tom was pretty clever—they found a mailbag with undelivered mail in it in his house."

"Yeah, Mike told me about that. How did Riordan manage that?"

"I asked him that—I visited him in the hospital. He became evasive, said he found it abandoned in the rain and took it home for safekeeping, then 'forgot' to turn it in. That was back in 1996—I know that, because the post office delivered the mail they found in the bag and I happened to get something delivered to my shop."

"What was delivered to your shop?"

"A lace-edged handkerchief. It came from a woman in Atlanta who wanted the shop to carry the pattern. Unfortunately, when I tried to contact her, I discovered she had died some years ago."

"That's sad, but not connected with this case, except peripherally, right?"

"True."

"So how did you get involved?"

"As I said, via Valentina Shipp, who came to me to help her round up volunteers to clean out Tom's house. She says you and Sergeant Malloy are building a case against her and she's asked me to help clear her."

"And you agreed to do that."

"Yes."

"So how are you doing?"

"Not very well. I have interviewed a man named Chester Teesdale, who stole a rifle—more actually *took back* a rifle Mr. Riordan had stolen from him some years back, which theft caused a very serious rift between Teesdale and his father. I am also taking another look at a report that appeared in our local weekly about other pieces of mail delivered from that bag. I'm hoping to find something of interest there."

"Send me a copy, okay?"

"All right, but I can tell you from their account of my receiving the handkerchief, their attention to accuracy is somewhat lacking."

# Chapter Twenty-eight

### ✦ ✦ ✦

OVER supper that evening, Betsy said to Connor, "Valentina is going to be arrested and charged with murder."

"Is there anything you can do?"

"Other than find out who really murdered Tom Riordan? No."

Connor cut a bite off his ham steak—he ate the British way, by using his fork in his left hand to hold the meat down while he cut it with the knife in his right hand, then putting the bite in his mouth without changing hands. Betsy remembered her father eating the same way. Her mother had thought it uncivilized. But there was something inefficient, even silly, about cutting meat on one's plate, putting the knife down, transferring the fork to the right hand, and then putting the meat into one's mouth. So lately she'd been doing it Connor's way.

Then he put down knife and fork and said, "Maybe we're

missing something. Maybe we're not seeing someone else as a suspect."

"Someone like who? Or whom?"

"Well, me, for one. I was alone in the house, remember? I came down the front stairs while the others came down the back and out into the backyard."

"What about Georgie?"

"Well, yes. She must have come down the front stairs ahead of me. But she went on through the dining room and, I assume, through the kitchen and out the back door."

"You're sure she was the only one to come down the front stairs?"

"Well, I heard the others go down the back, sounding like a herd of horses."

"Why would she come down a different way?"

"Does it matter? Or maybe she did come down the back with the others. And, for some reason she walked around the outside of the house and back in the front door."

"Why would she do that?"

Connor shrugged. "I have no idea. In fact, maybe she came down the back stairs, then, instead of going outside, she came into the living room to pick up something."

"Like what?"

The two fell silent while they tried to think of something that needed picking up.

Betsy said, "You're absolutely sure it was Georgie Pickering you saw."

"It was a woman wearing loose-fitting khaki trousers, a blue sweatshirt, and a yellow headscarf tied that clever way women have so the ends go to the back of their heads and tie under their hair. Look, she came upstairs along with everyone else to see the mailbag I had found, and she looked at the jewelry Phil had found and knocked us all over by declaring it genuine. I think I would have noticed if she and one of the other women were wearing the same clothing—and they weren't."

"She couldn't have come back in to take the box, though," Betsy said, "because she didn't know about the box until Emily told her about it over lunch."

Connor said, "That's right. I remember Emily started to tell us about it and Georgie said, 'Show it to me,' or words to that effect, as we were going back in."

"So it appears that nobody but Emily knew about it before lunch."

"That's right."

Betsy sighed and pushed the fingers of one hand into her hair. "As Goddy says, it's too many for me."

That night she dreamed that every man in town looked like Connor. She wasn't surprised at this—dreams are like that—but in her dream, she was anxious to find the real Connor. Her test was to ask for a hug, because she would know the real one by his strong, warm arms around her. But all the hugs were so frail she could barely feel them.

S HE told Connor about her dream the next morning. "What do you suppose it means?" she asked.

"Maybe you just need a hug," he said, and gave her a long, pleasant one.

"Ummmm," she said, comforted.

Down in the shop she told the story of the dream and Connor's terrific recommended treatment for the anxiety it produced in her.

Godwin said, "I think a hug is better than a kiss probably seventy or eighty percent of the time."

Then after a while, he came back to the topic of the dream. "Maybe your unconscious is trying to tell you something. When I remember a dream, a lot of the time it means something is bothering me."

"What's bothering me is that Valentina is going to be arrested. I don't see how dreaming about a hug is related to that."

"Maybe it's not the hug," Godwin suggested. "Maybe it's everyone looking like Connor, like his mother had a litter instead of just one baby."

Betsy smiled. "The only creature I know of who has a litter of identical babies is the armadillo."

"The armadillo has identical babies? Who told you that?"

"Connor. He says they're used in studies of leprosy."

"I'm not going to ask why, because I'm afraid you might tell me."

For some reason, Betsy's memory of the dream lingered. She often had a dream in which her unconscious mind tried to tell her something. Sometimes it was relevant, more rarely it was useful. She had a persistent feeling that this one wasn't about a scarcity of hugs from Connor.

She was nearly asleep that night when it came to her and she sat bolt upright in bed.

"What?" said Connor, who was a light sleeper.

"Twins, that's what it was about, twins!"

"What about twins?" He was still trying to get his bearings after being awakened from a sound sleep.

"The dream, it was about twins—I think you might be right, and I was wrong. Georgine and Grace are twins, maybe even identical twins. Georgine came into the shop the other day with the hood of her raincoat pulled up and I thought she was Grace." She smiled down at him. "But you came close, didn't you? You told me weeks ago that you thought there was only one of them, because they looked so much alike. And when I said no, then you said they might be twins.

"What I'm still thinking about is, why? Why would identical twins dress so that they look two sizes apart and tell people they are years apart in age?"

"Okay, why?"

"I don't know. I mean they sure didn't know it would come in handy at the Riordan house, did they?"

Connor sat up. "How did it come in handy?"

"They both dressed as Georgie to get that cinnabar box out of the house."

"They did?"

"They must have. Emily says she came down the back stairs with Georgie and out into the backyard and stayed with her the rest of the day. But you said you saw Georgie going into the dining room. No, you didn't; you saw Gracie. Or, maybe you did see Georgie, and they switched off earlier, and Emily spent part of the day with Georgie and the rest of the day with Gracie."

"Without noticing it? That seems odd."

"I'll talk to Emily tomorrow and see if I can get

something that will let me know if that's what actually happened."

"But why did they go to all that trouble to steal the cinnabar box?" asked Connor.

"They didn't steal it, they took it back."

"Then why the hole and corner? Why not just reclaim it?"

Betsy stared at him. She had a history of leaping to unwarranted conclusions. Was this another instance? "I don't know," she confessed. Yet somehow she was sure she was on the right track.

BETSY called Emily the next morning. She was determined to step carefully because she did not want to plant a false memory or cause Emily to try to guess an answer she thought Betsy wanted.

"I know I'm becoming a bore about this, but I'd like you to talk some more about finding that cinnabar box in Tom's house."

"Oh, Betsy, it *is* a bore!" Emily replied. "I'm so over that little box! And the etui, too. I looked them up on the Internet and all of them—the box, the needle cases, and the etui—cost hundreds of dollars. I'm sorry I saw any of them in that awful old house!"

"I know, it must be very frustrating to see something interesting mixed in with a lot of trash and then find out the something itself not only isn't trash but costs a lot of money. You kind of wish you'd stuffed it quietly into your purse and said nothing about it."

"No, I wish I'd never seen it. If I hadn't tripped over it in the first place . . ."

"You said it was under some magazines. Wasn't Georgie sorting those magazines? Why didn't she see it?"

"I don't know," Emily said crossly. Then she thought about it. "There were four or five stacks of magazines. She was just sorting through the second stack when Connor shouted."

"And when he did, she dropped the magazines and rushed to see what he found," said Betsy.

"Yes—wait, no. She asked me who shouted, and from where. I said it sounded like Connor, and that it sounded like he was upstairs, in the back of the house."

"So she went through the kitchen to the back stairs."

"Well, sure."

"And you went up the same way."

"Well, first I tripped over the box, and looked at it, and put it on the table."

"Under a magazine."

Emily abruptly changed the subject. "Wasn't that mailbag an amazing thing? I wonder how Tom got hold of it?"

"The mailman probably put it down over on Lake Street, where there's that big hill with steps going up to the houses. He must have had some packages to deliver to someone at the top and didn't want to carry the heavy bag up with him. He put it down for a minute, and Tom came along and picked it up and kept going."

"Yes, that sounds like it might have happened that way. Everywhere you went in town, rain or snow or sun, you'd see him out walking. He never took a bus and always said no if you offered to give him a ride in your car."

"Did you ever offer?" Betsy asked.

"Me? No, he was kind of strange, you know?"

"Poor fellow."

"Yes, poor fellow."

"But back to his house," Betsy said, trying gently to steer the conversation back to its original subject. "You saw Georgie upstairs looking at the mailbag?"

"Sure. You know what was even more amazing than that lost mail? Those pieces of jewelry. Phil took them out of his pocket to show Doris, and Georgie said, 'Let me see that,' and said they were real gemstones. Phil wrapped them in tissues and put them in his shirt pocket. Then Jill said Connor should take the mailbag over to the post office right away, and while he was about it, he said he'd buy lunch for everyone, so we all went out into the backyard and washed our hands and recited limericks."

"Who went back into the house?" Betsy asked. "Anyone?"

"Jill went back into the kitchen and brought out a dirty old bottle of Palmolive dish soap for us to use to wash up."

"How about Godwin, or Georgine?"

"No, only Jill."

They talked awhile longer, then Betsy called Jill.

"When everyone was in the backyard around noon that first day at Tom's house, you went back into the house to get that bottle of dish soap, right?"

"Yes, why?"

"Was everyone else in the backyard at that point?"

"Everyone but Connor, who went to take the mailbag to the post office and buy lunch for us."

"Did Georgie go back in the house, too?"

"No."

"Are you sure? You didn't, for example, see her coming through the dining room on her way into the kitchen?"

"No. What's this about?"

"Connor says he saw Georgie going through the dining room into the kitchen when he was bringing the mailbag down the front stairs."

"Oh, that's impossible! We were all in the backyard and stayed in the backyard while we ate our lunch—thank you, by the way, for paying for it. I can't believe that Connor is saying it—except it's Connor, and he's not often mistaken. What's the explanation?"

"He saw Gracie."

"No, Gracie didn't work in the house."

"Nevertheless, she was there," Betsy insisted.

"How could he mistake Gracie for Georgie?" Jill asked. "Did Gracie say she was there?"

"No."

"Well, then, who says she was there?"

"Connor."

"Come on, Betsy," Jill said, "they don't look all that much alike."

"If you take Gracie's wig off, they do."

"Wig?"

"Uh-huh."

"Oh," said Jill. Then, "Oh, for goodness sake! Is that what you're thinking? Have you called Mike about this?"

"No, not yet, but I will."

# Chapter Twenty-nine

❖ ❖ ❖

Betsy called the Pickerings' rented house.

"So?" one of the two answered—mocking the current fad for starting every conversation with that very word.

Betsy laughed. "Which Pickering am I talking to?" she asked.

"Me, Gracie. Is this Betsy?"

"Yes. Are the both of you there?"

"Right now, yes. But we're packing to leave. Why?"

"I want to pay a call on you, to talk about auctions. Connor's been going to a lot of them, and I think he's starting to think about getting into your line of work, buying and selling. I want to be able to talk intelligently to him about the process."

"Just the thing we need, more competition," she laughed. "But okay, sure. And when you come over, I can show you the progress I'm making on that lace edging. I can mail you the pattern."

"That would be wonderful."

Knowing better than to go to a suspect's house without telling someone where she was going, Betsy called Connor.

"I'm not going to make an accusation," she said. "I'm just going to 'take the temperature,' so to speak."

"Why don't you call Malloy?" he said in a worried voice.

"I did. He won't act without more evidence. But they're packing to leave. Maybe all I can learn is where they're going in case it's not home."

"Let him go take their temperatures. If they're guilty, what? They'll be running a fever?"

"More likely they'll be below normal, if they're the cold-blooded killers I think they are."

"If you seriously think they are a pair of murderers, then I seriously think you are behaving very foolishly. Can't you at least talk to Malloy?"

"I did talk to Malloy. He says I was wrong about Teesdale, so I must be wrong about the Pickerings. He says I'm flailing about, trying to cast suspicion on someone—anyone—other than Valentina. He says you're mistaken about seeing Gracie but because you're my boyfriend I have to stick up for you." Betsy gave a little sniff, whether of annoyance or sorrow, Connor couldn't tell. But she was determined to go.

He insisted on driving her over there. "I'll sit in the car, if you like, but I'm going."

"All right. In fact, I'm glad to have you along. Bring something to read."

The day was sunny, but the puddle near the curb by Connor's car was frozen. Betsy huddled deeper into her winter coat until the passenger cabin warmed up.

"It's been years since I lived in San Diego," she said. "You'd think by now I'd be used to this."

"You could sell that shop and move somewhere warmer," Connor said.

"Oh, who'd buy it?" she grumbled.

"Godwin would, in a heartbeat."

She would have disagreed with him, but a second's thought told her he was right. "Of course, he'd close up for two weeks every winter while he soaked up the sun in Mexico," she said.

"You could do that, too, *machree*."

She thought about that the rest of the trip, which didn't take long.

Connor parked up the street from the Pickerings' house, so a casual look out the window wouldn't show him sitting in the car. He took out his Kindle and was already settling down with it when she left the car.

She shook her head at him affectionately, although he didn't see her do so, and walked back to the house. It was an attractive single-family dwelling with a bay window in front and a sunporch on the second floor filled with mullioned windows, the architecture a happy if eccentric cross between Craftsman and English Country Cottage.

Betsy found the front door set deep under the sunporch and rang the doorbell. It was opened very promptly by Grace, who grinned and invited her in for a hug, her dark auburn hair sweeping lightly onto Betsy's cheek.

"Georgie, she's here!" Grace called. "Pour the tea into the pot!"

The living room was small and cozy, with comfortably padded chintz-covered furniture and a few too many little tables. The walls were papered in a small pattern of flowers.

Georgine brought in a wooden tray, put it on the coffee table in front of the couch, and they all sat down.

Monica Ferris

Georgine was wearing a pale blue jumpsuit and thick-soled blue clogs. Grace was in a long skirt checkered in lavender and white and a big-sleeved white blouse with a little stand-up collar. Both looked elegant and successful.

Georgine said, "Betsy, I just love you in purple. It's *your* color!"

Betsy smiled at the compliment. She did like the outfit she was wearing, a purple shirt with silver buttons and matching purple slacks. "Thank you," she said. And then, "I hope I'm not keeping you from something important."

"No, we're almost finished. We've been moving around so long we've gotten very efficient."

"How do you ship your finds?" Betsy asked, and soon they were engaged in a lively discussion of USPS, FedEx, and UPS—Betsy was venturing into mail order via her web site and not altogether happy about how much time it took to process orders for shipping.

Gracie poured more tea. "Shall I be mother?" she asked archly, a reference to a British custom. There was a selection of little cookies to go with the tea, served on a pretty plate.

"You're probably going to have to hire someone to run that end of your business for you," said Georgine. "We have someone who helps us back home. He works three days a week. Marvelous fellow!"

Betsy picked up a third cookie. It was as delicious as the other two. "Did one of you bake these?" she asked.

"Oh no, they're from Byerly's," said Grace, naming an upscale grocery.

"I understand you wanted to talk to us about auctions," said Georgine.

"Yes. Connor's been going to them, and he took me to one at Luther's—we saw you there, remember?"

"Yes, that's right," said Grace. "Did you buy something?"

"No, and neither did Connor—everything he liked, he got outbid on."

"If he still wants that peacoat, we'll sell it to him," said Georgine with a little smirk.

Betsy laughed. "Was it you two who got it? Maybe I'll buy it for him for Christmas—what size is it?"

"No, no," said Grace, laughing. "You don't want it. The lining is so badly torn it will need to be replaced. We have a tailor back home who does that sort of thing for us."

"Sounds as if you have quite an organization, a shipper and a tailor. Do you do restorations and repairs, too?"

"We have lots of contacts and know lots of people who can do things for us," said Georgine. "If Connor is serious, he'll find himself getting an organization, too. It's the only way to make a profit in this business."

"Do you sell things at auctions, as well as buy from them?" Betsy asked.

"Oh yes."

"I want to ask you how that works," said Betsy. "But first I want to visit your powder room."

"There's a half bath down the hallway off the dining room," said Georgine, pointing.

*Shouldn't have drunk so much tea*, Betsy thought to herself, walking down the short hallway.

There was a fresh roll of toilet paper in the holder, and Betsy, in a bit of a hurry, pulled sharply on the end. To her dismay, the entire roll flew out of the holder—whoever had replaced the roll hadn't made sure the spring-loaded roller was in place. The toilet paper uncoiled itself out of reach.

Betsy made a *tsk* sound of annoyance and reached for her purse, balanced on the edge of the sink, and pulled out a few tissues.

Then she adjusted her trousers and stooped to retrieve the toilet paper roll. The roller had disappeared and she, growing more annoyed by the second, got down on her knees to see where it had gone. Behind the stool? No. There it was, under the overhang of the sink's cabinet.

She got hold of it and was about to straighten up when she noticed that the quarter round molding running across the bottom of the setback under the sink cabinet had slid sideways, extending beyond the end of the cabinet.

She reached to slide it back in place, and instead it caught on something and came loose. She picked it up, and the thin facing board fell forward.

Beginning to mutter serious imprecations to herself, she saw that the thin board had been concealing a rough-cut rectangle cut in the drywall that the builder had used to face the foot of the cabinet.

And tucked inside the opening was a red box. Betsy reached for it, then yanked her hand back. The box was the exact size and color of the box taken from Tom Riordan's house.

She got up, washed her hands, and dipped into her purse for her cell phone.

"Connor," she said quietly, "I've found the cinnabar box. It's in an opening at the base of the sink in the downstairs powder room. Call 911, I'll stall them till they get here." She broke the connection.

She opened the door to the powder room and was startled to see the two Pickering sisters waiting for her. "We wondered what was taking you so long," said Georgine.

"That door is unfortunately—for you—very thin," said Gracie. "We heard things rattling around and then you on your cell phone."

"We're going out the back way, and you're coming with us," said Georgine.

"No, I don't think so," said Betsy, taking a step sideways, thinking to slide past them toward the front door. "Why did you keep it? Why didn't you mail it somewhere? Why did you have to kill poor Tom over it?"

The two women were moving to a place between Betsy and the front door. "Now, don't be afraid," said Grace in a tone of voice that sent a chill down Betsy's spine. "We aren't going to hurt you. But we have to move quickly. Come here. Now." She reached out a hand toward Betsy.

"Seriously," said Georgine, in the same tone.

"Stop," said Betsy. "Stay away from me."

"Or what, honey?" growled Gracie in a whole new voice, taking another step toward her.

Betsy made a dash to get around them. Her sudden move surprised them. She fled into the living room. The pair whipped after her. Grace slammed into her, knocking her off her path toward the door. Betsy ran behind the couch and the two separated, blocking her escape.

Betsy turned toward the pretty little bay window at the front of the house. She picked up a cut-glass lamp from a table and flung it into the window.

The windowpane exploded outward.

"What'd you do that for?" shouted Grace.

"Get 'er!" shouted Georgine. The two sisters rushed to take Betsy by the arms and drag her to the floor.

Betsy screamed in fright and kicked at them. One of them—Was it Gracie? In her panic Betsy couldn't tell—hit Betsy in the face and shouted "Stop fighting!"

"Let go of me!" yelled Betsy. She twisted an arm free and yanked at Gracie's hair—which came off in her hand. Betsy threw the wig away and cocked her arm to strike, but her wrist was taken by Georgine and pulled backward.

Things very quickly became confused. There was a lot of yelling and panting and struggling. Betsy was hit again, twice, in the face, and she kicked someone on the knee.

"That's enough!" shouted a man's loud voice.

It was Connor. He waded into the melee and pulled the two women off Betsy. "I said that's enough!" He shook them, hard, and held each of them at arm's length.

"Oh, Connor, oh, Connor, thank God!" gasped Betsy, breathless and panicked.

"She attacked us for no reason at all!" said Gracie, starting to cry. She began pushing at Connor's arm. "Let go, let go! You're hurting me!"

"She scared us!" said Georgine, trying to twist out of Connor's grip. "She threw the lamp at us and broke the window!"

Betsy got to her feet. Her shirt was torn, her hands were scratched, and she was pretty sure her nose was bleeding.

"Look!" said Betsy, pointing first at one, then the other. "They *are* twins!"

The sound of an approaching siren made everyone fall silent.

"Go out and wave them down, *machree*," he said. "I'll hold these two meanwhile."

\*     \*     \*

"THEY were serial thieves," said Betsy the next day at a special gathering of the Monday Bunch. "They traveled all over the country, buying antiques and collectibles wherever they went. And stealing from galleries and auctions. Then they'd sell whatever they got hold of on eBay or on consignment at other auctions, in newspaper ads, or even on craigslist.

"They had a clever ploy, using the fact that they were actually identical twins. They'd dress very differently and tell people they were sisters two, three, or more years apart. The blond sister, Georgie, would make her presence known in a room where witnesses were present, while Gracie without her auburn wig and dressed exactly like her sister, would commit the theft. If anyone noted something was missing and remembered Gracie being in the place where and when the theft took place, Georgie would supply an alibi. Gracie would change into her auburn-haired persona and join her sister in bidding on auctioned items or negotiating a price in a gallery.

"For variety, they'd do it the other way around, both starting out as auburn haired.

"They pulled a stunt like that on you, Emily."

"They did? When?"

"That day you found the cinnabar box. They knew it was there. Georgie, remember, was in the house for the walkthrough the day before. She must have been surprised to spot it, because it had been stolen from her weeks earlier—except of course she didn't know that Tom was the person who stole it. But that day, there were others around and she wasn't wearing one of those shoplifters' trousers or coats or skirts with the pockets on the inside to hide things in. So she dropped some magazines on top of it. The next day Gracie took her place, without her auburn wig and dressing in Georgine-style clothing—this time with the magic pockets—and waiting for the perfect moment to get you out of that dining room.

"They were probably thinking to make the switch at noon. But their chance came earlier, when Connor yelled from upstairs that he'd made a spectacular find. Jill and Valentina were in the kitchen. Georgie waited for them to leave, then went out the back door, came around the house, and signaled Gracie who was lurking by the big Dumpster. Then Gracie came in the front door and went upstairs to see what Connor had found. By then you were gone, and Gracie came in and went directly to the dining room. She must have been surprised not to find the box where she had left it. But she did eventually find it on the table, hid it in her clothing, and left the house."

Emily frowned. "You mean I was working with Georgie that morning and Gracie that afternoon? And didn't know it?"

"Slick!" exclaimed Godwin. "Heavenly days, that was clever!"

" 'Heavenly days'?" said Connor.

"Molly McGee's favorite expression," said Godwin.

"*Fibber McGee and Molly*," said Betsy to Connor. "Old-time radio show. I'll explain later."

"You didn't notice anything different between Georgie in the morning and Gracie in the afternoon?" asked Jill.

"Nnnnnno," said Emily, eyes squinched up, trying to think of something. "No, she seemed about the same."

"You'd think one of us would have noticed," said Valentina.

"We were working separately, remember," said Connor.

"Plus, it's an act they've been putting on for a long time," noted Betsy.

Emily said, "I guess I don't understand everything, yet. Okay, they—she—Georgie—saw the cinnabar box in Tom's house and decided to steal it. So they played that trick of switching places, like in that old movie *The Parent Trap*, right? But why? Was that thing so expensive it was worth the gamble?"

"Tom stole the box from them," said Betsy.

"Okay, so he did. And so, they stole it back. And then . . . they killed him." Her face reflected her puzzlement.

"Wicked, wicked," murmured Alice.

Betsy said, "When I went to see Tom, he showed me he had something like your eidetic memory. He bragged that he knew where every item in his house came from—even the stolen ones. And I made the mistake of repeating that to Georgie and Gracie. You see, Tom could have told me or Mike Malloy that he stole the cinnabar box from them. And that would have triggered an investigation that could have revealed they have stolen tens of thousands of dollars' worth of items from art galleries and auction houses all over the country."

"They have?" said Cherie. "I never read about a crime wave in the art world!"

"That's because the art world doesn't report thefts unless people are injured or the item taken is legendary—like the *Mona Lisa* or *The Scream*. They're afraid that if word gets out how often things are stolen, people won't donate art to museums or allow auction houses to sell their things anymore."

"How do you know that?" asked Jill.

"There's a book about thieves in the art world. I've been reading it." She smiled at Connor.

"Was the cinnabar box worth a lot of money?" asked Doris.

"Oh yes. It's about four hundred years old and worth somewhere between seven and fifteen thousand dollars. They really should have picked something other than cinnabar to steal."

"Why is that?" asked Cherie.

"Because the prosecuting attorney can prove the box I found in their house is the one taken from Tom's house."

"How?" asked Emily.

"Fingerprints. Tom's fingerprints are on the box."

"Aww, p'shaw!" scoffed Godwin.

"*Fibber McGee and Molly?*" guessed Connor, laughing at the mispronunciation.

"Yes," said Betsy.

"But don't crooks know to wipe things off?" said Emily. "Even I know that, and I'm not a crook!"

"They probably did," said Betsy. Then a little smile appeared. "But there's a tricky thing about cinnabar lacquer. If fingerprints are not wiped off right away, they become permanent. You can't wipe them off. Tom didn't know that, and so his fingerprints are all over that little red box. And probably the fingerprints of someone at Schwales."

Emily asked, "Were the needle cases in the box?"

"Yes," said Betsy. "And that awful mouse ball. They are all antique ivory."

"So there *is* a way to remove the brown color of old ivory," said Godwin.

"Sadly, no," said Betsy. "Ivory turns brown from handling. These pieces were put away soon after they were made, that's why they stayed white. Schwales is going to get them back after the trial, so they can try again to auction them."

"Why did they hold on to that box?" asked Phil.

"I think it was so they could frame someone else for the theft if it became necessary."

"Tell us again about that cute little hidey-hole in the bathroom," said Godwin.

Connor said, "Go to YouTube and type in 'DIY Secret Hiding Place.' There are lots of ways to turn a nook or cranny in your house or condo into a little secret deposit. Only problem is, burglars visit YouTube, too."

"Oh," said Godwin, deflated.

"Have they charged both of them with murder?" asked Valentina, who had been silent through most of this.

"Yes. Partly because they don't know which of them held the pillow down on Tom's face, and partly because they're fairly sure they pulled the 'which one of us is the twin?' ruse at the hospital, too."

"Why are people so wicked?" cried Alice, chin up, pressing her big hands down on the table's surface. "Why can't people be satisfied with what they can earn honestly?"

"I don't know, Alice," said Betsy. "I don't think anyone knows. If we did, perhaps we could find a way to stop people behaving like that."

Emily said, a little sadly, "I liked working with Georgie, even when she was Gracie. She helped me work as hard as she worked. Wait, did that come out right?"

"Yes," said several people, nodding.

Monica Ferris

"Plus, she knew interesting things. And she was funny."

"Tommy was like that, too," said Valentina, a little sharply. "He worked as hard as he could, and he knew things, and he told funny stories. He was a thief, but he didn't deserve to die just so those two could keep on being bigger thieves than he was."

"Damn," said Phil, softly. "Damn, damn, dammit to hell!"

And on that note, the meeting broke up.


THE Pickering sisters were found guilty of multiple felony-level thefts and first-degree murder. They were sentenced to life in prison.

About four months after the trial ended, Betsy received a thick envelope from Shakopee Women's Prison. Inside was the pattern for Viola van Hollen's handkerchief, carefully hand printed on three sheets of paper. With it came a note:

*I bet you thought I had forgotten all about this, but I hadn't. It gave me something to do during the trial and now at Shakopee. I'm not a bad person, I just did a bad thing. Georgie, too. We were having so much fun selling things we picked up, in honest—and dishonest—ways. We had a lot of fun being clever and we put a lot of money in the bank and bought a nice house, but all of it went to pay lawyers. Even the house. It was such a pretty house, near the beach. Defense lawyers are bloodsuckers; don't ever forget that. It's the worst part about being arrested.*

*Good-bye and keep on stitching! Regards, Grace Pickering*

# Crochet Pattern: Classic Lace

## Vivian Langford—August 2013

### SUPPLIES:

Linen or cotton handkerchief (11" square)
Size 80 tatting thread: 3 spools
Size 10 steel crochet hook

### STITCHES USED AND ABBREVIATIONS:

Slip stitch—sl st
Single crochet—sc
Double crochet—dc
Treble crochet—trc
Picot—pc (to form picot: ch 3, sl st in 3rd ch from hook)
Space—sp
Chain—ch
Treble cluster—tr cl (in this pattern, crochet 4 trebles, holding last loop on hook, thread over and pull hook through all 5 loops on hook)

# Crochet Pattern: Classic Lace

**Row 1:** Attach thread to any corner of hanky. Sc, ch 4, sc in same sp 3 times; this will make 3 loops in corner. Continue to ch 4, sc along side of hanky 1/8 inch apart to next corner. Make sc, ch 4 three times in same sp, making 3 loops in corner. Repeat this pattern around hanky and join with sc in beginning sc.

**Row 2:** Sl st in 1st loop, ch 4 and make shell in middle loop of corner as follows: 3 dc, ch 3, 3 dc in same loop. Ch 4, sc in next loop and continue ch 4, sc in loops along side of hanky to next corner. Repeat shell in corner loop and resume ch 4, sc along next 3 sides, making a shell in each corner loop. Join with sc in beginning loop.

**Rows 3 & 4:** Repeat row 2.

**Row 5:** Ch 4, shell in corner shell. Ch 4, sc in next 18 loops.* Ch 4; in next loop work 4-treble cluster as follows: (work 4 trebles, holding back last loop on hook, thread over hook and draw through all 5 loops on hook). In top of treble cluster work 3 picots as follows: (ch 3, sl st in 3rd chain from hook 3 times. Sl st in top of cluster). Then resume ch 4, sc in next 18 loops. In next loop repeat 4-treble cluster stitch with 3 picots in top of cluster. Resume ch 4, sc in remaining loops to corner. In corner loop work shell stitch. Repeat this pattern on 3 remaining sides of hanky. Join with sc in last loop before beginning shell.

*****Note:** Distance between clusters should be evenly spaced, so number of loops may vary between clusters, depending on size of hanky.

## Crochet Pattern: Classic Lace

**Row 6:** Ch 4, shell in corner shell. Ch 4, sc in next 9 loops. In next loop work 4-treble cluster stitch with 3 picots in top of cluster as in previous row. Resume ch 4, sc in loops to next cluster/picot stitch of previous row. Ch 4, sc in top of 1st pc, ch 3, sc in top of 2nd pc, ch 3, sc in top of 3rd pc. Resume ch 4, sc in next 9 loops. Work 4-treble cluster/picot stitch in next ch 4 loop. Resume ch 4, sc in loops to next tr cl of previous row. Ch 4, sc in top of 1st pc, ch 3, sc in top of 2nd pc, ch 3, sc in top of 3rd pc. Resume ch 4, sc in next 9 loops. Work 4-tr cl/pc stitch in next ch 4 loop. Resume ch 4, sc in remaining loops to corner. Ch 4, sc in ch-4 sp leading to shell. Work shell in corner shell. Ch 4 and resume pattern, working 3 remaining sides as first side. Join with sc in chain leading to beginning shell.

**Row 7:** Ch 4, shell in corner shell. Ch 4, sc in ch-4 sp. Ch 4, sc in loops to 1st tr cl of previous row. Ch 4, sc in ch-4 sp. Ch 4, sc in 1st pc of cluster, ch 3, sc in 2nd pc, ch 3, sc in 3rd pc. Ch 4, sc in ch-4 sp. Ch 4, sc in loops to next tr cl. Ch 4, sc in ch-4 sp leading to top of cluster. Ch 4, sc in 1st pc, ch 3, work 4-tr cl/pc stitch in 2nd pc, ch 3, sc in 3rd pc. Ch 4, sc in ch-4 sp. Ch 4, sc in loops leading to next tr cl stitch. Ch 4, sc in sp leading to top of cluster. Ch 4, sc in 1st pc, ch 3, sc in 2nd pc, ch 3, sc in 3rd pc. Ch 4, sc in ch-4 sp. Ch 4, sc in loops leading to next cluster. Ch 4, sc in ch-4 sp leading to cluster. Ch 4, sc in 1st pc; ch 3, work 4-tr cl/pc stitch in 2nd pc, ch 3, sc in 3rd pc; ch 4, sc in ch-4 sp. Ch 4, sc in loops leading to next cluster. Ch 4, sc in ch-4 sp. Ch 4, sc in 1st pc, ch 3, sc in 2nd pc, ch 3, sc in 3rd pc. Ch 4, sc in ch-4 sp. Ch 4, sc in loops to corner. Ch 4, shell in corner shell. Repeat pattern on next 3 sides and join with sc in last loop before beginning shell.

**Row 8:** Ch 4, shell in corner shell. Ch 4, sc in each ch-4 loop leading to 1st tr cl. Ch 4, sc in ch-4 sp leading up to cluster. Ch 4, sc in 1st pc, ch 3, work 4-tr cl/pc stitch in 2nd pc, ch 3, sc in 3rd pc. Ch 4, sc in ch-4 sp leading down from cluster. Ch 4, sc in loops to next cluster. Ch 4, sc in sp leading up to cluster. Ch 4, sc in 1st pc, ch 3, sc in 2nd pc, ch 3, sc in 3rd pc. Ch 4, sc in loops leading to next cluster. Ch 4, sc in 1st pc, ch 3, work 4-tr cl/pc stitch in 2nd pc, ch 3, sc in 3rd pc. Ch 4, sc in loops leading to next tr cl. Ch 4, sc in 1st pc of cluster, ch 3, sc in 2nd pc, ch 3, sc in 3rd pc. Ch 4, sc in loops leading to next tr cl. Ch 4, sc in 1st pc, ch 3, work 4-tr cl/pc stitch in 2nd pc, ch 3, sc in 3rd pc. Ch 4, sc in loops leading to corner. Ch 4, shell in corner shell. Ch 4, continue working pattern on next 3 sides as 1st side. Join with sc in ch-4 sp before beginning shell.

**Row 9:** Repeat row 7.

**Row 10:** Repeat row 8.

**Row 11:** Ch 3; in corner shell work 3 dc, ch 4, sl st in 3rd ch from hook (picot made), ch 1, 3 dc. Ch 3, in next ch-4 sp work 2 sc, pc, 2 sc. Continue working in each ch-4 sp with 2 sc, pc, 2 sc to 1st tr cl. *In 1st pc of cluster sc, pc, sc. In 2nd pc work sc, ch 3, 2 dc, ch 1, pc, ch 1, 2 dc, ch 3, sc (shell with pc made), ch 1. In 3rd pc, work sc, pc, sc. Continue working in each ch-4 sp with 2 sc, pc, 2 sc up to next 4-tr cl stitch. In 1st pc: sc, pc, sc, ch 1. In 2nd pc: sc, pc, sc, ch 1. In 3rd pc: sc, pc, sc, ch 1. Continue working the pattern in ch-4 spaces up to next tr cl. Work from * to next corner shell and work shell as 1st one. Continue working this pattern on next 3 sides and join in sc prior to first corner shell. Break off. Spray starch and press.